Praise for *The Assistants*

"Anyone who has ever been an assistant will appreciate Camille Perri's funny, honest, 100 percent relatable (and did I say funny?) debut novel about a band of exploited, entry-level strivers who even the score with their billionaire boss in the most ingenious way. After a long day at work, this is the book you'll want to pick up—and, after reading it, you'll never look at an expense report (or your colleagues) in the same way again."
                            —Elisabeth Egan, author of *A Window Opens*

"Camille Perri's *The Assistants* is a hilarious romp through the world of corporate greed and the people who assist them. It's also a great story of criminal redemption. It was a blast from start to finish."
                            —Lisa Lutz, *New York Times*–bestselling author of
                            How to Start a Fire and *The Spellman Files*

"A frothy debut."   —*O, The Oprah Magazine*

"*The Assistants* is wry, thoughtful, and funny as hell. I read through the night with a huge smile on my face as lovable Tina Fontana and her raucous band of disenfranchised assistants wreak some Robin Hood–style havoc on their corporate overlords. I had no idea income inequality and grand larceny could be this much fun! I'm so glad Camille Perri did."
                            —Eliza Kennedy, author of *I Take You*

"This delicious page-turner is a rallying cry for everyone squandering their twenties in thankless servitude to those who will never share the wealth—unless someone cleverly forces their hand."
                            —Nicola Kraus, coauthor of *The Nanny Diaries* and
                            How to Be a Grown-Up

"This isn't exactly the stuff fluffy romances are made of—it owes more to Robin Hood, or maybe Bonnie and Clyde, if Bonnie left Clyde in the car and distributed her spoils among her friends. . . . *The Assistants* is an economic fable, a story of class warfare dressed up as chick lit. . . . Powerful people of the world, take notice: The assistants will have their revenge." —*BookPage*

"An insanely fun ride that is as hilarious as it is smart." —*Popsugar*

"[A] raucous debut novel . . . It's great fun, and Perri freewheels enough millennial savvy, parenthetical asides, and clever repartee to give *Girls* a run for its money. . . . Just sit back and let a smart, funny writer entertain." —*Shelf Awareness*

"Reminders of the 1990s movie *Office Space* are present, with a millennial, feminist reboot . . . a fun, modern twist on a Robin Hood story." —*Library Journal*

"Assistant Tina Fontana and her cubicle coconspirators hatch a scheme to hijack their boss's expense account to pay off their student-loan debts . . . but soon their plot takes on a life of its own." —*Cosmopolitan*

"Fact informs fiction in *The Assistants*, a fantasy-fulfillment novel for all the underpaid workers who make important people's worlds go round." —*Elle*

"Attention readers fed up with their jobs: call in sick tomorrow and dive into this [crackling] debut. . . . Perri's writing is quippy and the pace breezy . . . enjoy the sweetness of plotting revenge over cocktails (expensed, of course). You'll feel better after reading, promise." —*Kirkus Reviews*

the assistants

Camille Perri

G. P. PUTNAM'S SONS

New York

PUTNAM

G. P. PUTNAM'S SONS
Publishers Since 1838
An imprint of Penguin Random House LLC
375 Hudson Street
New York, New York 10014

The Library of Congress has catalogued the G. P. Putnam's Sons hardcover edition as follows:

Perri, Camille.
The assistants / Camille Perri.
p.   cm.
U.S. Edition ISBN: 9780399172540
1. Office workers—New York (State)—New York—Fiction.   2. Office practice—New York (State)—New York—Fiction.   I. Title.
PS3616.E768A88   2016   2015025081
813'.6—dc23
International Edition ISBN: 9780399576935

First G. P. Putnam's Sons hardcover edition / May 2016
First G. P. Putnam's Sons international edition / April 2016
First G. P. Putnam's Sons trade paperback edition / May 2017
G. P. Putnam's Sons trade paperback ISBN: 9780399185175

Printed in the United States of America
1   3   5   7   9   10   8   6   4   2

BOOK DESIGN BY KATY RIEGEL

the assistants

prologue

You've probably heard of my former boss. And even if you haven't heard of him, he has influenced you, I promise. Ever watched the all-day news or seen a big blockbuster summer movie? Him. Do you read the newspaper? What about one of those glossy magazines with magenta cover lines like *Dirty Talk Hot Enough to Make His Boxers Combust*? Him. Odds are, if you exist in the modern world, Robert owns all or a portion of the media you consume. He hovers around number thirty-five on the *Forbes* billionaire list. I was his assistant.

All important men have assistants.

That's the first principle I want you to remember.

Do important women also have assistants? Yes, of course. But men rule the world. Still. That's the second principle I want you to remember. Men still rule the world. Not because this is some feminist manifesto, but because it's a simple fact essential to how this all started. And that's what everyone wants to know—the reporters, the bloggers—what they all want to know is how we did it.

How Did Two Little Girls Outsmart the Most Powerful Man in New York? That was the *Upworthy* headline. I'm thirty years old; Emily's twenty-eight. My five feet four inches on tippy-toes brings down the average, but Emily is a solid six foot something in heels. Not so little. What *Upworthy* meant was "powerless."

A BuzzFeed story read: *Modern-Day Robin Hoods Look More Like Charlie's Angels.* They Photoshopped us into swimsuits and put guns in our hands.

Gothamist dubbed our network the *Secretary Sisterhood of Thieves!* (Exclamation theirs.)

Rumors, all of it. Internet chatter. No one knows for sure what actually happened.

So, let me make this perfectly clear. It wasn't stealing, really. And it was almost by accident that we discovered just how much money there was out there for the taking.

That's the third principle I want you to remember. There is enough money.

There is so much money.

1

HERE'S HOW this whole mess started: Robert had to be in LA for a big meeting with his West Coast Titan Corporation execs and his Boeing's engine had the gall to malfunction.

"Tina!" he yelled from inside the soundproofed glass cube of his office.

Robert isn't a yeller by nature, but he had no other choice in order to overcome the soundproofing, forcing his voice to travel through his open office door. I knew it was my name he'd called by the tone. We each had our own tone. If it had been his deputy he'd wanted it would have been a gruff monosyllabic bark; for his senior editor it would have been a throaty holler; his executive producer called for a higher-pitched squawk. My skill at deciphering these subtleties was critical because it was my job to fetch whomever he called. When he wanted me, his voice dropped to a quieter bellow that bordered on a plea. It was a more intimate sound because with me Robert's needs were always personal—he had an upset stomach and required TUMS, he'd forgotten a birthday and needed a last-minute gift, or he couldn't for the life of him figure out how to upload this new software onto his iPad. Robert's vulnerable call for me was a daily assurance that I was essential to the success of this castle of a man—a man whom half the world considered to be a monster because they could never come within earshot of understanding him.

In less than a second I was at his desk, notepad in hand. Behind me a wall of flat-screens flashed the news being broadcast by Titan and its so-called competitors. Robert had the uncanny ability to devote a small portion of his gaze to each screen simultaneously. In all he owned nine satellite television networks, one hundred seventy-five newspapers, one hundred cable channels, forty book imprints, forty television stations, and one movie studio. His total audience reached around 4.7 billion people, which came out to around three-fourths of the population of the entire globe. But *the news* was his baby. He was never not watching it, analyzing it, shaping it. That's why he situated his office at Titan News headquarters, where he could keep close watch not only on his wall of flat-screens but also on his journalists. A man as powerful as Robert could have hidden himself anywhere, pulling at the strings of the world from a lounge chair in the Seychelles, unseen by his employees—but he needed to be here at the center of it all, at the hub.

Our office didn't look like a newsroom that you'd imagine from movies or TV drama series. The floors below ours were more like that—the broadcast, print media, and digital newsrooms, each of which could have easily passed for something out of *The Matrix*.

And there was an entire floor of flashy studios used for our non-stop news coverage and thrill-a-minute opinion shows. But our office on the fortieth floor was far less exciting, just row after row of desks and cubicles. Still, we were the brain of the whole operation, the source from which all orders trickled down. Titan's chief editors and all of Robert's most trusted deputies had desks on our floor so Robert could pull them into impromptus with the business leaders and celebrities he met with—and so he could foster relationships between them and the political-party representatives (yes, from both parties) who came to lobby him. I guess what I'm trying to say is, what the fortieth floor lacked in flash it made up for in influence.

Robert had his shirtsleeves rolled up and was rubbing his dark-haired head with both hands like he always did when he was upset. For a man his age, Robert had a surprisingly full, thick head of hair, which he attributed to a hearty diet of smoked meats and aged bourbon.

"I need to be on the next flight to LA," he said. "And have them bump the seats around mine."

Robert made requests like this as if he were ordering a pastrami on rye at the corner deli, or in his case, maybe braised brisket on a roll.

"You're flying commercial?" I asked.

"Don't get me started. The Boeing died and they tell me there aren't any jets available for the rest of the afternoon. Can you believe that shit? Not one. I used to be somebody in this town, you know that?"

In the six years I'd worked for Robert, not once had he ever flown on a commercial airline. I glanced at the clock. In order for him to make the LA meeting on time, he'd have to be on a flight in the next two hours.

"And make sure they comp me," he said.

"The airline?" What amounted to buying out half of first class on a flight that would be leaving almost immediately, Robert wanted for free. And he expected it to be done as simply as saying "hold the mustard."

"Okay," I said.

Robert brought his hands down from his head, placed them flat on his desk, and looked at me amiably with his big brown eyes. "Thank you," he said.

That's something people who haven't met Robert can't understand—his graciousness. They see a seventy-year-old media tycoon accused of evading every tax and law imaginable to expand his multinational domination. They see a sinister businessman accused of single-handedly making a mockery of news journalism. They see a one-percenter with a "Don't Mess with Texas" bumper sticker on the back of his Mercedes. But actually, Robert's a very nice man.

So I called the airline, used my executive voice, and politely explained our crisis situation.

"You do understand this will cause a great disruption to our other first-class passengers," the phlegmy-voiced woman on the phone said. "But because Mr. Barlow is such a valued customer we're happy to accommodate him." She sounded like one of Marge Simpson's chain-smoking sisters.

"Thank you," I replied, perfectly mimicking Robert's amiability.

All sweetness and light, Robert always said. That's how you

have to talk to people, all sweetness and light, but tough as stewed skunk.

She clicked away on her keyboard. "The total fare will come to nineteen thousand, one hundred forty-seven dollars."

I had the urge to gasp. That was a high enough figure to make flying in a private jet sound fiscally reasonable.

"Ma'am?" I said. "I do understand this is terribly short notice and you're going to great lengths to accommodate Mr. Barlow's sizable request, but I was wondering if it would be possible for this fare to be complimentary."

Silence.

"Hello?"

More silence. Then laughter, then the clearing of mucus, then finally—"You've got to be fucking kidding."

"Excuse me?"

"Who does this guy think he is?"

"Ma'am," I said again, which always made me feel slightly Southern in spite of my New York roots, and also a little bit like an asshole, "did you just curse at me? I'd like to speak to your manager immediately."

"There is no way we're comping Robert Barlow," she said.

I glanced at the time and then at Robert's desk. He'd already left for the airport, unable to even fathom that his request would be denied. Jesus, no wonder he never flew commercial if this was the treatment he got. Asking to fly for free or not, where were these people's manners?

"Fine," I said. "We'll pay the fare. But as soon as I hang up this phone I'm filing a complaint with your customer service department."

"Credit card number, please."

I recited Robert's corporate Amex number from memory as obnoxiously as possible.

Two seconds later the woman replied, "I'm sorry," like she wasn't sorry at all. "That card's expired."

"Impossible."

I could hear her grinning through the receiver. "That card is expired."

Shit. Fine. How could I be losing this battle of wills so terribly? I fished through my bag, found my wallet, pulled out my own credit card, and read off the number.

Titan didn't allow assistants to have corporate cards, so it was my personal card that I had to use.

"One moment, please," she said.

I listened to her breathing, which sounded like Darth Vader performing an anti-tobacco PSA, and then she came back with: "I'm sorry. That card's also been rejected. You've exceeded your credit limit."

I pretty much set myself up for that one. None of my credit cards had a limit over eleven thousand dollars. "Can I split it between two cards?" I flipped through my wallet.

"No," she said.

"No?"

"No."

"I would seriously like to speak to your manager immediately," I said. "I'm not even kidding now."

"Okay, fine. You can use two cards." My nemesis was growing bored of sucking the life out of my day; I was obviously harshing her mellow disengagement. "But this isn't customary. I'm doing you a favor."

"I appreciate that," I said, because at heart I'm a total weakling.

I read off the number to my second credit card, got "one moment"-ed again, but—at last—tragedy was averted.

I hung up the phone and took a deep breath.

Of course I filed an expense report the moment I received an e-mail confirmation for the fare. Twenty thousand dollars was half of my yearly salary.

People often assumed I made more as the assistant to one of the richest, most powerful men on the planet, and I let them. It was less humiliating that way. Maybe there was a time when "executive assistants," also known as "secretaries," were "taken care of," but those days are long gone, at least in the media industry. They went out with lunches at the Four Seasons, smoking indoors, and the existence of the middle class. Every assistant I knew made under fifty K a year. But the new hires made only thirty-five K, so it wasn't really my place to complain.

YOU KNOW HOW sometimes when you call to order something over the phone, like plane tickets, let's say, a recording might come on just before a real person answers that says, *This call may be recorded for quality assurance purposes?*

Well, my call with the hater from the airline was one of those lucky calls. I'd never filed a complaint the way I threatened to; I'm way too lazy for that sort of thing. But a few days after the incident, I received a call from the airline's head of customer relations apologizing for the "confusion" of the attendant on the phone. She'd been "let go," I was told, also known as fired. The airline retroactively comped Robert's flight and they were sending a gift for his troubles.

"Would Mr. Barlow enjoy a bottle of good red wine?" the groveling woman asked.

"Why, yes. Yes, he would."

Things like this happened to Robert all the time. Before I worked for Titan, I never realized that very rich people didn't pay for stuff.

(Let's call that rule number four: Very rich people don't pay for stuff.)

I was so naïve. This sucking-up from the airline would have at one time struck me as shocking and unbelievably unfair, nonsensical even. Why wouldn't a billionaire have to pay for something a poor person would absolutely have to pay for? But I'd grown used to it in the past six soul-crushing years, so it no longer fazed me. I immediately filed the whole incident under forgotten, went home, watched some Netflix, and fell asleep ignoring the unpaid bills piling up on my kitchen table, per usual.

A few days later I was g-chatting with Handsome Kevin Hanson from legal (that's what every female in the office called him, or just Kevin Handsome for short) while shoveling spoonfuls of Pinkberry into my mouth. I was enjoying an intense brain freeze coupled with the rush I always experienced while chatting with Kevin, when Billy the mail guy (aka "Patchouli," on account of his stinking to high hell of the stuff and dutifully passing it on to all of our parcels) dropped a white, hippie-infused envelope onto my desk that read: *Travel & Entertainment Reimbursement.*

Suddenly I remembered.

I signed off g-chat, made sure Patchouli Billy was at a safe distance, and then sliced open the envelope with my silver letter opener. And there it was. A crisp green check in the amount of $19,147 with my name on it.

Of course. My credit cards were billed. My credit cards were unbilled. But T & E had already filed the claim. I'd already been approved for the reimbursement.

I couldn't stop looking at that beautiful, blossoming number. Nineteen thousand, one hundred forty-seven dollars. It was so much money to me. It was nearly, to the dollar, the exact amount of my student loan balance, and I'd been struggling to pay that down for almost a decade. (Thanks for nothing, NYU.)

I folded the check in half, then in half again, and shoved it deep into the black-hole darkness of my bag.

Later, I would recognize this as the moment that I faltered, my pivotal turn. But at the time it seemed innocent enough. I would just, you know, bring the check home and then tear it to shreds.

Sure, I could have torn it up right then and been done with it, but I wanted to look at it some more first. To sit with it in my moldy one-bedroom Brooklyn apartment, with its leaky roof and rats in the walls. I needed to take the check home to bed with me, for just one night, before discarding it.

So I did.

One night then turned into a week that I slept with that gorgeous green-patterned piece of paper on my nightstand, weighted down by my half-empty orange pill bottle of Lexapro. Then I had a nightmare that one of the rats in the walls made it into my room when I wasn't home and ate the check, so I weighed it down with a mousetrap instead. Not one with cheese in it, just the trap, set and ready, cocked like an armed security guard.

While gazing into the check's fine crosshatched surface, I'd let my eyes go soft and compose scenarios of cashing it and then being caught. What would I say? *Oh, that check? Didn't I cancel that? I'd never intentionally take money that didn't belong to me. That's just not how I was raised.*

Which was true. I was raised Catholic by what they call old-school Italians. (Or what Robert in his native Texan twang would call Eye-talians.) My parents were the kind of people who favored the vengeful, Old Testament God over the more forgiving, non-violent version from the "Americanized" (their word) New Testament. My father would threaten to cut off my pinky finger himself for a lesser offense than stealing. But then again, wasn't my angry Geppetto of a dad's most favorite phrase *God works in mysterious ways?*

What if this was that mysterious way?

And didn't I "secret" this exact type of scenario when I read that self-help book *The Secret? Twenty thousand dollars*, I remember saying to the universe. *That's all I need. It's not that much money, but for me it would be a life-changer.* Nineteen thousand, one hundred forty-seven dollars was pretty damn close to twenty thousand dollars, and only a fool would refuse an accurately answered prayer from the universe.

Before long, I found myself becoming absentminded. I would catch myself leaving the house without shoes on or forgetting where I put my keys. I was *this close* to brushing my teeth with hemorrhoid cream when I realized what was going on. I was in love. I'd fallen in love with the idea of not having student-loan debt, and all the swooning and fantasizing that accompanied love was making me scatterbrained.

While drinking a cup of coffee or riding the L train, I'd slip into daydreams about how my life would change for the better if I let myself keep the reimbursement money. I could have savings, I thought. I could start hoarding my money in one of those things they call a *savings account*. All at once I would become less anxious and more generous. Maybe I'd get a dog—one of those adorable new mixed breeds, like a Cheagle. Maybe I'd start going to the gym with all the extra time I'd have not debating between eating the slightly off leftover burrito in the fridge and splurging on some groceries from C-Town; between getting the cavity in my molar filled and having that funky paramecium-shaped mole on my back looked at. And, sure, I could get one more wear out of this pair of socks before I go to the Laundromat. And look at this sheath of aluminum foil, it's still good as new, I'll just give it a little rinse. No. No more of that. Instead, I could be living the good life of enjoying dire necessities *and* bountiful comforts. I could pay my phone bill *and* go to the movies *on the same day*.

The next thing I knew, I'd come to in Canarsie.

This is the last stop on this train. Everyone please leave the train.

Something had to happen. I had to rip up that damn check!

Okay, fine, I told myself. *I'll do it.*

Back in the safety of my bedroom now, blinds drawn, check in hand, I was poised to end this thing once and for all. But maybe I would just, you know, take a picture of the check first. Not a selfie or anything, just a snapshot. And not the kind that disappears thirty seconds after you take it, or whatever—just an old-fashioned photograph, to remember the check by.

And then I remembered that app on my phone, the one where all you have to do is click a photo of a check and—poof—it's deposited into your bank account.

Damn you, technology.

Technology made it so easy to deposit that check, I could have done it by accident.

It wasn't an accident—but it could have been.

First I had to open the magical check-depositing app and log on with my username and password. Then I had to snap a picture of the check's front and the check's back. *Make sure the entire check is inside the box and touch the camera icon when you are ready.*

Was I ready?

No, but the novelty of this process was so fascinating that I continued on anyway. Depositing a check with my phone? Who knew I'd ever see the day? It was just unreal enough to feel imaginary.

It wasn't an accident when I logged on to my student-loan account either. But that was the cunning whimsy of technology at work, too, because if I actually had to leave my house at any point—or even just sit down at my desk and write out a physical check, and stuff that check into an envelope, and walk that envelope to the mailbox to mail it—I don't think I could have done it. But quietly typing alone in my dark bedroom felt so innocuous, so anonymous, and even potentially undoable. There's something devastatingly permanent about dropping a letter into a public mailbox, isn't there? The way the envelope is in your grasp one minute, and then it's gone, followed by that heavy metal lash of the door. You open the door again just to make sure, as if in the history of all letters there was ever one that didn't make it down. And then there's that split second of panic. *Did I remember the stamp? The return address? It's too late now.*

But just clicking Send? There would always be *Cancel. Edit/Undo.*

I stared at the words on my computer screen—*Pay in Full*—for a long time before making the decision. Earlier in the day, Robert had had an argument with his wife about whether the peppers growing in their garden were jalapeños or habaneros. He turned out to be wrong, so he had me run out to buy her the diamond bracelet she'd had her eye on from Tiffany. Total cost: $8,900.

So $19,147 was roughly only two lost arguments to Robert.

And it wasn't even his money, was the thing. It was the Titan Corporation's money, and Titan had billions—literally billions and zillions of dollars. Could anyone really blame me for not giving this minuscule-to-them-yet-life-changing-for-me amount of money back to the Titan Corporation?

It had already been three weeks since the reimbursement check was issued to me, and nobody had missed it. Nobody had missed it! Meanwhile, I could have fostered a family of Cambodian children for what I was paying in interest alone on my student-loan debt each month.

One click. *Pay in Full.* That was it, that was all it took, and it was done. I was free.

2

Days of anxiety-induced nausea, accompanied by acute acid reflux, passed. Every time Robert called me into his office an angel somewhere would lose its wings and I would throw up a little bit in my mouth. I thought I would feel a great sense of relief once I deposited the check and paid off my loan—and there was an initial rush—but then, instead of relief, what followed was more worry. Except it wasn't the low-level, all-pervading, quiet hum of money-related worry I was accustomed to. This was more concentrated and pointed, like an in-your-face cystic pimple. Instead of *Shoot, rent's due this week, is there enough in my account?* or *Fucking-a, Time Warner raised their rates again?*, it was: *I stole.* Robert asking me when his peak-lapel tuxedo would be back from the cleaners? *I stole.* Robert asking me to research the political donations made by his three o'clock appointment? *I have no morals.* Robert just back from Georgia, dropping a bag of peaches onto my desk because he knew how much I loved them? *I could take my own life.*

Then Emily Johnson summoned me up to the forty-third floor.

For most purposes, our office on the fortieth floor could have been considered the building's top floor. The three floors above us were all business-related—the bean counters—strategically positioned to remind every employee below them that these folks were watching, omnipresent, like an all-knowing god from above. Forty-three was Corporate Governance's floor, composed of barely used rooms filled with plush couches that were reserved for the tight buttocks of Titan Corporation board members. And it was T & E's floor.

What is T & E, you ask? Not to be confused with T & A (Google it; NSFW), *T & E* stands for "Travel and Entertainment." At some companies it might stand for "Travel and Expenses," which makes a little more sense, but Titan higher-ups were generally more entertainment focused. It would have made the most sense if everyone simply called it BE, short for "Business Expenses," because on the most basic level that's what these reimbursements were supposed to be for—expenses you incurred while conducting business. But such an acronym was probably way too metaphysical for everyone involved.

Anyway, the forty-third floor looked exactly like you'd expect it to. All slick brass and polished wood. It smelled like nothing. Like if nothing were a scent that could come in a bottle, it would smell exactly like the forty-third floor. And it was quiet, so quiet they pumped in white noise from overhead vents. For privacy, supposedly, but I think it was to keep people from going ballistic over the impossible nonexistence of the place, to keep the operating officers and bookkeepers from disappearing into its cool vacuum, convinced they were invisible.

The director of Travel and Entertainment was a middle-aged man who wore a bow tie every day and listened to opera with headphones on inside his office. His final approval had to be stamped on every expense account filed within the building—even Robert's. But it was his assistant who actually waded through all the forms and approved them with the loopy script of Bow Tie's signature, while he hummed along to Puccini.

All important men have assistants. The T & E director's assistant was Emily Johnson, a blond-haired, blue-eyed bitch from Connecticut.

Emily was the type of girl who would reject my reports if I failed to arrange all the scanned receipts facing the same way. "I can't read this chaos," she'd say over the phone in her Waspy lockjaw accent. The accent of East Coast boarding schools. "Upside-down receipts give me vertigo."

But Emily had never before summoned me up to the forty-third floor to speak face-to-face. My guts went limp the moment I read her e-mail and I ran to the bathroom.

Hovering over the spotless marble sink, I looked in the mirror. Stupid. What a stupid anemic face I had, even paler now with guilt. It had been a little over a week since I used the flight reimbursement money to pay off my student loan. Why didn't I just hold on to it for a while longer? Now I couldn't even give it back. I was certainly about to be fired, or interrogated. Or worse, prosecuted. And Robert. Most horrible of all would be Robert's disappointment in me, the way he would raise his hands to his head, or begin restlessly turning his UT class ring—his other nervous habit. He was away on business today, thank god, but it was only a matter of time now.

The bathroom door swung open and in stepped two freelancers with toothbrushes in hand. There was a strange obsession with oral hygiene in our office that permeated all the way to the temp staff. I slipped past them with my head down, dodging the trappings of restroom small talk.

My heart raced and I could feel two sweat stains pooling beneath my underarms as I made my way to the elevator bank's centralized kiosk. Out of habit I pushed the down button and then had to wait for the system to sort out its digital confusion when I immediately switched to the up button. The kiosk directed me to elevator D, then to E, and finally to A—which I dashed to before it could complete the ominous spelling of the word *dead*.

Emily was waiting for me behind the forty-third floor's sliding glass doors when I stepped out of the elevator. She wore a white blouse over white pants and white high heels. It was still the tail end of winter, but already her skin had somehow tanned to a beachy golden brown. She watched me, smiling.

The doors were locked for security and my ID card couldn't open them, so I had to wait for Emily to scan her card and let me in. Just for fun, she kept me standing there, helpless and waiting, hyperventilating.

When she finally relented and scanned her card, the doors unlocked with a metallic clank much like the release of a prison cell gate. So many aspects of our building struck me as prisonlike—our ID cards may as well have been one of those house-arrest ankle bracelets the way they tracked our every move. Not to mention all the security guards leering around each corner. Why in the world did I think a place like this would just overlook nearly twenty thousand dollars?

Emily led me to the northwest conference room and hermetically sealed us inside. She sat opposite me and soundlessly slid a manila folder across the glass tabletop.

I looked away. The view outside was so much more beautiful from up here, even though it was only three floors higher. The windows went from floor to ceiling with no obstructions, so even from where I was sitting I could see the frantic procession of tiny people and yellow cabs struggling down Eighth Avenue.

"I know what you did," Emily said. And before I could muster up any false confusion she added, "Don't deny it, Fontana; you'd be wasting my time."

It was strange hearing her call me by my last name. That's what everyone in the building called me, except for Robert, but how did she know that? We weren't friends.

"I understand why you did it," her lockjaw said.

She *understands*? This girl didn't understand the first thing about me. She was Connecticut Barbie. I was Skipper, and not even the modern Skipper of recent years with larger breasts and a new face mold. I was the juvenile Skipper of the sixties, the one perpetually on the brink of becoming a woman. Emily Johnson and I would never understand each other.

"In fact," Emily continued, standing up from her chair, coming around to my side of the table, and leaning her perfectly toned lower body against its glass edge, "I think you did the right thing. They wipe their asses with twenty thousand dollars around here." Her WASP accent dropped like a curtain. Gone were the intonations of Katharine Hepburn and Bette Davis. "You get me?" she said.

"Um," I said, startled, "I'm not sure."

"I think you do." Emily opened the manila folder and gestured for me to read it.

She waited.

It was an account statement with her name on it from American Education Services.

"Why are you showing this to me?" I asked.

Emily tapped her French-manicured fingernail on a number. The total statement balance. Seventy-four thousand, three hundred twenty-three dollars and twenty cents.

"You think you're the only one with money problems?" she said. "You think you're the only one who's trained herself not to sound like a truck driver from the Bronx?"

I stood up now, too. "Aren't you from Greenwich? Don't you have a pet horse named Dancer?"

"I'm from the slums of Bridgeport and my parents work for the post office. I just pass real well. Now sit yourself back down."

I was so caught off guard that I obeyed her. She pulled her long blond hair back into a ponytail and I swear she transformed into a completely different person. Emily was still stunningly beautiful—she couldn't not be—but her rich-girl pretension had altered to a thuggish toughness.

"So here's what's going to happen," she said. "I'm not going to rat you out and you're going to use Barlow's expense account to pay off my student loan. Then we'll be even."

"Are you out of your mind?" My voice hit an octave that caused Emily to glance quickly at the glass door, forgetting the conference room was safely soundproofed. "No way," I said. "Forget it. We'll get caught."

She flashed a pearl smile that resembled the Emily I knew before. "You already got caught. By me. And I'm surely not going to catch myself."

She slapped the manila folder shut and hugged it to her chest. "Be creative filling out the reports. Scatter it around. A few thousand dollars here and there. I'll take care of the rest and in a few weeks' time this will all be over."

"I can't do what you're asking," I said. "It would really be stealing. It's wrong."

Emily fiddled with her diamond-stud earring, definitely no cubic zirconia. What of her was real, and what was fake? I no longer had any idea.

"That's so typical," she said. "Of your kind."

"My kind? What's that supposed to mean?"

"Come on, Fontana. That chip on your shoulder you lug around all day? Like you work harder than the rest of us."

"You don't even know me! You've never once made eye contact with me in the cafeteria; you ignore me when we're the only two people in the elevator." Emily freed her golden hair from its knot and shook it down to a cascade upon her shoulders. A long-limbed man in a double-breasted suit walked by us in the hallway. Emily laughed out loud and waved to him through the glass like Miss America.

Then her face got serious again. "You'll do it, Fontana. Because above all else, you're a survivor, just like me. And I know you're not really as dumb as you look."

Before I could protest, Emily went to the door and opened it. "Enjoy the rest of your day," she said, with her accent back on track.

3

I HAD NO IDEA how to go about this.

Okay, that is a blatant lie. I knew exactly how to go about this. Everyone who filed expenses at Titan was aware of the tiny box at the bottom of our Travel & Entertainment forms labeled *Out-of-Pocket Expense, Miscellaneous.* You checked this box if you paid for a business-related purchase *out of your own pocket.* Pretty straightforward, right?

What's that you say? Why not just make it all up?

Because the trick with out-of-pocket expenses was that you had to provide documentation, to prove they were legitimate—those damn scanned receipts that Emily Johnson insisted all face the same direction lest she become dizzy and nauseated.

It was Friday afternoon, three p.m. I glanced at the rectangular light on my desk phone to see if Robert was on a call. He wasn't, so I crept to his door and gently knocked on the inside of the glass.

Robert looked up and his sternness softened at the sight of me. "Tina!" he shouted, like I'd surprised him. "What can I do for you?"

"Receipts," I said.

"Is it the end of the week already?" He shuffled around some folders on his desk, gathering crinkled slips of white and pink paper from the depths of numerous piles. He dug his fingers into the Longhorns coffee mug that he kept on the credenza behind his chair specifically for this purpose. He went to his closet and searched through the pockets of a few suit jackets. Then he handed the whole jumbled, crumpled pile over to me. One or two of the tiniest slips floated down to the floor and I let him pick them up.

This was all customary. This systematically chaotic gathering of the receipts, the retracing of steps to manifest the paper trail of everything he'd bought that week using cash. It was the same every time.

You'd be amazed by how much money the man could shell out in a seven-day stretch. Don't let his outward grit fool you; Robert enjoyed his comforts and luxuries. And I think he must have gotten a kick out of reaching into his vest pocket, pulling out a wad of bills, and fanning them like a winning hand of poker onto the table at Per Se or Porter House. Otherwise why not just charge everything?

In fact, I bet Robert would have paid for all his purchases using gold bullion if only he could carry that much gold bullion in the vest pocket of his Armani suit jacket. Once I overheard his senior VP ask him if his Mercedes was a lease, and Robert nearly spat on the carpet. "I like *owning* things," he replied. I imagined a similar situation whenever a clerk or attendant innocently asked Robert,

"Cash or credit?" I could see the way he'd glare at them just before throwing down a rubber-banded brick of hundreds.

It was nothing but more work for me, the weekly process of collecting the receipts, scanning them, and sending them to T & E for approval. But today it would be my lifeline. Today I filed Robert's out-of-pocket expense report in the usual way, methodically, robotically. Then I hit replay and did it again. Same receipts. Two reports. One for him, and one for me.

How did this plan dawn on me?

I'll tell you: In the past six years there had been many days I thought, *Wow, Robert Barlow really trusts me!* Because I had serious access to this man's identity. Account numbers, passwords, when he was due for his next prostate exam. I knew all his secrets. On the worst days my thinking was more along the lines of, *Wow, I could rob Robert Barlow blind if I really set my mind to it!*

But this was a working-class girl's fantasy not so different from my childhood wish that I was actually a foundling whose real parents were the royal king and queen of all the land . . . The truth was, I took great pride in the trust Robert had in me. I was flattered by it, and by simply being associated with him. On my own, as a person, I wasn't so important. But as Robert Barlow's assistant, maître d's and hoteliers knew me by name. I couldn't afford to frequent their establishments, but they still knew my name. They sent fifteen-pound panettones addressed specifically to me at Christmastime.

Robert made me worth something. I would no sooner have stolen from him than I would have from my own peasant-stock mother and father.

But now this. Emily fucking Johnson. Beneath Emily's pomposity I had never believed her to be very intelligent. I'd assumed she was just another dumb blonde with an expensive education. Now I didn't know what to think. She was obviously smart enough to outsmart me.

From today onward, for however long it took, this would be my method: duplicate Robert's out-of-pocket expense receipts (totally illegal), get reimbursed for the false receipts (all lies), cash the reimbursement check (no turning back now), and hand the cash over to Emily. (What were the odds she'd even say thank you?)

Filing the same receipts twice, the second time with my account information plugged in instead of Robert's, was by no means an ingenious plan. If Emily weren't the one doing the approving, I would have gotten caught on the first false report. I cannot stress this enough. The reason we could actually get away with this is because the men who made the big bucks passed off the responsibilities they couldn't be bothered with (like signing their own names) to their assistants.

A few weeks' time, Emily said it would take—which was highly optimistic. So I added an extra thousand dollars here and another few thousand there to the report on my computer screen—each time clicking the box for *Receipt Lost or Damaged*. That would speed things up a bit. Usually you needed to provide a receipt for any expense over one thousand dollars, no exceptions, but (a) this was Robert's company, and (b) Emily didn't give a damn either way.

I hesitated before hitting *File* and then just closed my eyes and went ahead, because if I'd learned anything from reading *Hamlet* in my senior-year Shakespeare colloquium, or from consuming ceaseless Nike commercials throughout the midnineties, it was to just frigging do it already.

Ten grand. Boom. Filed.

Just then, Robert yelled something from inside his office and I understood he was calling for his senior editor.

I popped my head above my desk's dividers like a mole peeking out of its hole and called out over the plain of cubicles. "Dillinger! Robert wants you."

Everyone on our floor addressed one another by their last names, Longhorns football style. It was a habit nobody who worked outside of a male-dominated office could really understand.

Dillinger, whose first name was Jason, rushed to Robert's office and closed the door behind him. When I returned to my seat, I noticed the lower right-hand corner of my computer screen had come alive.

Lunch today?

Kevin Handsome was g-chatting. By "lunch" he meant heading down to the cafeteria at the same time to buy our lunches, and then riding the elevator back upstairs together to eat separately at our respective desks. In all it was a ten-minute date, five minutes tops of uninterrupted conversation. A minimum of three minutes of palm sweats and me obsessing. *What does this guy want from me?*

Kevin wasn't called Kevin Handsome for nothing. Genetics had been good to him. He had a mop of dark hair and round brown eyes in an all-American style. He was tall and fit with just enough dork mixed in to make him approachable. I sometimes imagined him jogging or boating, or playing touch football with his brothers à la the Kennedys.

A guy like Kevin could only be this nice to me because I was

Robert Barlow's assistant. It had happened before with other guys, albeit less attractive ones. Eventually the flirtatious male would ask for some favor—a slot on Robert's calendar or an invitation to some event. But manipulation or not, he was cute.

I agreed to lunch. *It's build-your-own-burger day,* I replied, to emphasize that I was in it solely for the red meat and unlimited fixings, not Kevin's company. *See you down there.*

I should mention that the Titan cafeteria wasn't really a cafeteria. It was more of a food service Pangaea, connecting all imaginable menu options together in one space. There was a grill station, a soup station, an international station that changed according to obscure holidays and days of observance no one's heard of, and—a crowd favorite—the "action station," in which a line of chefs cooked up your meal in fast-action. Of course there was also sushi, pizza, specialty sandwiches, a salad bar, and a celebrity chef's table. Don't even get me started on snack time, which ran from three to four p.m. and encompassed more dessert options than the Viennese hour at the last Italian wedding you attended. But the pinnacle of all, to me, was build-your-own-burger day. I loved build-your-own-burger day so much that each month when it rolled around, I'd enter it onto my Outlook calendar ahead of time. Once, in my excitement, I accidentally entered it onto Robert's calendar instead of mine—with the requisite triple exclamation points and all. (This is why no one person should ever oversee more than one calendar, but such is the assistant's burden.) The exclamatory note sat there for about a week before I discovered the error, but Robert never mentioned it.

Kevin was already on line at the burger station when I arrived.

I admired the fact that he wasn't looking at his phone, like everyone else on the line. He just waited, with his hands in the pockets of his gray suit pants, soaking up the atmosphere, as they say. His eyes brightened when I made my approach.

"I saved you a spot," he said, letting me cut in front of him.

I knew the woman behind us wouldn't complain about my cutting because Kevin had that soothing effect on people. People, mainly women, yearned to do him favors.

"How's Wiles today?" I asked.

Glen Wiles was the head of Titan's legal department, and Kevin's boss. He was also the only man at Titan more feared than Robert—not because he had more power, but because he was by far the bigger asshole.

"At the moment, Wiles is turning the office thermostat all the way down to make his assistant's endowment perk up. You know . . ." He gestured toward his own pectoral nipples. "So business as usual, really."

"Yeah, Robert would never do that to me," I said, looking down at my non-tits beneath my sweater.

Kevin cleared his throat and politely looked away. Fortunately, it was our turn to build our burgers.

LATER THAT NIGHT, the guilt really hit hard, the way it tends to do when the distractions of the day all fall away and you're finally left alone with yourself. Until this point—rational or not—using Titan's money to pay off my student-loan debt had felt like something that happened to me more than something I'd done. But this was deliberate. I'd chosen to do this for Emily, or with Emily, instead of turning myself in, and that was wrong no matter how you looked at it.

Things are going to hell in a handbasket, Robert would have said. His voice was always in my head. I couldn't help it. So much of my daily energy went to thinking about Robert, thinking *as* Robert, anticipating his needs, responding to his requests, manifesting his every wish. It wasn't possible to just turn his voice off at the end of the day.

A couple sandwiches shy of a picnic, he would have called my thinking now. *Crazy as a bull bat.*

I stared up at the rain bubble that hung down from the ceiling over my bed—a white plaster water balloon threatening to plunge onto my head at any moment. It was an anomaly of nature that defied all logic considering I lived on the ground floor of my apartment building, but there it was every time it rained, taunting my limited comprehension of both plumbing and architecture.

It was storming outside, and the roaring thunder and flashing lightning only reinforced my notion that God was angry with me. I watched the bubble swell with each passing second, stretching like a waterlogged belly. The Internet had gone out in the storm and I didn't own a television, so tracking the bubble's growth was my only active form of entertainment. I could have gone on that way all night, but the buzz of my doorbell shook me back to consciousness.

It was just after midnight. Who could be at my door?

A rumble of thunder crescendoed to a crash. My windows rattled and I realized it must be death at my door, a scythe-wielding reaper, come to massacre me in my blue-and-white-striped paja-mas as punishment for my crimes.

Actually, it was a soaking-wet Emily Johnson.

"What are you doing here?" I said. "How did you know where I live?"

Emily looked like she'd just stepped out of a *Sports Illustrated* swimsuit issue, if the swimsuits were replaced by the designer nightclub-wear Westchester girls partied in to get laid. She was all drenched and disheveled. Her eye makeup ran down her face in crooked inky streams.

"Are you crying?" I asked.

She pointed up at the sky like I was a moron. "It's raining."

"Right. But what are you doing here?"

"My date tonight was a bust," she said, in a way that sounded like she might actually begin to cry. "And I can't make it back to Bridgeport in this storm. Some asshole smashed the driver-side window of my Range Rover with a goddamn brick. I covered it with a plastic bag, but there's no way I can sleep in there tonight."

"You sleep in your car?"

"It's not a car, it's a Range Rover."

"You have a Range Rover but no apartment?"

"Fontana, I have nowhere else to go. Can I come in or not?"

I was still so disoriented, trying to relate this Emily Johnson to the one I knew from work. That version of her was a wire pulled taut. This girl on the brink of tears in my doorway was slack and loose, unguarded. She was vulnerable. Real. And a little insane looking.

"I don't have much space," I said. "It's not like I've got a guest room. I barely have a living room. And how did you know where I live? Did I already ask you that?"

"Don't you have an air mattress?" She stepped past me, through my doorway.

"No, actually." I followed behind her to the kitchen as she began to disrobe.

"I brought this," she said. From her oversize Coach hobo bag she pulled a bottle of Jameson. "To say thank you for letting me crash here."

I was suddenly transported to the most significant moment of my adolescence: seventh grade, when the queen bee, Dana Vandorn, was surprised by her period in the bathroom stall next to mine. She came out sheepish, searching her purse for a dime in order to vend a pillowy maxi pad from the machine. But who carried dimes? I just happened to also be experiencing menses that week and I knew this was my moment. I knew I could have let Dana Vandorn suffer—lord knew she deserved it—but I chose instead to take the high road and offered her a Playtex Sport from my bag. She thanked me with an expression exactly like the one Emily was wearing now. Gratitude pregnant with shame. And you know what? After that day, Dana Vandorn never called me a dyke again.

"Are you a lesbian?" Emily asked.

Had I been thinking out loud?

She was standing in pasties and a black thong. Her dress and accessories lay in a damp puddle at her feet. "It's cool if you are," she said. "But I want to be clear that I—"

"I'm not a lesbian." It was just like a pretty girl to assume everyone wanted her.

"Are you sure?" she asked. "Because your clothes." She pointed to my white Hanes T-shirt and striped men's pajama bottoms.

"Positive. I'd probably get a lot more action if I was, but sadly no."

Satisfied, Emily pranced into my bedroom. "Do you have another pair of man pajamas for me to wear?" she asked, and then stopped in her tracks. "What the hell is that?" She pointed, horrified, at the rain bubble hanging down from the ceiling. "It looks like a tit." She jumped up on my bed and poked at the bubble with her pinky.

"Please don't touch it," I said.

"Look, it's even got a little nipple. We should stick it with a pin and milk it."

"I said don't touch it!"

I tossed a clean pair of pajamas at her and went to the kitchen to let her get dressed in private.

This was so not the tightwad bitch I knew from the office. I couldn't get over the fact that she'd actually used the word *tit*. I returned to the bedroom carrying the Jameson and two souvenir shot glasses.

Emily tilted her head at me and frowned. When she blinked, her blond bangs caught onto the tips of her eyelashes. "How old are you?" she asked. "Are we on spring break in Fort Lauderdale? Don't you have any rocks glasses?"

I dashed back to the kitchen and returned with the only other glassware I owned besides coffee mugs—old jam jars with the labels torn off.

"That'll do," Emily said, unscrewing the cap from the whiskey.

I also brought out my coveted box of Thin Mints from the

freezer, a sure way to impress any houseguest—not that I was trying to impress Emily Johnson, but still.

"Want one?" I asked, holding an icy-cold cookie out toward Emily.

She shook her head no, but I noticed her smile.

"You live here alone?" Emily scanned my cramped yet sparsely furnished space. "I figured," she added, before I could answer. She pulled her golden hair back into a ponytail. "You seem like the loner type. It's probably because you have low self-esteem."

Why exactly had I let this girl in from the rain? She was a textbook example of why I never invited anyone over.

As Emily got drunk, her eyelids grew heavy and her speech pattern slowed, but she didn't get any friendlier, as some people do. "You shouldn't feel self-conscious about being a thirty-year-old assistant," she said. "At least you're good at it. Not everyone could handle how demeaning it is."

Thanks, I thought. This was the Emily Johnson version of a compliment.

"So what's your deal?" I asked, once I sensed she was inebriated enough. (I'd been waiting for her to become inebriated enough to ask.) "If you're as broke as you say you are, then what's with all the fancy clothes and jewelry? How do you pay for it all?"

Emily brought her Connecticut lockjaw back into play for her response. "I live by the kindness of others," she said. "The kindness of men."

Pure Hollywood. I countered with my best Blanche DuBois impression. "Whoever you are," I drawled with a Southern accent, brandishing my whiskey like a prop, "I have always depended on the kindness of strangers."

Emily lifted her eyebrows, bleary-eyed. "I don't know what the hell that was, but please don't ever do it again."

"Sorry." I set my glass back onto the nightstand.

I was finding Emily's sense of humor difficult to pin down. I'd heard she'd gone to Harvard, but that couldn't have been true. No one familiar with the *Harvard Lampoon* would have scoffed at a literary reference that way. Not to mention the fact that Emily was basically a professional con woman.

"Where did you go to college again?" I asked, with a bit too much nonchalance.

"When a man's kindness comes up short," Emily said, irrespective of my question, "and I don't have it in me to drive all the way to my parents' house, I sleep in the back of the Range Rover. Even that was a gift."

"Some dude gave you a car?"

"Do you understand that a Range Rover isn't just *a car*? It's a one-hundred-K full-size luxury SUV." Emily reached over me to refill her glass. "The guy who gave it to me was a famous plastic surgeon. After we broke up I tried to sell it, but it turned out to be a lease, so it's mine for another year."

"Can't you just get one of these dumb guys to pay off your debt," I asked, "so we don't have to resort to grand larceny?"

"It doesn't work that way." Emily finally gave in and reached for a Thin Mint.

"I approved your first expense report today," she said, changing the subject. "Ten Gs, not a bad start. I like how you got really creative in the notes section and threw all caution to the wind in terms of attaching receipts."

Remembering the money made my stomach lurch. Sweet

Jesus, Mary, and Joseph (this was my mother's voice in my head now, not Robert's), how had I gotten myself into this? This was so not me. I didn't even download music illegally. I'd never in my life ingested an illicit drug. I crossed the street only at crosswalks. And you know what else? It was true that I didn't have many friends, as Emily so assiduously pointed out, but that was because I didn't really like people all that much. Other people were usually more trouble than they were worth, so I preferred to be alone. Yet here I was having a slumber party with one of the stars of *American Hustle*. She was in my bed!

Emily pointed her cookie up at the ceiling rain bubble. "Think it'll pop?"

Hell is other people.

In my mind I recited a whiskey-infused poem: *What happens to a rain bubble deferred? Does it just sag like a heavy load? Or does it explode?*

The tribulations of being a former English major.

"I kind of hope it pops," Emily said. "Even though it'll make a huge nasty mess."

4

In the weeks that passed from that first night Emily Johnson knocked on my door until the morning Margie Fischer cornered us, I learned a number of things. I learned how easy it is to acquire a calculating blond girl as your roommate, especially one who doesn't pay rent and likes to boss you around. I learned that pretty blond girls don't always wake up so pretty, and in the evenings they often have gas. And finally, I learned that Emily Johnson, the portrait of popularity, was secretly as friendless as I was—otherwise why else would she be spending so much time with me all of a sudden?

The air mattress had just appeared on the floor one day, wedged between the radiator and my dresser, fully inflated, covered in pink sateen sheets and a white comforter. But I still woke up most mornings to find Emily sleeping beside me like a sneaky pet, her bony elbow or knee digging into my side.

I was supposed to be an island. An island unto myself, like John Donne famously said, or was it Buddha? John Donne might have said no man is an island, but whatever, either way, I was not into having somebody else around all the time—somebody who tried to ride the train with me to work every morning and who interrupted me, without fail, every time I settled in at night to catch up on the latest episode of something on HBO GO. "Who's that?" Emily would ask, commandeering my bowl of popcorn. "Why's he so mad?" "What's with all the bad wigs on this show?"

"Shouldn't we avoid showing up to work together?" I would argue. "Wouldn't it be better to avoid being associated with each other in any way?"

I even tried: "If you start watching this show now, you're going to get a major spoiler."

But Emily wasn't worried. I was the worried one.

Emily wanted to talk about it constantly—what she adoringly referred to as our *scheme*, like it was our love child, like we were its baby mamas. She was all *us*es and *we*s, cooing googly-eyed at her rapidly dwindling student-loan balance.

It occurred to me (probably much later than it should have) that it was highly unlikely that Emily would let me put a stop to the *scheme* even after the last of her debt was paid off.

But it turned out not to matter, because Margie Fischer happened.

The morning that Margie Fischer cornered us, Robert was really in a huff. Around eleven a.m. he screamed to me from his office in a tone of voice that could only be called desperate, while pantomiming a drinking motion with his hand. He pointed at red-faced Glen Wiles, who was seated across from him perched forward in his chair, poised to have a heart attack at any moment, and then at himself.

"With lime," he mouthed through the glass walls of his office. That meant tequila. Before noon. It was going to be a long day.

A lesser man than Glen Wiles would have crumbled beneath the stress of such a meeting, but fortunately Wiles, like Robert, thrived on pressure, ambition, and cutthroat competition. On money, basically. So much money. Glen Wiles was a blundering brute, whereas Robert was a stickler for good manners, but aside from that, they were pretty much on the same page. Politically, they were two sides of the same coin, and that coin had better be free of government regulation of any kind.

When I brought them their drinks Robert had been talking about the islands—which he abruptly stopped doing the moment I entered the room.

"Thank you, Tina," he said, and then waited for me to exit before finishing his sentence.

I didn't understand half of what upset Robert about *the islands* on a daily basis, but taxes were his only true archenemy—that much I understood. Reporters from the liberal papers were always criticizing Robert for his "offshore tax havens" and "abuse of tax loopholes," so I knew not to discuss the Caymans or Bermuda with anyone. I'm pretty sure it was in my employment contract that just uttering the words *Cayman Islands* or *Bermuda* in a voice louder than a whisper could get me fired immediately.

I returned to my desk, watching the tiny rainbow speckles in the carpet, imagining myself as one of those hear-no-evil monkeys with his nimble monkey thumbs lodged in his ear holes. A g-chat message from Emily was waiting for me when I sat down.

I have to talk to you about Kevin Handsome, she'd written.

And when I hadn't written back, she'd added: *Seriously.*

Almost immediately Kevin then g-chatted me. *Hiya.*

Hiya, I wrote back, as I always did.

Then Emily chatted again. *I won't be ignored.*

I blocked her because this was more social multitasking than a woman no longer in her twenties could handle, but a second later my phone started to ring.

"I'm going to kill you," I said aloud while reaching over to smack the silence button—but my fingers came to a halt. It wasn't Emily. My caller ID informed me of the worst: it was Margie Fischer.

Margie Fischer was the Titan Corporation's long-suffering head of accounting. She controlled Titan's purse strings. That was her job, watching the numbers, and everyone did their best to stay out of her way (even Robert, I was pretty sure). Margie was gruff and couldn't have cared less what was appropriate in terms of social interaction, which made people very nervous. You could never be sure what would come out of her mouth, but more often than not, it would be a scolding of some sort. Once she'd caught me in the Titan cafeteria taking a whiff of the half-and-half before pouring it into my coffee and she boomed from behind me, "What are you sticking your nose in that for!"

I stuttered an explanation of how I was only checking to make sure it was fresh, but Margie wasn't having it.

"You think anybody wants to use that now that you've stuck

your face into it?" Her voice was like a cannon blast. Heads from as far away as the action station turned.

Never one to think clearly under pressure, the best defense I could come up with in the moment was, "Nobody but me uses the half-and-half anyway. Everyone around here uses skim."

Margie's face dropped.

This was the absolute wrong thing to say for a slew of reasons, not the least of which was that Margie, who had in fact been waiting for the half-and-half, was on the heavy side. A less-polite person might describe her as *very fat*. I wouldn't have dreamed of calling Margie fat to her face, or even behind her back—but I may as well have done just that with my half-and-half comment. She'd had it in for me ever since.

And now she was calling me for no good reason I could think of.

Shit. Shit. Shit.

I pressed my desk-phone's mute button ever so gently and watched the accusatory red light above the keypad blink on and off like a soundless alarm. I must not have moved or breathed for a full minute after the blinking stopped because I was light-headed and seeing spots when my cell phone's vibration snapped me back to reality.

It was a text message from Emily: *Margie Fischer from accounting jst called me. We're fkd.*

I immediately texted back: *What did she say?*

Emily wrote: *I didn't answr.*

So how do you know we're fkd? I was about to write back, but of course we were. How could we not be? If there was anyone at

Titan capable of figuring out our expense account scheme, it was Margie.

Kevin's chat momentarily averted my attention: *Coffee break later today?*

Then a burly voice behind me said, "Knock knock."

My cell phone was still in my hand. Margie pointed at it with her thick, stubby pointer finger. "You must be texting with Emily," she said. "Is that why neither of you could answer your desk phones?"

I slipped my cell into my bag and glanced quickly at Robert, who was still busy barking at Wiles in his office, then swiveled my chair away from him to face Margie. "Hi there," I said as cheerfully as I could while resisting my gag reflex. "What can I do for you?"

I guessed Margie Fischer was probably in her sixties, but it was difficult to tell because she dressed like an old Jewish man from Long Island, which adds a decade no matter what your age.

"I was calling to confirm our lunch date today at Michael's," she said. "Is one o'clock still good for you and Emily?"

I swallowed hard. My cell phone kept vibrating inside my bag. I could only imagine all the *WTFs* Emily had written.

Margie's thick gray hair was pulled back in a low ponytail that was so tight, the skin of her face was pulled back with it. The way she was hovering over me now I couldn't help but think of a sumo wrestler. A smiling Jewish sumo wrestler in high-waisted pleated khakis.

"Lunch?" I asked.

"Yeah, lunch. Unless you'd rather I speak to Robert directly about his T & E reports."

Still smiling.

"Tina!" Robert called to me from his office. He held up his empty glass and shook it back and forth.

I swiftly rose from my chair. "Emily and I will see you there at one."

"KEEP IT TOGETHER, FONTANA," Emily said. "We have to stick together; we have to deny everything." We were marching down Sixth Avenue on our way to meet Margie for lunch. Emily was in a pink Stella McCartney dress and matching heels and I was in my usual pants from the Gap and a V-neck sweater over a button-down. I guess I shouldn't hold it against anyone who mistakes me for a lesbian, or an adolescent boy wearing a Catholic-school uniform.

"You could have at least changed into something less designer," I said to Emily. "Didn't you have anything from the Gap or Old Navy in your office closet?"

"I'm wearing a pair of your underwear that I'm pretty sure are Hanes Her Way," Emily said. "Does that count?"

When we arrived, the avian-looking hostess eyed me up and down and I could tell she was trying to figure out if I was someone famous. Only a very famous person would show up at Michael's in clothing so carelessly uncurated. I spotted Margie across a sea of power lunches, already working on some appetizers. She wiped her mouth with a cloth napkin and waved us over.

"Betty and Veronica," she called out. "Over here."

We walked toward her with our heads down, sat, and waited.

"Glad you could make it." Margie gestured to the appetizer plate in front of her. "Oysters and littleneck clams on the half shell. Help yourself."

A waiter wearing a black tuxedo jacket approached us and leaned in closer to me than any waiter I'd ever known. He had obviously been given instructions by the hostess to figure out if I was anyone worth sneaking a photo of. Emily and I each ordered a glass of wine and a house salad without looking at our menus.

Margie laughed and leaned back in her chair. "Would you believe I've eaten here only once before? Fancy place like this. Can't afford it. But today's a special occasion because I figure you'll be expensing this meal. Both of you."

There it was. She knew everything.

Her eyes bounced back and forth between Emily and me, eager for a reaction.

I didn't know what to say. But Emily as self-righteous WASP would not go down without a cornea-scratching, ponytail-pulling fight like those witnessed on field-hockey grounds across New England.

"I'm not sure what you mean, Margie," she said. "Do you care to tell us what this is all about?"

"You're not sure what I mean." Margie cocked one eyebrow up and looked at me. "She's not sure what I mean. Ha." She slammed one massive hand down on the table, causing all the glassware to rattle. "I mean you girls are stupid! How stupid can you be? And you just kept going."

"We were about to stop," I blurted out.

Emily shot me a look that promised she would murder me in my sleep later that night.

"We were just trying to pay off our student-loan debt," I said. "That's all."

"That's all?" Margie tilted her head.

The waiter appeared with our wine and some more appetizers. Grilled asparagus and an avocado salad.

Margie pulled both plates closer and dug in. "It's partly the generation you were born into, I don't envy you that. But you don't expect me to just turn my head and pretend I don't know what I know, do you?"

Emily uncrossed and recrossed her legs. "Okay, Margie, fine. What do you want then? You must want something or you wouldn't have brought us here."

"Do you even know what I do for the company?" Margie asked, ignoring Emily and pointing at me with her fork. "Aside from the general accounting. Aside from keeping the books clean and making sure nobody's stealing."

For a moment I thought Margie might spontaneously stab me in the face with her fork, and I was totally okay with it. I wanted her to, to take me out of this misery. What other way out was there?

"I also oversee all of Titan's charitable donations," she said, and then paused to slurp an oyster. "For tax breaks, that kind of thing. I used to be a grant writer, back when I thought all it took to change the world was to get enough good people to do something good. My parents instilled that in me; they were career activists, so it goes without saying they retired frustrated and penniless."

I wondered where Margie was going with this. Emily was right that she must have wanted something, or else we would have already been dragged out in handcuffs.

"Cut to the chase, Margie," Emily said. "How much will your silence cost?"

Margie cracked up laughing loud enough for a number of

finely groomed heads to turn and stare. "This one watches too many cop shows."

She leaned back in her chair again, then rocked herself forward and brought her voice down to a mannish whisper. "I don't want any money and you don't have any to offer me, princess. All you've got to offer is access."

The salads arrived, and for Margie, the waiter set down a grilled lobster.

"Ah, lobster," Margie said. "They say they're the cockroaches of the sea, but man-oh-Manischewitz are they delicious."

Emily and I left our salads untouched.

"First things first," Margie said. "I'm not part of this. I have enough hard evidence to put you both in jail tomorrow, so don't fuck with me. Being pretty isn't going to help you here. Understand?"

For a split second I was actually distracted and flattered by the fact that she'd implied I was pretty.

"You're not part of *what*?" Emily asked.

Margie smiled wide. "There's an assistant in Accounting, her name doesn't matter. She's the best kid I've ever known, smart as a whip. Works really, really hard, never had a break in her life. You're going to help her pay off her debt just like you've helped yourselves."

"How much?" I asked.

"Eighty thousand; a real bargain, considering she had no help from her parents. She's been dutifully making payments since graduation."

Emily's neck was speckling with hives as pink as her dress.

"You're insane. You think Robert Barlow isn't going to notice all this money disappearing?"

"You weren't so concerned about that when it was for your own benefit," Margie said.

"I was." I raised my hand. "That's why we were about to stop. I think Emily's right, this is going too far. And Robert doesn't deserve this."

"Robert," Margie said, "is a warmonger, neoconservative imperialist. He's a bully with no interest in helping anyone but himself. And more than all that, he's a thief. A bigger thief than any of us in a million lifetimes could ever be. Trust me, I know. I keep his books."

"I think you're exaggerating just a bit," I said, offended on Robert's behalf.

"Oh, you think so? You think I'm exaggerating?" Margie slid her plate in closer and cracked open her giant lobster. "Want to talk about his tax shelters?"

"Not really," I said.

"I didn't think so." Margie was acting smug, but she was wrong. In spite of what Robert's most vocal critics claimed, all of his island accounts were perfectly legal. He was just smarter than everyone else, and people resented him for it.

"Do you honestly think a man like Robert would do something as dumb as cheat on his taxes?" I said. "With so many people watching him?"

But Margie was finished with that argument. "Look," she said. "This is the deal I'm offering you. You do this for me or I turn you in. It's as simple as that."

I turned to Emily and had never seen her looking so pale beneath her suntan. "I really don't understand," she said. "Making us do this. What's in it for you?"

"Nothing," Margie said. "Can you imagine that?"

"There has to be something," Emily said. "Your assistant can't be that good."

Margie looked directly at me. "Because the game is rigged and nobody does anything about it; not to mention, I know you can get away with it. And I guess the honest-to-God truth is, I've always dreamed of being a class hero."

Then she let out a roaring burp for all of Michael's to hear.

5

THE NEXT MORNING, Emily and I both called in sick. Instead of facing the horror of going to work, we lay on my bed side by side in our pajamas, me in my leisurely stripes and she in her lace Chanel two-piece. Emily had trickled her stuff into my apartment from the back of her Range Rover little by little so that before I knew what hit me, "we" owned stemware, kept a hair dryer in the bathroom, and drank mimosas for breakfast.

"I know we're in a situation that will most likely lead to life in prison for both of us," Emily said, swirling the juice in her glass. "But can we talk about Kevin Hanson for just a minute?"

"What about him?"

Emily sat up. "He doesn't like me, no matter how much I flirt with him."

"You're twenty-eight years old," I said. "You're due. Humbling rejection comes with the Saturn Return; you'd better get used to it."

"You don't understand. I think he likes *you*, Fontana. He's seen us together and keeps asking about you."

The look we shared was one of mutual bewilderment, like we'd just encountered a talking cat or one of those Sudoku puzzles—or even something not so bafflingly Japanese. "That can't be right," I said. "He must need me for something, from Robert."

"I thought that, too, at first. But how would that explain his dis-interest in me?" Emily said it like the *dis* had been painfully extracted from the *interest*.

She had a point.

We both jumped at the sound of my buzzer, spilling a little mimosa over the side of our crystal flutes. I peered through the dusty horizontal bars of my venetian blinds just in time to catch a black Grand Marquis pull away from the curb. "I think the FBI is here," I said.

"When the FBI comes for us, they won't need to be buzzed in." Emily topped off her glass.

The buzzer rang again and it seemed useless to fight anything at this point, so I got up to see who it was.

A uniformed FedEx deliverywoman shoved an envelope into my chest. Then she held out a digital notepad for me to sign with a pretend pen. I initialed an illegible scribble-scrabble and carried the envelope back to my bedroom.

"Special delivery," I said, tearing it open. "No return address."

"Is it anthrax?" Emily asked, not bothering to raise her head from my pillow.

It was not. The envelope contained a stack of crisp white

papers—neatly collated and studiously stapled—photocopies of my and Emily's fake expense reports. Every single one. On top of the stack was a yellow sticky note that read: *In case you thought I might be bluffing.*

The note was handwritten by Margie; I could tell by the heavy-pressed wide loops. A spasm shot through my gut. "We are so screwed," I said. "We are so screwed!"

Emily tore the papers from my grasp, gave them a quick once-over, and set them aside. "Maybe not." She handed me my mimosa. "Think about it for a minute. With Margie in on this now . . ."

"There is no *this*," I said.

"I'm just saying, there's not really anyone left to catch us at this point. Not if we're careful. We could probably even—"

"No." I set the glass down on my nightstand. "No, no, no, no, no."

"You don't even know what I was going to say."

"Yes I do. And the answer is no."

"Consider the apartment we could get instead of this one." Emily was up on her knees now, tugging on my pajama shirt. "Bigger, better, sans rats." She banged on the wall with the palm of her hand and there was a claw-toed scurrying behind the drywall.

"We're not really a we," I said. "And this is *my* apartment."

"That hurts my feelings, Fontana, it really does."

"You don't have feelings."

Emily reached over me, apprehended my mimosa from the nightstand, and swallowed it down. "I would if I could afford psychotherapy. Or a weekly massage. Or a hot tub. I'd have lots of feelings then."

Observing the change in my expression, Emily paused. "I'm kidding," she said.

But I knew she wasn't really. I moved to the other side of the bed, like Emily's copious greed might be contagious.

"You got over seventy thousand dollars of student-loan debt to disappear," I said. "Do you understand how long it would have taken you to pay that back? You'd have been in dentures and a housedress by the time you paid that back. Platform shoes would have gone in and out of style, like, six times by then. Isn't that enough for you?"

"I don't think you really want me to answer that." Emily pointed her glass at the ceiling rain bubble.

I knew what she was up to. She took it for granted that with enough bullying and harassment, she could convince me of anything—but I wasn't really as weak as I appeared. I am from the Bronx, after all. I hail from a neighborhood where the local library had a metal detector, and a household where the heat was never turned up higher than fifty-three degrees in winter. I was raised by parents whose approach to discipline relied heavily on the level swing of a wooden macaroni spoon. So I could handle a little pestering from doll-eyed Emily Johnson without losing my will.

Sure, the part of Bridgeport where Emily grew up was known for its high frequency of muggings, violent crimes, and easy accessibility to drugs. And her childhood home did get broken into by that meth head that one time. But she was still softer than I was.

"I'm just saying." Emily adjusted her timbre—she was shooting for reasonableness now. "It wouldn't take that much money to significantly raise us up, you know, to a position of real self-sufficiency."

I reclaimed my empty crystal flute and held it out to Emily for a refill. "I have no intention of going to prison because you want to live like a Kardashian, so put it out of your mind. We'll help Margie's assistant, whoever she is. We'll pay off her debt—it'll take a few weeks, maybe a few months—and then this will all be over. For real this time."

Emily smirked as she filled my glass to its brim. "We'll see."

"We're stopping once we get Margie off our backs," I said. "I'm serious."

"We'll see," she said again.

But we would not see. I admit that Emily was growing on me, or maybe it was just that I'd gotten used to having her around, but I wasn't going to budge on this. I wasn't about to lose sight of the fact that as white college graduates living in New York, poor and disillusioned as we were with our negative net worth, we were still relatively high up on the socioeconomic food chain. If I learned anything of value at NYU, it was that. So, no, Emily would not convince me to keep this scam going so she could have a weekly massage and a hot tub. If I lost my new best / only friend over it, so be it. At least I'd still have what was left of my dignity.

Emily fluffed the pillows behind her and propped one at the back of her neck. "So what are you going to do if Kevin asks you out?" she asked.

"Do you think that's a real possibility?" I inched a bit closer in from the small corner of the mattress that still belonged to me. "Should I be preparing for that?"

"Yeah, preparing." Emily outstretched her legs, lifting one, pointing and flexing her toes to check her pedicure, and then the other. "You should be stocking up on bottled water and duct-taping the windows."

Emily was missing my point. Kevin was a Titan lawyer. He worked with Glen Wiles.

I leaned over the side of the bed to retrieve Margie's photocopies from where Emily had dropped them. "With all this going on"—I shook the papers at Emily—"you think it's wise for me to go out with Kevin?"

Emily checked her manicure then, one fingernail at a time. "You're forgetting that Kevin is also by far the best-looking man who'll ever be interested in you in your entire life, so if I were you, I'd take what I could get when I could get it. Now give me those." She flicked her fingers at Margie's photocopies, which I dutifully handed over.

She rose from the bed, papers in hand. "Let's go burn these on the stove right now."

"There's no gas." I followed behind her, toward the kitchen. "It got turned off."

"Seriously?" Emily turned around on me, inexplicably incredulous.

"I didn't pay the bill."

"What if I wanted to heat up some soup or something?" Emily said.

And then we both burst out laughing. For whatever reason, Emily standing over a hot stove, stirring a steaming pot of Campbell's minestrone, was the most hilarious and unlikely image in the world.

"I'm sure we've got a match somewhere in this place," I said, wiping the laugh-tears from my eyes. I appreciated the momentary reprieve from our humorless reality: that we were in fact in a situation that would most likely lead to life in prison for both of us. If the burning of documents didn't tip us off, nothing would.

6

It was the tail end of a blessedly uneventful week when I noticed that Robert had taken to expensing his shoe-shines. Was he testing me? Perhaps he was reassessing my loyalty to him or my talent for creative nonfiction. I would not fail him now. *It's commensurate with Mr. Barlow's position to maintain freshly shined shoes*, I wrote in the comments section of the reimbursement form. It's not like Emily was about to reject any claim that I processed. I should have written: *It's commensurate with Mr. Barlow's position to have someone touch and rub and smack around his feet on the regular because he gets off on it, but like most men he will never admit this is the real draw of shoe-shines.*

Filing Robert's expense reports had taken on new meaning since Emily and I had teamed up. I began to see every one of Robert's company-paid-for $500 dinners, every pair of center-stage theater tickets, every penthouse hotel room, in terms of real paper money—which, for whatever reason, I'd never done before. Like: What I needed to pay the Roto-Rooter man to unclog my ancient toilet, Robert used to play a round of tennis at the country club. What I needed to buy a computer that didn't spontaneously shut itself down, he used to have his Mercedes waxed with a rare special formula that was probably composed of the placenta of baby dinosaurs. My monthly MetroCard was a single *RM*-monogrammed handkerchief, which Robert considered to be use-and-toss disposable.

The Oprah Magazine would refer to this as an "aha moment."

(Yeah, I read *O, The Oprah Magazine*, so what? We all need some sort of religion in our lives.)

As I scrolled through Robert's corporate-card-statement, I grouped his purchases by category: entertainment, travel, food, lodging, etc. It was a game of solitaire I could play in my sleep, but then a rogue charge suddenly caught my attention.

He dropped $2,400 at the Bel Air Pro Golf Shop?

I hated having to knock on Robert's door to question a transaction; it always felt like I was accusing him of something. But this wasn't the typical cost of a "golf meeting," which I was pretty sure Robert coined as a business-expense term in the first place—this was for stuff he bought in the shop. It might appear suspicious if I *didn't* question him about it.

I shot a look to his office. He was watching the wall of flatscreens across from his desk and he was alone, for once not on the phone. I had to go now.

"Um, excuse me, Robert . . . ," I said, entering invisibly and pointing to the charge, which I'd highlighted in the statement printout. "Does this look right to you?"

"Yes," Robert said. "That was my golf meeting with Gary from the West Coast office. I forgot to have my clubs and shoes sent over from the hotel so I had to buy a new set."

"Of course." I nearly bowed and crept back to my desk.

Of course? Really, Tina? Do you hear yourself?

Something had been stirred in me that I'd never felt before. Rather than going back to the hotel, or even sending a lackey back to the hotel, he'd just bought a whole new set of golf clubs? What the—

Hiya, Kevin chatted. *Lunch?*

I took a deep breath. *Sure. Meet you down there in five?*

How about out front?

Wait. What? Like leave the building?

It's sunny out today, he wrote, followed by a smiley face, which gave me pause. I was all for gender equality and all that, but let's put it on the record here that no self-respecting man should implement the smiley or any emoticon, ever.

! I wrote back. *Ok.*

This is going to sound crazy, but I'd never seen Kevin outside in the light of day before. When we came face-to-face in front of the building, his eyes did this sparkly thing that reminded me of the attractive vampire from *Twilight,* and for a few seconds I was rendered utterly speechless. He wasn't wearing his suit jacket and his shirtsleeves were rolled up the way Robert kept his, except Kevin's arms were a golden brown with just the right amount of dark hair covering them. The sun also brought to light that I had a ketchup stain on the front of my pants from yesterday's hamburger.

"You okay?" Kevin asked. "You look a little confused."

I nodded.

He started walking forward and I followed. "What do you think of burgers and shakes from Lucky's?" he asked.

I think I'm in love, I thought.

We took our food order to go, in greasy paper bags, and walked across Columbus Circle to Central Park. He helped me up the giant prehistoric-looking rock just off the playground and shooed away some bratty kids having a water pistol fight. It was all too good to be true.

"Is this an occasion of some sort?" I asked, unfolding the waxy wrapping on my burger.

"No, not really." He was already chewing his first massive bite. How did guys do that? I was no slouch when it came to rushing greasy meat into my mouth and he still had me beat by a solid thirty-five seconds.

"Not *really?*" I said.

"No, I just . . ."

Here it comes, I thought. *The part where I find out what he wants from me.*

"Emily Johnson," he said. "She . . ."

I knew it. He was intimidated by Connecticut Barbie and was calling on fainthearted Skipper for assistance. I wanted to stand up on that brontosaurus rock, raise my fists, and scream out all the way to Sheep Meadow: I knew it, you predictable motherfucker!

"She told me she's been staying with you," he said, staring down at his fries. "Which I found surprising because Emily can be kind of . . ."

He was fiddling with his food the way guys who are sexually frustrated peel at the labels of their beer bottles. I took this for a tell: he wanted to bone Emily.

"Well," he said, fiddling on. "From my perspective, it wouldn't seem like you two would be friends, but I guess I was wrong about that."

"You wanted to sit down to lunch so you could unravel the mystery of my and Emily's friendship?" I asked, sounding really bitchy.

"Ha." His laugh was perfect, damn him. "No, I guess it just made me realize that I don't know you that well." He raised his eyes to mine. "But do I really need a reason to lure you out here into the fresh air and sunlight?"

I turned away for fear of being compelled, seductive vampire style. "We're working on a project," I said. It was the best lie I could come up with on the spot. "That's why we've been spending so much time together."

"Oh." He pushed his soda straw in and out of its plastic lid, causing it to squeak like a slide whistle, and this was somehow not that annoying coming from him. "A project for work?" he asked.

"Not really."

"Not really?"

"No," I said. "It's not. It's a . . ."

I was scrambling. If it wasn't a project for work, then what was it? A book group? A knitting circle?

"It's sort of a . . ."

For the love of God, Tina. Think.

"It's sort of a *consciousness-raising* project?" I said.

A little background: In college, like many freshmen venturing into the liberal arts for the first time, I was besotted by electives with titles like "Feminism and the Body," "Passionate Politics: Emotions and Social Movements," and "Gentrification and Its Discontents." A girl I met in "Gender, Race, and Class," who wore a leather corset as a shirt, convinced me to join the Women's Center. (Technically, it was the Womyn's Center, but let's not even.) There, flannel-clad girls with names like Andy and Grover introduced me to private-school-tuition-worthy terms like *hegemony*, *social constructionism*, and *consciousness raising*. Finally, this hard-earned education was paying off.

"Consciousness raising about what?" Kevin asked.

Robert's new set of golf clubs popped into my mind.

"Inequality, mostly," I said, like a true expert on the subject.

Kevin stared at me for a moment and I could almost see the preconceived notions he had of me shifting around in his beautiful brain.

"You okay? You look a little confused." I was mimicking the crack he'd made at me in front of the Titan building, but I don't think he got it.

"I'm impressed," he said. "What sort of inequality are you focusing on?"

"All kinds." I stuffed my mouth full of french fries.

"Is it a nonprofit?"

"Yup. Exactly."

"You're really keeping this close to the vest, aren't you?" He said it lovingly, or I would have struck back at him with my scorpion claw.

"It's still in the early stages," I said, after swallowing my fries. "I guess I just don't want to jinx it." Which made no sense at all, but Kevin, well-bred as he was, politely replied, "I get that. That makes total sense."

Brought up by animals as I was, I lunged at the chance to impolitely change the subject. "So what was it like growing up in

Massachusetts? I bet your parents are really proud of you. Being a lawyer is second only to being a doctor, right? And you don't have to be around germs."

"Massachusetts?" Kevin appeared perplexed. "I'm from DC."

A piece of hamburger bun caught in my throat. "Sorry, I must be mixing you up with someone else." *Like the Kennedys.*

He kindly ignored the grotesque choking sound that escaped from my mouth. "To be honest, my parents don't love that I've chosen to work for the Titan Corporation, and I don't either. I'd much rather move out of the corporate world and into public service—I'd love to work for a nonprofit. But I'd have to take a significant pay cut, and that's not really an option right now."

What was this? Was Kevin Handsome snowing me to make himself appear more human? My cell phone vibrated in my bag before I could decide.

It was Robert. "Barlow can't find me anywhere," I said, reading his text. "He's not used to me leaving the building. I should get back."

"Doesn't someone cover for you when you're out?" Kevin asked.

"An intern. But she's not me." I said this with the utmost pride, because when you're the second-most-pecked chicken in the coop, you have to take pride where you can find it.

This was a common Barlowism, by the way, explaining social hierarchy and laws of dominance in terms of farm animals, namely fowl.

Kevin stood up and gathered our trash. "Maybe we can have dinner sometime."

I wasn't certain I'd heard him right. He'd been bending down to grab a napkin that had caught in the breeze, but just in case, I said, "Sure."

Back at the office, it turned out all Robert needed was for me to remind him of the name of the restaurant "with the good view, on top of that hotel."

It was Asiate, at the Mandarin Oriental, and he asked me this at least once a week. If only my useless fill-in (*dumb as a prairie dog,* Robert might say) could have gotten it together and remembered such critical information, I wouldn't have had to cut short my lunch with Kevin. Fortunately, I'd brought my leftovers back to the office with me.

I reached into the now fully-greased-over paper bag for a cold french fry. It was just as well that lunch got abbreviated, I thought. It could have only gone downhill from there.

LATER THAT NIGHT, I was sitting on my bed, eating pad thai out of the carton with chopsticks from the Chinese restaurant (my favorite Thai place never gave out chopsticks; apparently real Thai people don't use them) and flipping through the pile of mail that had accumulated on my nightstand, a paper mountain of bills and useless notifications, when I came across an envelope from my old friend Sallie—Sallie Mae, the former title holder of my student-loan debt. Who knew how long this letter had been there, buried between various credit card offers and multiple supplications from the World Wildlife Fund.

I was alone in the apartment—Emily was out on a date—but I

still set my chopsticks down like a secret I didn't want anyone to hear before slitting the envelope open.

It was a letter of congratulations, informing me that my debt had been paid in full. It boldfaced my final statement balance: double zeros.

Well I'll be damned, Sallie Mae.

I released a shocking and spontaneous orgasmic breath. It wasn't right, how thrilled I was at the sight of those zeros. The sensation that washed over me was like nothing I'd ever felt before, except maybe, appropriately, when I found out I'd gotten into NYU.

I returned the letter to its envelope and set it down onto my nightstand, then inexplicably stashed it beneath my pillow.

It was done. I had a clean slate. A new start, like I was eighteen and hopeful again, but this time I was smarter—too smart to sign my life away to a school I knew nothing about.

The only reference I'd had for NYU when I decided I had to go there was that Theo Huxtable went there in season five of *The Cosby Show*. I could have chosen a cheaper school, like my parents wanted me to. But cost was no issue, my Doc Marten–boot–stomping self insisted. This was my college education we were talking about! I wanted to go to the best school I could get into, the school I'd seen on television.

Not since then had I been this free.

Emily's key rattled in the front-door lock, so I returned to my dinner and tried to appear normal, or at least regular. My mouth was full of noodles when she appeared in the bedroom doorway, kicked off her high heels, and said, "I brought you a hamburger."

I glanced down at my mostly eaten pad thai and attempted an

instant calculation of how disgusting it would be to eat both. Then I recalled the hamburger I'd already eaten for lunch and had to re-calculate.

"My date sucked," Emily said, crossing the room. "And I have no intention of ever seeing that jerk again, so when he went to pee, I told the waitress to give me a burger to go."

Emily dropped a plastic satchel that looked more like a swag bag from the Oscars than a restaurant's to-go carton onto my nightstand. "It's actually quality meat, so you'll probably think it tastes weird."

She sat beside me and started removing her jewelry, piece by shiny piece. "What's wrong with you? You look like you're hiding something, or like you just had sex. What are you hiding?"

How did she already know me so well? I pushed my Thai food aside and allowed myself one nibble of burger, seeing as it was still warm. "I got a letter confirming the untimely death of my student loan."

Emily's doll eyes popped. "Let me see it. I bet I'll be getting one of those too, soon. When I do, we should frame them side by side and hang them on the wall like diplomas."

I retrieved the letter from beneath my pillow to show her. "My diploma is buried under a dozen rolls of wrapping paper in the bottom drawer of my parents' china closet."

Emily put her hand on my shoulder, squeezing as she scanned the letter from top to bottom. "This is way better than a diploma anyway," she said. "I'll get the champagne."

"Hang on a sec." I caught her by the wrist. "You've still never told me, where did you go to college?"

"Harvard," she muttered, yanking her wrist free and turning quickly away. She scurried to the kitchen.

"How did you get into Harvard?" I called out after her, striving not to put too much emphasis on the *you*.

Emily returned with a bottle, not bothering with glasses. "Hartford. H-a-r-t-f-o-r-d," she said, spelling it out for me. "It's in Connecticut."

I should have known. Only Emily Johnson would choose a college based on its likelihood to induce favorable misunderstanding.

"You know everyone at Titan thinks you went to—"

"I know." She uncorked the bottle.

"What was your major?"

"Don't get me started." She took a long slug of champagne and handed it off to me. "I wanted to be an actress; that was my biggest mistake. But who knows, maybe there's still hope for my starring role in *Busted: A True Crime Story of Not Getting Away with It*."

My stomach churned, not from the Thai food mixed with my second burger of the day, mixed with champagne, but from the realization that we were in fact an Oxygen network original series waiting to happen.

"Do you think it's our own fault?" I asked. "That after all these years, we're still just assistants?"

"You've got a few years on me, don't forget."

"Two. Two years doesn't even qualify as a few."

"But you're thirty, and that counts extra."

"I guess it's all our own fault," I said.

But wasn't there something wrong with the fact that I'd still have been paying for a college education that got me nowhere if I hadn't stolen my way out of it? When all my life I'd done every-thing I was told?

My phone bleeped before I got very far in hypothesizing an answer. It was a text: *Got your number from Emily. Hope you don't mind. Just wanted to say lunch was fun, how about dinner this Saturday night?*

"Oh," Emily said. "I forgot to tell you something."

"You gave Kevin my phone number?" It occurred to me that I was yelling. "Kevin asked for my phone number?"

"I know, right?" Emily shook her head in disbelief. "Though he's kind of a pussy for not asking you for it himself, don't you think?"

I was feeling a feeling, but I wasn't sure which one. Shock? Doubt? Diarrhea?

"What are you waiting for?" Emily said. "Text him back before he comes to his senses."

"I don't know, Em. Don't you think this has prison stripes writ-ten all over it? What if he starts asking questions?"

"You're impossible." Emily grabbed my phone and texted something with the lightning quickness of a late-millennial, then tossed my phone onto the bed.

I scrambled for it. "What did you write?"

Emily smirked. "I wrote, 'Let's skip dinner and get right to dessert.'"

"Are you kidding me?" I retrieved the phone and tapped furi-ously at its screen. "Is that supposed to be sexual innuendo?"

She was messing with me. What she actually wrote was: *Yes!*

"Damn it, Emily, you used an exclamation point? I would have never used an exclamation point there. Of all punctuation, it's the neediest."

"You're so lucky I entered your life," she said. And then waited a beat. "It's the only way we're gonna get Kevin to enter you. Right here!" She raised her hand for a high five.

"Or turn me in," I said, passing on the hand slap.

7

What do you wear to dinner with the perfect man?

I Googled just that, but the top hits were all from ask-any-idiot-anything dot com, and they all suggested "comfort" as the most important component of a proper outfit, which I wanted to be true from the bottom of my heart but knew had to be false. My striped manjamas, as Emily called them, could not be the correct attire for my date with Kevin, so I went with my go-to black dress, which the salesgirl at Forever 21 had assured me was right for any occasion.

Hair down. Contacts, not glasses. Makeup? Regular. I'd learned the hard way on previous dates that trying something fancy with my makeup always ended in disaster. Keep It Simple Stupid, or KISS, which was a rule I also applied to kissing itself, though it was doubtful tonight would end anywhere near the arena of tonsil hockey.

I carefully applied my mascara with my mouth open, as I always did. (I'm not the only one who engages in this nonsensical act, am I?) No need for blush since I was already a little anxious-pink beneath the surface. For a full-blooded Italian, half-Sicilian on my mother's side, I was implausibly pale and quick to go red. If not for my dark brown hair, dark brown eyes, and penchant for rigatoni, I could have easily been mistaken for Irish—or, more likely, what some nefariously referred to as Black Irish.

My cell phone bleeped and I was sure it was Kevin canceling, but it was only Emily wishing me luck. Actually, her exact text was: *don't fk this up*. But I knew what she meant. There was something suspect about this night, something I was missing and therefore bound to fk up. This may sound to you like the idling hum of low self-esteem, but it wasn't. It was an indisputable fact that Kevin Hanson and I were not on an equal plane of hotness. Every eligible woman and half the eligible men at Titan would have entered the Hunger Games for the chance at a date with him. Why was he pursuing *me*?

We met at Nougatine, which Emily had explained to me was "the more casual sister of Jean-Georges," which sounded not so impressive to me at first. Was I not good enough for the fancier, more formal sister? Should I read into the fact that Kevin had opted for the Edith Crawley restaurant over the Lady Mary? But Emily assured me that Nougatine was in fact a respectable and highly regarded first-date choice—and no, its name had nothing at all to do with the nougat of a Snickers bar.

Kevin was waiting out front when I arrived, which I appreciated because I was five minutes early. I would have been fifteen minutes early had I not ducked into a Duane Reade to check my hair in the cosmetics-aisle mirror. I also helped myself to a squirt of hand lotion, so what?

Kevin was wearing a tailored blazer over crisp jeans and a dress shirt. He waved when he saw me walking up the block, and I waved back, and then there was that terrible five or six seconds where you don't know what the hell to do with yourself before you reach the person. I tried to smile wide enough so he could see it and fought the urge to do something goofy—a battle I lost when I goofily brought my hands to my mouth and called out, "Helloooooo," as if he were very far away.

He played along, waving his arms to and fro high above his head and shouting, "I'm over here!"

This was a good man.

After we were seated and starting on some wine, Kevin ordered for us—from the tasting menu, which turned out to be an unexpectedly large amount of food considering it sounded like a practice dinner before the real one.

The last guy I had gone on a date with (more than a year ago, a guy I met at my corner bodega while debating between a pint of Cake Batter Ben & Jerry's and Birthday Cake Oreos) had brought me to a restaurant / bowling alley called Bowlmor. Yes, it was a restaurant literally inside a bowling alley. We could hear pins crashing around while we chewed. He did not pay for my chicken wings and then got pissed when I beat him by a spare. So you could definitely say I was trading up.

Kevin's dark hair looked so thick and healthy beneath the restaurant's fine lighting that it took all the self-control I had to not reach out and run my fingers through it. I wondered what he washed it with. Certainly not the no-frills brand I used. This had to be some sulfate-and-paraben-free stuff they didn't even carry at Duane Reade. And his teeth were so white and clean, and perfectly straight. I could have watched him eat for hours.

"So tell me more about this project of yours," he said, after plate number eleven was set down before us.

"Let's not talk about that," I replied, striving to appear coy.

"Are you kidding? That's all I want to talk about. I was just being polite by waiting till now to bring it up."

I giggled the way I hated when other girls did it. Between my first-date-with-a-beautiful-man jitters and the all-encompassing dread related to my recent embezzlement habit, I couldn't control any of the words or sounds coming out of my mouth.

"You're just trying to flatter me, aren't you, ha ha ha, no really though, let's not talk about that, tell me more about your folks. Are they still in DC?"

What was I saying? Folks? Why was I talking like Pa from *Little House on the Prairie*?

Kevin blinked his long eyelashes twice, maybe three times, in rapid succession and then nodded.

"What do they do?" I reached for my wine.

He craned his neck sideways and smiled at me. "Don't you know it's rude to ask?"

I was about to catapult into a motormouthed apology when Kevin said, "I'm kidding. It's fine. My father's also a lawyer, actually. So is my older brother. And my mother's in politics."

"Politics?" (Is it rude to ask one-worded questions that aren't actually questions?)

"She had been a social worker," Kevin said. "But she got frustrated and decided to take matters into her own hands."

"Is she, like, secretary, of state or something?"

"Ha." (That laugh of his. I could die.) "No, but she does work for the State Department, and people are always comparing her to Hillary Clinton. So I guess you can say I'm used to having a strong woman around telling me what to do."

I choked on my Chablis.

"Sorry," he said. "That was supposed to be a come-on, but it sounded more like I was flirting with my mother."

A come-on? Was he implying that I was a strong woman who would tell him what to do? Man, was he way off. My cheeks were turning red; I could feel them burning up, the bastards.

At least Kevin was also blushing. "Seriously though," he said, "I want to hear all about this nonprofit you're working on. Talking with you the other day reminded me how stupid my job is, and how much happier I'd be doing something meaningful."

"You do remember my real job is being Robert Barlow's slave, right?"

"Aside from that, though. You give a fuck." He stunned me with his sudden use of profanity. "That's not something I've found in most of the women I've met."

He was really going for it.

I smiled and looked down modestly.

"So come on," he said. "Tell me more about it."

When I looked up, he was pitched forward with his eyes wide. His whole demeanor seemed to be crying out, *Touch me, pet me, love me.* He was obviously a mama's boy and possibly part Labrador retriever, but so what? This guy really liked me, or the idea he had of me. I had to keep that idea alive.

"Well . . ." I found myself stuttering as I searched my brain for all those smart-sounding words I learned at NYU's Women's Center meetings. "The thing is, we, as in our generation, we've tried to do everything right but we're still . . ."

Kevin was holding his wineglass suspended in midair, so rapt he was by my manifesto.

". . . People say we're lazy and entitled. But the truth is, the deal we were promised growing up, if we work hard and get a good education, it's really not working out. The dream we were sold, and the job market we encountered . . ."

I was killing it and not in a good way, but Kevin didn't seem to notice.

He was nodding his moppy head, eyes intense, locked with mine.

". . . And what about the people who aren't even fortunate enough to go to college? How are they supposed to . . . if we're struggling this much, what about them? It's like, like institutionalized classism."

Aha. There we go. Good liberal-arts vocab word, *institutional classism*.

Kevin set down his wineglass and reached across the table for my hand. "I couldn't agree more. We are absolutely living in the midst of a new Gilded Age."

His hands were softer than mine, I'm not even kidding. And they smelled of . . . what was that? . . . Drakkar Noir? Hadn't anyone ever told him that was the scent of every girl's eighth-grade boyfriend?

"I'd love to get involved in some way," he said. "If there's anything I can do."

I had him, I really did, pubescent cologne and all. But no, he could not get involved. (*That dog won't hunt*, Robert would have said.)

I fiddled with my napkin.

"It's sort of my and Emily's thing right now," I said.

"Of course." Kevin's eyebrows settled in disappointment and then rose again in eager-for-purpose anticipation. "Though, you may need legal advice sometime."

God forbid, I thought, and then waved to the waiter for more wine.

8

I NEVER IMAGINED myself as someone who would be wined and dined by a man like Kevin Hanson. Then again, I never imagined myself as someone who could ever be blackmailed either, because didn't you have to have a terrible guilty secret in order to be a blackmailee? Who would have thought I'd have something more shameful to hide than the renegade hairs that sprouted on my chin every few days, or the way my breath smelled when I woke up, or that I sometimes ate a bag of Doritos for dinner?

But here I was, siphoning money to Margie Fischer to keep from being outed, just like I'd done for Emily, who—let's give credit where credit is due—was really the one to pop my blackmail cherry.

The process continued on in the same way: I would duplicate Robert's expense receipts and file them twice, once for him, and a second time for me, plugging in my own account information in place of his. Emily would approve the false receipts and issue me a reimbursement check, which I would then cash and hand-deliver to Margie, concealed in an interoffice delivery envelope.

Again, the secret to our success was Emily doing the approving in lieu of Mr. Bow Tie. And now with Margie involved, we had one more layer of protection—though *protection* feels like the wrong word. Margie was like a mad dog that might turn on you at any moment, if you looked it in the eye the wrong way, or if you happened to smell like a rib-eye steak or whatever.

This was not a lifestyle that suited me. I am in no way an adrenaline-seeker. I'm much more of an irritable bowel syndrome kind of gal, really. And rest assured, my bowels were highly irritated by all the stress. They'd become like the Jerry Seinfeld or Larry David of bowels.

Emily and I didn't know whose eighty thousand dollars of student-loan debt Margie was paying off, but we'd narrowed it down. Margie had three accounting assistants in her department: (1) a middle-aged woman with a penchant for flamingos (she had flamingo earrings, flamingo office supplies; her skin even emanated a pink Floridian hue), (2) a nerdy young Russian named Yevgeny, whom everyone lazily called Eugene, and (3) the Lean Cuisine Lady—the crackpot who sat alone in the cafeteria every day, tending to the separate sections of her plastic tray with such measured movements you could just tell she counted how many times she chewed each bite of baked chicken before swallowing it down.

Emily and I knew it had to be one of the women, and regardless of whether it was Flamingo or Lean Cuisine, we were sure she wouldn't be told a thing about where the money came from. Margie would probably just surprise her one day with a big check, like

Ed McMahon used to do for Publishers Clearing House. And then we'd all go our separate ways.

It was the Wednesday after my date with Kevin, just past noon, when I was in the D elevator on my way up to Margie's office, clutching to my chest an interoffice-mail envelope full of hundred-dollar bills. Aside from a few texts, I hadn't spoken to Kevin since he hailed me a cab outside Nougatine—after I'd declined his offer to have one more drink, and he leaned in (ostensibly to give me a kiss good night) and I instead shook his hand.

"Thanks for dinner," I'd said. "See you Monday."

I shook the man's hand.

After relaying this story to Emily, she asked: "Do you have some sort of brain damage? Did your parents hit you in the head with a frying pan when you were little?"

Even I had to wonder.

Naturally, I'd been dodging Kevin ever since, so when elevator D stopped on the way up to Margie's floor, it goes without saying that it was Kevin standing there when the doors opened.

"Well, hello," he said. "What are you doing traveling above the fortieth floor?" His eyes shot to the envelope I was hugging to my chest.

"Just making a delivery," I said.

"Isn't that what messengers are for?" He stepped inside and the doors sealed shut.

"Robert doesn't always trust the messengers," I said.

"Really? Even with all the cameras around?"

My bowels stirred.

"There's one now." Kevin pointed up at a convex lens on the

elevator's ceiling. "Smile." He pitched his head close to mine, like we were posing for a selfie.

Sweet Jesus, Mary, and Joseph, I was being careful enough, wasn't I?

The letter envelopes I used for the cash were the un-see-through kind, and I brought them from home already sealed—there was nothing suspicious about that, was there?

"This is you. Forty-two." Kevin woke me up to the fact that the elevator doors had opened again. "Be careful now; you're not accustomed to being up so high. Ha."

I stepped out soundlessly.

He was staying on to forty-three. "Talk later?" he said.

I nodded as he disappeared between the closing doors, wondering: was he trying to tell me something? All this talk of cameras and being careful.

I considered the envelope inside the envelope in my hands. It would only look more suspicious at this point if I changed my mind and returned to my floor without delivering it, right? So I forged ahead as planned to Margie's office; handed her the envelope; recited my line, "Robert would like you to look at these documents right away"; and then bolted back to the elevators, before she could get a word out in response.

Back on forty, the moment I stepped through the glass doors, I knew something was amiss. Desk after desk, cube after cube, in our open-office space had been abandoned. Computer monitors flaunted screen savers of aquarium fish and outer space. Desk phones blinked red with unheard messages. Only a few unimportant women remained working at their stations, along with a couple of interns. Then I noticed everyone else, fifteen or so guys, gathered around the big screen in the south conference room.

I should note here that the "few unimportant women" still at their desks were the other three women who worked on the fortieth floor besides me. None of them held any significant position of power, so they were as good as invisible in terms of access to Robert—or anything interesting going on in the conference room.

At first I thought it must have been a sporting event that had the guys so intrigued, but then I recognized one of the faces on-screen—it was Jason Dillinger, from our very own office. He was on one of those news shows where all the guests have totally opposite political views and they're just supposed to duke it out till one of them gets their mic cut.

Dillinger must have scored a point because Robert threw up his fist and the rest of the conference room cheered.

I paused to take in this scene for a moment because I'd recently finished binge-watching *Friday Night Lights* and was still particularly susceptible to the nuances of male bonding rituals. It was so clear to me (and perhaps only me) how every man in that conference room looked up to Robert, how they tried to talk like him, think like him. They rolled up their shirtsleeves to just below the elbow like he did, and wore their dress shoes, like him, without socks in the summer. When he threw up a fist, they cheered.

To the outside world, Robert had a terrible reputation. His ways of doing business were not always considered "politically correct" or "fair" or (if Margie Fischer was correct) "entirely legal." But in this office, he was a role model, a maker of men—good old-fashioned, quintessentially American men. Men like they just don't make 'em anymore.

Hats off inside. Tuck in your shirt. Hold a door. Know how to change a tire, and for Chrissakes change your own oil. No Titan man who worked directly under Robert would ever be found *sitting* on the subway when a woman, child, or elderly person was in view; in fact, he would most likely be found standing even if the entire car was empty.

To the outside world, Robert's traditional ways could be misinterpreted as sexist, but really it could all be boiled down to a single maxim: *Don't be a wuss.* And it applied to everyone across the board, man or woman. Genitalia aside, if you weren't self-sufficient, if you weren't tough (*tough as stewed skunk, tough as an old boot*), Robert had no time for you. Which I believed was why he'd taken a shine to me. I wasn't one to ask for help when I needed it, just like a good ol' boy.

Robert spotted me gawking at the conference room then and waved me over.

I stepped just inside the doorway.

"Will you order us some sandwiches from the Eye-talian place?" he asked. (He meant Mangia, the pasta and panini restaurant on West Fifty-Seventh Street.) And before I could even grab a pen and a piece of paper, the guys all started calling out their orders, most of which I already knew by heart anyway.

Mozzarella and tomato on a brioche roll for Hayes. Salami, provolone, and roasted peppers on a baguette for Cooper. Don't forget to say "no watercress" on McCready's smoked turkey on ciabatta. Dillinger, had he not been on television at the moment, would have wanted the herb-roasted chicken breast on Tuscan flatbread—just like Robert—except with tomatoes.

My college degree never covered this sort of material; there was no "Introduction to Remembering Breads, Toppings, and Condiments 101" at NYU, but it was cool—I could always recite a verse from Milton's *Paradise Lost* to impress the Mangia delivery guy if I wanted to.

I returned to my desk to place the order, and there I found a g-chat message from Kevin: *Another dinner date soon? I'll share all my secret camera knowledge if that sweetens the pot.* The message was followed by a winking smiley face that I did not like the looks of one bit.

Was I being paranoid or was Kevin trying to communicate to me—using a complicated flirtation code—that he had heard something, noticed something, or figured something out?

Just the thought was enough to make me forget if Evans wanted basil chicken salad or basil Parmesan chicken salad.

END OF DAY, Robert had Jason Dillinger in his office for a drink, to celebrate his successful television appearance. They were seated opposite each other on the living-room-like furniture across from Robert's desk—Dillinger sitting up straight and rigid on the couch, and Robert lounging all the way back in his armchair, with his legs crossed. On the glass coffee table between them, there was a crystal ice bucket that I could see needed refreshing. Robert had no patience for watery ice.

So I stepped in, said, "Excuse me," and reached for the bucket.

Robert was midsentence: ". . . and we put down new flagstone pavers and added lighting under the porch. It looks nice, real nice." Then he paused, like he'd just noticed I'd entered the room. "You've never been out to the ranch, have you, Tina?"

I hugged the sloshing ice bucket close to my chest. "No, I haven't."

No, I hadn't, but I'd heard all about it. Around the office, Robert's upstate ranch was spoken of in language so ardent and enthusiastic that, taken out of context, one might think it was hell on earth: *It's fucking sick. It's ridiculous. It'll make you want to kill yourself.* Of course, among the Titan men of the fortieth floor, this was the highest form of praise.

Unlike work parties, for which I always did the legwork, Robert's ranch get-togethers were all his own. They were special, coveted. And I probably don't need to tell you that Robert wasn't an all-for-one, one-for-all type. No. He'd pick and choose who got an invite, seemingly at random—some of the guys had been invited many times over, others never once—but as with everything Robert did, everyone assumed there was a cunning methodology to it. For this reason, an invitation to the ranch became just one more carrot for everyone to compete for.

"Well, why don't you come out this Saturday then?" Robert said. "I'm having a little barbecue. You can ride the train up with Dillinger and his wife. Do you . . ."—he stumbled on his own words for a moment—". . . have a significant partner?"

A significant partner? The phrasing alone reminded me how little Robert actually knew about me. It was easy to forget because I knew everything—literally everything—about him, right down to his underwear size (42–44) and his favorite sock brand (VK Nagrani).

"No," I said. "I'm alone, I mean, I—"

"You fly solo." Robert grinned. "All right then. So you'll ride the train with Dillinger and his wife."

"Okay," I said. "I'd love to. Thank you."

So bowled over I was by this surprise, this un-fucking-believable carrot dangled in front of my face, that I forgot for a moment that I was stealing from this man.

"You ever shot a gun, Tina?" Robert asked.

"A what?"

"Do you shoot?" He must have noticed a terrified look on my face because he added, "Not at people. I mean, skeet, cans."

"No," I said.

"Well I'm gonna teach you then. By the time I'm done with you, you'll be able to shoot out the eye of a needle."

"You'll love it," Dillinger said, never one to like being left on the outskirts of a conversation. "Robert taught me my first time out."

Kiss-ass.

"I can't wait," I said, and then just stood there awkwardly.

Robert's attention diverted to his phone, and I realized the ice bucket I'd been holding too close had seeped a wet island across the front of my white button-down.

"I'll be right back with fresh ice," I said, and made my escape.

9

JASON DILLINGER and his wife, Kathryn, sat facing me in our cozy Metro-North four-seater, so that I was moving backward. Dillinger had brown hair, brown eyes, and the palest, most translucent skin you've ever seen. He was tall, with long legs (thankfully hidden beneath powder-blue summer chinos) that took up all of what little floor space there was between us. Nobody in the office worked harder or longer hours than Dillinger, hence the never-seeing-the-sun thing. He was only thirty-five, but his interoffice competition was already complaining about how he was most likely to be Robert's successor.

"So this is your first one of these," he said, making meaningless conversation.

I nodded. "You've been before?"

"Three times. But this is the first time I'm bringing Kathryn."

Kathryn, who sat huddled against the window, was lost in her

Kindle and gave no reaction to the sound of her own name. She was good-looking, I'll give her that, like J.Crew-catalog-model good-looking. A surprising percentage of guys in the office had extremely attractive wives—wives who, as Emily would say, were not on an equal plane of hotness. It wasn't that these Titan men were wealthy, because most of them weren't, but working in media—news media especially—still maintained a certain cachet, in New York at least. Plus, nerdy guys were having a moment, weren't they? It was simply the right time in history to be a pale dude who wore glasses and had a really big brain.

"I was blown away the first time," said Dillinger, who at least had the decency to wear contact lenses. "You really get to see a new side of Barlow. Though, you probably know him better than any of us ever will."

"Probably," I said proudly, for this was the one thing I had on all the guys with hot wives in the office. My access to everything Robert.

"Got any good stories about him?"

Nice try, Dillinger. Of course I had good stories about him, but if I'd learned anything in my six years of servitude, it was discretion. Robert trusted me because I was good at keeping my mouth shut. (*No ten-gallon mouths around here.*)

However, I did keep in my conversational arsenal a few choice tidbits that I'd toss to the needy in moments such as these.

"Well, I do have one favorite story," I said, leaning in and lowering my voice in such a way that even Kathryn stirred. "Did you know he once got into a fight with George Clooney on a golf course?"

This was a safe story to tell, because I knew Robert loved people to know about it.

"I heard that once." Dillinger's pallid face pinked. "Is it true?"

I nodded. "Apparently, Clooney left a bunker unraked after he'd bumbled his shot, and Robert is a real stickler for smoothing out the sand. So he marched right up to Clooney and told him to get back over there and get to raking—and don't leave any furrows either."

I should mention here that when I first started working for Robert, I would spend my nights searching the Internet, diligently looking up all the words, names, and places he'd thrown at me during the day that I didn't understand. In time, I figured out how to talk about all the things Robert cared about. Golf, tennis, boating, Texas sports teams, luxury vacation spots, fine wines, and rare liquor. My knowledge was shallow, but it was enough to sound like I knew what I was talking about—which is all most people need anyway.

"So what happened?" Dillinger asked.

"What do you think happened?" This was the best part of the story. "Clooney got his ass over there and smoothed out the sand."

Dillinger shook his head, rosy with admiration. "I could totally see that happening."

"I know, it's so Robert," I said. "But obviously never repeat that."

"No, no, of course not." Dillinger leaned back, silently deciding who would be the first person he'd relay it to.

"You know," he said, "I asked Robert yesterday, what should we do if it rains today, because the forecast was predicting a storm, and he answered, matter-of-factly, 'It doesn't rain when I have a barbecue.' Then I remembered the last three times I came out were all beautiful days. And now look."

Dillinger pointed past disinterested Kathryn, through the sunny train window, to the clear cerulean sky. On top of everything else, he now accepted as fact that Robert could control the weather.

When we arrived at the Poughkeepsie station, we took a ten-minute cab ride to the house—or the estate or whatever. To say it was vast would be an understatement along the lines of calling the Great Wall of China or Michael Fassbender's penis "long."

The cab took us uphill along a gravel driveway, where the house—a white two-story colonial with dark trim—appeared to the left, upon another small hill. To the right there was a barn, and past that, a far stretch of grass that disappeared into a forest.

We stepped out of the cab just off the house's front porch, and there was Robert welcoming us, glass of bourbon in hand, wearing khaki shorts, loafers, and a striped polo. I'd never seen his knees before, and I was having serious trouble focusing on anything else. His wife (Avery, a former Texas Longhorns cheerleader) was at his side. She was the same age as Robert but didn't look a day over fifty-five, dressed casually in white cotton shorts, sandals, and a sleeveless top. Her auburn hair looked like she'd just stepped out of the salon.

"Y'all have a smooth ride getting here?" Avery Barlow had been to the office on a few occasions so this wasn't my first time meeting her, but when I looked into her bright hazel eyes, I still couldn't help but think: *You are married to Robert. You knew him when he was nothing but a brassy college boy who read too much James Lee*

Burke. You married him before his first billion. What was he like back then? Did he always speak in commands? Was he even the natural leader of your friend group?

"Getting here was a breeze," Dillinger said in response to Avery's question. "The train ride was a pleasure."

Already he was laying it on a little thick.

Robert pointed toward the backyard with his drink. "Come on around back."

We did as we were told, and, reaching the backyard, the stunning swimming pool was the first thing to catch my eye—followed by red-faced Glen Wiles lounging poolside, smoking a cigar.

Shit.

Wiles struggled up from his chair and over to us. He was wearing a T-shirt, which he'd already mostly sweat through; cargo shorts; and no shoes. I thought Robert's knees were bad. Glen Wiles's feet were like two ham hocks past their sell-by date.

I was beginning to wonder what the hell I was doing here.

"Tina, you're hanging with the big boys now, huh?" Wiles gave me a smack on the back with his big bear-paw hand. "That's my wife, Carolena, over there, she's catching some sun. Say hi, honey."

Carolena, in a gold lamé bikini that she absolutely had to have bought at a store for strippers, looked like a *Real Housewives of New Jersey* reject. Her skin was the blackened bronze of a tarnished penny, the kind of pennies I used to dunk in Taco Bell hot sauce to make them shiny again. She peeked at us over her enormous sunglasses, waved, and then turned over to sun her back.

"She's not a big talker, that's why I like her," Wiles said, before re-pacifying himself with his cigar.

I followed Dillinger to the patio bar and poured myself a glass of white wine. Dillinger had bourbon because Robert was having bourbon. Kathryn, who'd finally stowed away her Kindle, disappeared into the house with Robert's wife for a tour—because that's what women did. They looked at house stuff. Though biologically I, too, was a woman, I had zero interest in oohing and aahing over period details and antique linens, so I stayed put and took a seat at the patio table.

Robert pulled up a chair beside me, slid my wineglass aside, and placed a tumbler of bourbon in front of me. "You want this," he said.

I looked at him with owl eyes.

"That's twenty-three-year-old Pappy Van Winkle's Family Reserve." Robert urged the glass to my hand. "Best bourbon you'll ever drink."

I took a sip. He was right; it was good. And I wondered how he got it.

During the workday, Robert would often shoot me an e-mail along the lines of: *Can you run down to the liquor store and get me a bottle of Famous Grouse forty-year-old blended malt . . .* And I would then spend the next four hours calling every liquor store in New York trying to locate the rare bottle, which I'd go pick up myself or have rush-messengered. He had no idea how much effort went into fetching such things, or how much money it ended up costing. All he knew was by six p.m. the bottle was on his desk.

So it blew my mind when Robert stood and fired up his own barbecue grill. He planned to do all the grilling himself, just like a regular person. And his wife started bringing out side dishes—carrying them herself—from the kitchen. Avery Barlow was serving us? I was expecting maids and butlers, white gloves. Maybe even someone on standby to chew the bigger pieces of food for us, I don't know. Instead, Robert ordered Dillinger and me over to the grill to show us exactly how he buttered the steak.

"You have to do it this way," he said, dipping a brush in a bowl. "This here is a mixture of butter and oil." He painted each slab of thick meat on both sides, while Dillinger snapped photo after photo of the process with his phone.

I couldn't for the life of me figure out why now, after six years, I'd finally been invited here to be fawned over and schooled in the essentials of barbecue grilling. And why I thought it was okay to come given the present (criminal) circumstances.

Robert turned each steak over with a pair of tongs. "You flip once," he said. "That's it. You flip too much and you won't get a well-seared crust."

What if Robert brought me here to soften me? To knead me with kindness, leaving me no choice but to come clean? He was such a brilliant manipulator, anything was possible. Then again, it was entirely plausible that it simply hadn't occurred to Robert until now to invite me out here. Like most powerful people with a lot on their mind, that's how he worked. The world around him functioned according to his whims.

"Now, you paying attention?" Robert removed all the steaks from the grill and set them on a cutting board. "You let them rest for about five minutes, it gives the juices time to circulate. And in the meantime you can refresh your drink."

He stepped past me to the bar cart. "Another bourbon for you, Tina?"

"Yes, thank you," I said.

When the five minutes of juice circulating were up, we all sat around the patio table to eat. I was seated between Robert and Dillinger, and across from Glen Wiles. It was difficult having to look at Wiles while I ate, but the steak was so unbelievably delicious that—

"This steak is unbelievably delicious," Dillinger said.

Robert nodded, pleased with himself. He was so much more relaxed here than at the office. Some of the wrinkles in his forehead had taken the day off, and his face had a glow about it. He told the story of how he and Avery first met. *She was the prettiest cheerleader on the fifty-yard line, pretty as a pie supper, and I knew right then we'd get married. It'll be forty-nine years in October.*

Then he told another story, and another, and another.

Let me tell you something about crawfish . . .

We had a ranch hand once who . . .

My daddy back in his wildcattin' days . . .

And like Aesop's fables and the oeuvre of Eminem, many of these stories concluded with a moral.

There ain't no such thing as the wrong bait.

And that's why you never insult another man's wife.

Just because a chicken has wings don't mean it can fly.

I wiped the juice dripping down my chin with my cloth napkin. This was better than NPR's Story of the Day podcast.

"See that barn over there . . ." Robert gestured in the general direction of the barn, which was actually too far away for any of us to see from where we were seated. "You know who painted that barn? Billy from the office, the mail carrier."

Dillinger halted midbite. "Are you talking about Patchouli? The guy who skateboards down the building's handicap ramps?"

Robert laughed. "He told me he used to paint houses, so I

hired him. I paid him well, and I gave him a bottle of vodka. It was a three-hundred-dollar bottle of vodka, and he drank half the bottle before he left. That boy got drunk as a skunk, couldn't see straight."

Wiles forked at what was left of Carolena's steak, which was all of it. "If that kid had any clue how much that vodka cost, he probably would have sold it."

Yeah, to pay his rent, I thought, but everyone was having such a good time, I kept my mouth shut.

Robert refilled my glass again. "Tina, I have to say, I'm impressed by your tolerance. You can drink just like one of the boys."

Wiles reached across the table and lifted the side of my empty plate, bloody with the memory of a buttery steak. "She eats like one of the boys, too."

"I'm sorry, Glen," I shot back without thinking. "Were you hoping to finish my leftovers?"

The table roared. Maybe the bourbon was having an effect after all.

Wiles was stunned to momentary silence, but Robert was clapping his hands. "Thatta girl," he said. "You tell him!"

Robert's overjoyed reaction kept Wiles quiet, but you could see in his eyes that he was seething. He didn't have the self-confidence to take a joke.

I didn't either, obviously, but whatever.

"All right now. That's enough fraternizing." Robert stood up. "We've got to get shooting while the light's still good. Tina, Jason, you ready? Glen, you coming?"

I'd forgotten about the forthcoming guns-and-ammo element to this visit.

"Nah." Wiles lumbered toward the pool. "I might be too tempted to teach Tina a lesson for mouthing off to me that way."

Okay. Was that his way of, like, saying he wanted to shoot me?

"Leave her alone, Glen," Robert said. "You had it coming." He turned to Dillinger and me. "It's just the three of us then. The truck's already loaded up; come on."

I admired that it didn't even cross Robert's mind to invite Dillinger's wife along as we made our way across the property to the truck. Probably because she didn't eat or drink or insult Glen Wiles like one of the boys. And because as far as I could tell she was mute.

I so wanted Robert's truck to be a dusty old pickup, but it was just a regular shiny SUV, the kind that may have had bulletproof glass. Which could surely come in handy considering my deftness at sharpshooting.

Dillinger sat up front with Robert, who was driving. Driving. Robert. It was so insane seeing him perform such a normal, mundane activity. And he didn't even drive like a grandpa. He drove like he gave orders, with precision, and not so much patience.

We sped around the side of the house, along a path to another field that wasn't visible from the driveway. It, too, was ringed in forest. Robert and Dillinger conversed about work, while I silently tried to gauge on a scale of one to ten just how drunk I was. One being too drunk to hold a gun straight, ten being way too drunk to hold a gun straight.

We arrived in the middle of nowhere, stepped out onto the grass, and Robert opened the tailgate. Inside it looked like something out of the movie *Goodfellas*.

Robert tossed a rifle to Dillinger but strapped the one intended for me over his own shoulder. Then we walked a good distance away from the truck.

"Now, Jason, you just hang back," Robert said. "Because I know you know what you're doing, but Tina here needs a lesson."

Dillinger sulked off to the side and kicked a rock, jealous that I was the recipient of all of Robert's attention.

"Now." Robert got organized. He demonstrated how to load the rifle, how to hold it. He showed me how to aim it, toward the forest. Then he held it out to me like an offering. "Go ahead now, give it a try, I'm right here, don't be scared."

I took the gun into my hands and tried to mimic his exact position, gripping it just as he'd gripped it, holding my body just as he'd held his.

"Good." He arranged my arms and shoulders, reminded me to keep my feet planted. "Now, when you pull the trigger, you've got to be strong. Not weak, you understand? You're like a sturdy oak tree."

I swallowed hard. I could hear my own heartbeat.

"Firing a gun is all about power. You've got to acknowledge the power and harness it. You control it. You're in charge. You can't be a chickenshit with a gun in your hand," he said. "Can you feel it, Tina? Can you feel the power?"

I did. And in that moment I wanted to turn it on myself.

"Now go on," Robert said. "Fire."

10

The week following the trip to Robert's ranch, I felt like I was being wrung out and twisted dry every time Robert's eyes met mine, every time he pointed at me with his fingers shaped like a pistol and called me shooter. If only he hadn't been so welcoming and so protective of me during that visit. It made delivering this week's envelope of cash to Margie Fischer worse than ever, not because of the cameras—I decided there weren't enough security guards in the world to actually watch all the footage those Titan cameras recorded—but because all I could see when I looked at that envelope of money was Robert with his hand on my back, pouring me another bourbon and saying *thatta girl* in his unguarded twang when I swallowed it down in a single gulp.

I needed to be done with this. I needed to get Margie's blackmail debt settled and have this be over, because after the bonding we'd done at the ranch, I would literally die—from shame more than guilt—if Robert found out what was going on.

Midweek, Kevin and I met for lunch at the chopped-salad station in the Titan cafeteria and he drilled me with questions: How many acres is the ranch? Were there horses? What did you think of Wiles's wife? She used to be a stripper, that's how they met, can you believe that?

"I can totally believe that," I said. In fact, the first thing I'd reported back to Emily upon returning from the ranch was: "Glen Wiles's wife looks like a former stripper; I bet that's how they met."

Kevin shook a bottle of balsamic over his spinach salad. "Come on, Tina, give me something, some gory detail. Were the toilet seats made of gold? Was the main course an endangered species?"

I took comfort in the fact that Kevin's tone was more curious than snooping, which calmed my paranoia somewhat. This was no official investigation.

He passed me the Russian dressing. "Did Robert make you slice the limes for everyone, or did he have a servant to do that?"

"Screw you." I slammed the bottle of Russian dressing down too hard, causing it to spurt orangey-pink nastiness into the air. I looked down to find the front of my navy-blue sweater speckled with the stuff, but I ignored it. "Robert is really good to me. Slicing the office limes is just part of my job."

Kevin was taken aback by this sudden turnaround. In the past I'd always been glad to rag on Robert for an easy laugh.

"Sorry," he said, after the longest twenty seconds of all time. "I didn't mean to . . ."

"It's fine." The chopped salad attendant offered me a napkin and I addressed my sweater. "It's just that Robert was a model host and—"

"I get it," Kevin said. "He's your boss, you're right, I was out of line."

He didn't get it at all. But it was better that way.

We made our way back to the elevator bank, awkwardly silent.

"We still on for Saturday night?" he asked, sheepish, like this one flub might have blown it between us forever.

I nodded. "Let's go to the movies."

"Great idea," he said.

And it was: the less talking I had to do, the better.

KEVIN AND I were set to meet at the Chelsea Bow Tie cinema on Saturday night for a seven fifteen p.m. showing of the new Jennifer Lawrence movie. The Chelsea Bow Tie was my favorite theater in the city because it was often filled with peacocking gay men wearing bow ties, and I just couldn't resist the obviousness of that. Plus, in the case of a film starring a diva icon—Cher, Barbra Streisand, Sarah Jessica Parker, James Franco—full tuxedos or outlandish costumes were never out of the question.

I got to the movie theater a solid half hour too early and panicked about whether I should buy the tickets, so I decided to circle the block in the humid, ninety-degree heat, walking slowly (to the chagrin of all the fast-paced, pathologically tardy New Yorkers behind me) so as not to whip up a sweat. This was the first of my and Kevin's dates to which I wore jeans and sneakers, and my trusty Converse One Stars were coming in handy now.

On the third lap, I spotted Kevin standing in front of the theater. He was wearing a short-sleeve collared shirt, jeans, and *sneakers*.

Yes. No dress shoes. We were outfit-synced. (I was equally thankful he had not chosen to wear a bow tie.)

Kevin held up the tickets as I walked toward him, and when I reached him, he tapped a finger on his silver wristwatch. "You're right on time," he said.

I beamed like a person with impeccable timing.

Then he laughed and wrapped his arm around my shoulders. "I have to confess. I saw you circling the block."

"Damn it!"

He drew me in tighter, not allowing me to escape the humiliation. "I appreciate the gesture," he said. "Lots of other girls would have just stood there watching the clock, making me feel bad for being late."

"But you're fifteen minutes early," I said.

"I meant late according to Tina Fontana time," he said, smiling.

We made our way inside, and Kevin let me break free from his hold at the refreshments counter. "Popcorn or candy?" he asked.

Was this a trick question?

It was our first time at the movies together, which was no simple ordeal for me. I had very specific needs when attending the cinema. Get stuck midrow, up too close to the screen, or too far back, and it was over for me. I may as well have just headed home. I preferred—no, required—a centrally situated aisle seat, the most coveted location among the anxious and weak-bladdered.

"How about popcorn *and* candy?" Kevin grabbed for his wallet.

Good man.

"Surprise me," I said, trying to sound spontaneous and non-chalant. "I'll go save us seats."

Which I did, but the theater had already filled up—the only aisle seat available was a single—so I settled for two midrow seats, closer to the screen than was comfortable, and tried to not be a little bitch about it. The theater went dark a few seconds before Kevin appeared, looking around like a retriever pup when you pre-tend to toss his ball but keep it in your hand. He hugged one arm around the most gigantic vat of popcorn I'd ever seen, and the other around a soda so enormous it would have sent former mayor of New York Mike Bloomberg into instant diabetic shock. I waved him over.

Somehow he managed not to douse anyone as he climbed over the knees separating us, or if he did, they just let it slide because look at this sweet Labrador of a man so eager to please his female guest.

He handed me the twenty-pound-bucket of popcorn, sat, and whispered, "God, I hate sitting in the middle of a row, but that's all on me; next time I'll make sure to arrive earlier."

Then he pulled two supersize boxes of candy from I don't even know where because they couldn't have possibly fit in the pockets of his crisp jeans. "I wasn't sure if you'd prefer Butterfinger Bites or Twizzlers, so I got both," he said. "Also, I got Cherry Coke. I hope that's okay. I never drink Cherry Coke, except—"

"Except at the movies, with popcorn," I said, finishing his sen-tence, which was actually my sentence.

"For the salty and sweet," he said, tilting his head and smiling so bright his teeth sparkled white even in the darkness.

This shit might actually work out, I thought.

The trailers charged ahead, one after the next, "In a world . . ." and all that, and Kevin reached for my hand.

I looked at him, and right then he went in and touched my lips with his. Just like that. It was a kiss so soft and sweet, and salty, too, that I didn't even have the chance to think: *Do people on dates still kiss in the movies? Especially a first kiss.* Nope. By the time my brain had the capacity for critical thinking, the kiss had already happened and the movie had started.

We both turned to watch the screen, but I couldn't focus on anything but my panic.

This was a bad idea—as I'd been repeating to myself every time Kevin made some obvious, yet still unbelievable, gesture toward liking me. Bad, bad, bad. Now wasn't the time to let anyone get close. Especially someone so connected to the situation. I'd spent so much of my life alone, loveless, sexless, under my bedspread binge-watching away my loneliness. And now—*now?*—I strike upon a potential boyfriend? A man who isn't certifiably insane, or an active alcoholic, or an unemployed drummer in a noise band—a man who recognizes the intense synergistic effect Cherry Coke has with movie popcorn? WTF, as they say.

Kevin moved his hand to my knee. He gently, almost imperceptibly, stroked a soft circle up my thigh.

Not smart, Fontana. Bad, bad, bad. But, goddamn, it felt good.

11

A<small>T LAST</small>, on an overcast day in late July, we finished paying off Margie's blackmail debt. Kevin and I had been dating for reals for about three weeks. There was never a conversation like, *Are we boyfriend and girlfriend now?* But after our movie date it became obvious to me that we were soul mates—as long as he never found out about, you know, the embezzlement thing.

During the days and weeks that followed, we went to fancy Upper East Side restaurants and took in the pretension. We went to Lower East Side dive bars and took in the hipsterdom. We went to the Guggenheim and took in the art. When we stayed in, we took in each other—though not literally, to Emily's horror. Kevin and I had not yet slept together, but like the popular girls in my high school used to say, *we'd done everything but.*

The truth is, I was still testing him. I had a natural inclination to mistrust people who had a lot of money—people who grew up with money—because how could anyone who's never suffered be depended upon to suffer through me? I am not a low-maintenance girlfriend. I'm more like a fixer-upper in a dicey neighborhood.

Kevin came from money, but the weeks of testing were conclusive that he didn't act like it—and he didn't seem to care that I didn't. In fact, the more time we spent together, the more it dawned on me that Kevin liked that I didn't come from money. I hadn't told him much about my immigrant parents or the tiny Bronx apartment I hailed from, but whenever I'd slip and forget myself—like the time I lost my r's and g's saying, *Aw you fuckin' kiddin' me?* when a car cut us off in front of a crosswalk—Kevin would throw his head back and laugh. He'd pull me in and smack my low-rent cheek with a kiss. It was all kind of perfect . . . too perfect.

I kept waiting for the moment when teenage Freddie Prinze Jr. and the rest of the cast from *She's All That* would jump out from the shadows, pointing and laughing, revealing this was all a cruel joke. But it never came.

Kevin and I shared a mutual appreciation for Freddie Prinze Jr. movies—*I Know What You Did Last Summer, I Still Know What You Did Last Summer, Scooby-Doo Knows What You Did Last Summer*—and anything and everything by John Hughes. We once acted out the entire first half of *Ferris Bueller's Day Off*. We once acted out the post-prom kiss from *Pretty in Pink*. I knew we would sleep together soon. Kevin had managed to gradually wear me down, to get me to let go of who I thought I was supposed to be and instead just be who I am. So doing the nasty had to be the next step.

But on this particular overcast day in late July, I did everything in my power to push Kevin out of my mind as I rode the elevator up to Margie's office with her final payment—the last bundle of cash stuffed in an envelope, stuffed in a bigger envelope. *Dear God, please let this really be the end*, I prayed while squeezing the envelope close to my thumping bunny-rabbit heart. That I was in no position to be asking God for jack shit didn't stop me from trying anyway.

The elevator doors opened and I marched, head down, to Margie's office, handed her the envelope, and recited my line: "Robert would like you to look at these documents right away."

Margie picked her head up and fastened her eyes to mine, and it occurred to me that no one else was around. The bespectacled accounting underlings who usually buzzed around Margie's desk were nowhere to be found. Had she arranged that? If this were a movie from the late nineties, now would be the moment when some ambient, concern-inducing Radiohead music would start to play.

Margie rested her meaty hands flat upon the envelope.

"Okay?" I said.

She blinked her round eyes a few times but said nothing.

"So we're good?" I said.

Margie leaned back in her chair, and it squeaked formidably. As much as I knew this was supposed to be the end, part of me never believed it. Whether I was conscious of it before this moment or not, I'd been afraid all along that Margie wouldn't let us go.

"You and Emily had your fill?" she asked. "You had enough?"

"Yes, ma'am," I said, out of nowhere morphing into an obedient Southerner, because maybe it made me sound more sorry?

Margie erupted with a full-belly laugh. "You've been spending too much time with that redneck boss of yours." She gave a nod to the door. "Get the hell out of here; I've got work to do."

I flooded with relief and bolted before she could change her mind—the music would now change to some buoyant, joy-inducing Radiohead song, whatever that would sound like.

In the elevator, I began to see spots. My hearing went under-watery and my head spun. But I was safe.

It was done.

My body felt floppy all of a sudden, loose, like a balloon let go to deflate and swirl around. And by the time I was back at my desk, I'd already begun considering possibilities for myself in a way that I hadn't since college. I remained debt-free, after all—through all of this, that hadn't been taken away from me. So what would I do now? How could I be a positive force in the world? What was my true life purpose? I was suddenly thinking in Oprah-speak now that I was no longer hyperventilating.

At lunchtime, Emily insisted we go to the bar down the street with the booze-lunch special to celebrate. Have you ever made a new friend who's a vegetarian and found yourself eating more veg-etables? I was beginning to wonder if Emily was an actual alco-holic and if I was gradually becoming one by proxy, so my first reaction was to suggest we put off the celebration till after the sun began to set. But Robert had a twelve p.m. lunch meeting at Marea, followed by a two p.m. lunch meeting at La Grenouille, which meant he'd be out of the office till at least four, so there was really no good reason for me to decline Emily's offer. Even my useless fill-in could hold down the fort in a Robert-less office.

Emily and I ordered two-for-one dirty-pickle martinis with blue cheese–filled olives off the lunch-special menu, which almost qualified as real food, and hunkered into a shadowy booth in the bar's corner.

I raised my glass. "To the end," I said. "To this nightmare finally being over."

Emily ignored my heartfelt toast and got right to drinking. There was something on her mind. I could tell by the way she kept glancing left and right all shifty, like she was peeking through a newspaper with eyeholes cut out.

"I heard it's got bulletproof glass," she said. "And a rocket-detection system. To keep him safe from all the people who want to murder him."

I set down my cloudy glass of lunch. Emily was referring to the luxury yacht Robert had just purchased. His fifth. Because four wasn't enough.

"I heard it's got a helipad and a swimming pool. And an aquarium." Emily shook her head. "An aquarium. On a boat!"

"Is there something you're trying to tell me?" I asked.

She brought her face in close to mine. "I want a boat with an aquarium," she whispered, as if it were a secret. "Or, at the very least, a house with an inground, temperature-controlled, saltwater swimming pool. Don't you?"

"I thought we came here to celebrate," I said.

Emily leaned in even closer. "I do have something to tell you. Don't be mad."

Just then I noticed a tall redhead approaching our table, and I knew I'd been tricked.

I recognized this bombshell of a woman from the Titan building. She always wore bold-colored skirt suits and six-inch heels, even on dress-down Fridays, which made me despise her a little. Okay, a lot.

"This is Ginger Lloyd," Emily said. "She's *Glen Wiles's* assistant."

"Huh," I said, because Glen Wiles's assistant and I e-mailed each other, like, fifty times a day. But I'd never matched the woman to the name.

Of course her name was Ginger. How did the parents of all the Gingers of the world know their little ones wouldn't grow up to be blondes or brunettes? Or was the name itself so powerful it actually oxidized the hair follicles over time, to match the name by adulthood?

Ginger strong-armed me into a firm handshake. "We finally meet face-to-face."

"After Robert, Glen Wiles is the company's highest-paid executive," Emily said, and I could see the inground, temperature-controlled, saltwater swimming pool in her eyes. "After Robert, Glen Wiles has the company's highest-allowance expense account, and what does he even need an expense account for? Lawyers shouldn't need expense accounts."

I had a feeling I knew where this was headed.

I stood up to go, but Emily grabbed me by my shirtsleeve, pulling me back down. "Just hear her out. She wants to join us, and she has a lot to offer."

"No, I'm not doing this." I shook my sleeve free. "I can't believe you. I can't believe you told!"

If there had been anyone else in the bar drinking their lunch, they would have turned to look to see which adult woman was throwing the tantrum.

Ginger sat down beside Emily and made herself comfortable. She removed the silk scarf that had been modestly wrapped around her ample chest, and for a split second I felt my eyes bulge out like Bugs Bunny's.

"I heard one of the fish in Robert's yacht aquarium cost eighty thousand dollars," Ginger said with a devious calm. "One fish. I heard he had it flown in from Singapore."

That was true. I'd overseen the flying in of the fish myself.

"I owe one hundred sixty K," Ginger said. "The equivalent of two fish."

There wasn't a hint of desperation to Ginger's tone. She hadn't come to beg.

"That's a lot of money," I said. "Is it all in student loans?"

"I went to Brown." Ginger tied her silk scarf to the strap of her purse with an elegant knot. "Then Columbia Law School."

"Shouldn't you be a lawyer, then?" I asked. "Instead of a lawyer's assistant?"

"I dropped out of law school," Ginger replied matter-of-factly. "It was all wrong for me, not that where I've ended up is any better, working for Glen Wiles of all people. No one is worse than he is. No one. Except Robert." Ginger had a glint of crazy in her eye that made me nervous. "Nobody deserves to make that much money," she said. "That's why I want to join you and Emily. Imagine what the three of us could accomplish if we joined forces."

I turned to look at Emily and she was good as gone. Her mind was off planning a stable for her pet horse.

Ginger leaned back, crossed her long legs, and the emerald in her crazy eyes glistened into something more pointed. "Glen Wiles is in the pool of executives who make so much money they buy West Village mansions just to house their art collections."

Emily moaned at the word *pool*.

"That's a true story," Ginger said.

It was. I'd read about that sale in the *Times*. Wiles needed the mansion for his new Picasso.

Emily waved to the bartender and ordered us a bottle of chilled champagne with three glasses.

"We're not doing this," I said, for Emily's benefit as much as Ginger's.

"Don't listen to her," Emily said.

"No, I'm really not doing this," I said. "I'm going back to work."

Emily retaliated with a lockjawed severity I hadn't heard since that first morning up on the forty-third floor. "Not for anything, Fontana, but what makes you think we can't just go ahead without you?"

I'd already stood up to go, to storm out brandishing my self-importance like a flag. What made me freeze in place? Was I really shocked that Emily would be so quick to disregard our weeks of collusion and bonding, the bottles upon bottles of Asti Spumante we'd shared—that she'd drop me in a second for an upgrade to a shinier partner in crime? Since when did I believe in friendship?

"I'm leaving," I said.

"Bye then," Ginger said.

Emily called to my back, "I want you with us, Fontana; that's why I set up this meeting. But if you're not with us, I'm certainly not going to let you stop us."

I kept walking, without turning around, all the way back to the office.

12

I MUST NOT BE cut out for genuine alcoholism because a liquid lunch just did not do it for me. So before returning to my desk, I beelined to the cafeteria's sandwich station to grab a BLT.

One might wonder how I could eat at a time like this, but I needed to eat because I needed to think. Fucking Emily Johnson. We'd done it, we had crossed the finish line, and she had to go and screw it all up by telling someone. Ginger Lloyd, who was obviously terrible.

This was what I got for letting my guard down, for thinking Emily was my friend. And for believing, even for an instant, that anything could go right, ever.

I ordered my BLT as usual—heavy on the B, light on the L and T—then scanned the table area for the standard sights: the four sharp corners of suited power lunches, the anxious outer perimeter of interns unpacking brown-bag PB&Js, the showy center of look-at-me fashionistas picking nuts and berries off plates of lettuce, and off to the side, in her no-man's-land table for one, sat the Lean Cuisine Lady, who always ate alone.

It was by accident that our eyes met. Or so I thought.

Then a light came on behind her thick, pink-tinted grandma glasses (which I had the sense to understand were not intended to be ironic) and she raised her fingers.

Was she waving? I checked behind me, saw that my BLT was ready, took it in hand, said thank you, and when I turned back around, she still had her fingers raised.

The Lean Cuisine Lady was waving me over. The plastic-tray-loving crackpot who assisted Margie Fischer in accounting. But what could I do but make my way to her table? Allowing her to continue waving from across the crowded cafeteria, even if I pretended not to see her, would only draw more attention.

"Hi," she whispered when I reached her, in the exact voice you'd expect from someone who wore a salmon-colored cardigan over a salmon-colored turtleneck all summer.

"I think you may be confusing me with somebody else," I said.

She adjusted her glasses. "Oh aah well." She made sounds that weren't quite words. She had to be a practical joke, right? "I don't think so," she whispered. "I'm Lily Madsen. I work for Margie Fischer." She gestured awkwardly at the empty seat across from her. "Would you join me for a moment?"

So *she* was the one Margie blackmailed us for. She had to be.

I sat, because standing there for even a second longer would have gotten the entire cafeteria straining their eardrums to hear our conversation.

"I only wanted to say thank you," Lily said. "And, oh aah well"—this was apparently a repetitive vocal tic of hers—"I was wondering if you might also be able to help my friend. Oh aah well, she's not really my friend, but she works here at Titan."

"Wait." I pushed aside my untouched BLT so I could better grip the table's edge. "So you know it was me who helped you?"

Lily nodded. "You and Emily Johnson."

"And you know *how* we helped you?"

Lily nodded with more vigor.

"Margie Fisher told you all that?"

More vigor still.

"And then you told someone else?"

Lily stopped nodding.

"For fuck's sake!" I said, and Lily's face went red so fast I thought I would have to smack her across her tiny mouth to get her breathing again.

"I'm sorry, is that bad?" she asked with a gasp. "I'm sorry."

"Who is it?" I asked. "Who did you tell?"

"She won't say anything, I can assure you. I can honestly assure you. She hardly speaks at all."

"Who is it?"

"Wendi Chan."

"Wendi Chan from Digital?"

"Yes."

Wendi Chan was one of Titan's digital assistants. Like most of Titan's digital team, Wendi Chan was Chinese, but unlike most of Titan's digital team, she wore black combat boots, a wallet chain, and dark eyeliner, and she regularly dyed two hot-pink "horns" into her bangs.

It was true that Wendi Chan usually said very little. She was more of a starer than a talker, a creepy, Gothic starer who always looked a little bit like she was on the brink of knifing someone to death. Once when I called her up to my desk because my mouse ball was no longer working, she leaned over me, knocking her heavy wallet chain against my hip; picked up my mouse; spit on its ball; rubbed the thing down on her combat pants; tossed it back onto my desk; and barked, "Now it works."

"Well, fuck, Lily," I said. "You told crazy Wendi Chan? Is she the only person you told?"

Lily began to partially asphyxiate once more. "Yes. I'm sorry, I'm sorry, I'm sorry."

I covered my face with my hands.

"Oh dear," Lily said. "Oh aah well, I realize I've upset you, but would you be willing to speak to her?"

"I don't know," I said into my palms, which still smelled of pickle brine from the bar. "I need to think."

"Oh aah well, but would it be all right if I give you her address?" Lily pulled a slip of paper from her cardigan pocket and passed it to me. "She wanted me to tell you that she'll be home tonight and she'd like you to go see her."

How was this my life? I was supposed to be an island. Hell is other people. Hell is other people!

I had lost all control of this situation, and I *needed* to be in control.

"That's Wendi's address there," Lily whispered. "Please go and see her tonight if you can."

I STEPPED INTO my apartment after work to find Emily and Ginger Lloyd on my kitchen floor surrounded by markers, glitter, glue sticks, and towering stacks of various Titan magazines. *Home Beautiful, Architecture Digest, Lush Décor, Mode, French Mode, Mode Teen, Mode for Men, Yachts and Yachting, Fancy Fish.*

"Are you guys making dream boards?"

"You've got to be able to see what you want in order to have it," Ginger called to me while gluing down a picture of a Marilyn Monroe look-alike in a fur coat driving a red Ferrari. She had arranged it so that the Ferrari was headed straight for a picture of Glen Wiles. And she'd creatively pasted the Target logo over Glen Wiles's receding hairline.

Emily held her board up for me to see. It was far less ordered than Ginger's, less of a homicidal narrative and more of a Jackson Pollock–like splatter of jewelry and swimming pools.

"It's not too late to change your mind," she said. "I got you your own piece of paperboard just in case."

I was inexplicably touched that Emily had considered me while stealing art supplies from the Titan office supply room.

"And look at this." She reached across the floor to a copy of *Millennium Foodie* and turned to a page she'd marked with a glitter pen. "This is the FleurBurger 5000," she said. "It's a hamburger they have in Las Vegas that contains foie gras and a special truffle sauce. It's served with a bottle of Château Petrus, poured into Ichendorf Brunello stemware. It costs five thousand dollars, but we'll be able to afford it!"

Staring down at this full-page spread of charred meat on a brioche bun made me realize something vitally important: Emily and Ginger were going to run their scheme with such moronic ostentation that they would get themselves caught in a matter of days, possibly minutes. And then *I* would be caught because the paper trail of forged documents would lead right back to me.

"Don't you like it?" Emily asked.

I took the issue of *Millennium Foodie* from Emily's outstretched hand, closed it, and set it down on the kitchen table. "You have to stop this," I said as gently as I could. "Don't you think if the two of you start showing up to work draped in blood diamonds and Birkin bags that people are going to start asking questions?"

Without warning, Emily grabbed the nearest issue of *Ultimate Houses* and chucked it at my feet. "I picked that burger out for you myself!"

"I appreciate that, Emily, but I can't let you do this. You'd be putting me at risk. Even if I don't cooperate with you."

I ducked out of the way of a soaring glitter pen, then a glue stick, and, most egregiously, a pair of scissors. In Emily's defense, they were at least safety scissors.

"You put yourself at risk when you cashed that check!" Emily Frisbeed a double issue of *Fine Wines* straight for my forehead.

Fortunately, I was a seasoned flying-object dodger on account of my parents, so Emily had yet to land a blow. Ginger, meanwhile, was calmly cutting the crotch out of another picture of Glen Wiles. It was a known Titan fact that Glen Wiles was a serial sexual harasser, so I could only imagine what it was like for someone with Ginger's cup size to be his assistant—but still, she was a little too entranced by rendering him a eunuch.

"You're killing our good-energy vibe in here," Ginger said without looking up. "I think you should take your negativity elsewhere."

A box of crayons ricocheted off my collarbone and I knew I had no choice but to go. Only after I slammed the door shut behind me did I realize I'd just been driven out of my own home.

My cell phone tinged and I was sure it was Emily calling me, to tell me that her psychotic break had ended and it was now safe for me to reenter my own apartment without a helmet.

Instead, it was a text from an unknown number: *I'm waiting for you—WenDi.*

How did Wendi Chan get my cell phone number?

Immediately following that text came another: *I'm still waiting.*

Then a third: *Still waiting. I've got all night.*

Lucky for Wendi Chan, I had nowhere else to go anyway.

13

Wendi chan lived in Bushwick, Brooklyn—Williamsburg's grittier, less gentrified younger sibling. (It should be noted that given the warp speed of gentrification in present-day New York, Bushwick is already becoming a coveted neighborhood on par with the city-as-luxury-good at large—but trust me when I tell you that Wendi's apartment building was an enduring, gentrification-resistant hellhole.)

No wonder she was so ornery. She worked all day in the creepy Titan basement surrounded by computer screens, doing god knows what with zeros and ones, and then she came home to here, the bowels of a broken building on Knickerbocker Avenue. I was surprised the doorbell worked when I pressed it.

She buzzed me in and I descended the stairwell, following the sounds of drums and screeching to the only apartment door that was propped open. I was free to let myself in to what I realized was band practice.

There were four of them, all Wendi look-alikes, set up in the middle of the living room. Honest to god, they could have passed for an Asian gothic version of Jem and the Holograms.

I stood awkwardly, straining not to cringe as the singer hit her high notes. Then Wendi called cut.

None of the girls acknowledged my presence before disappearing into one of the two bedrooms.

"You all live here together?" I asked as Wendi propped her bass up against the wall.

She nodded. "Four Chinese girls from Flushing living in a Bushwick basement."

"That should be your band name," I said.

Wendi made a sour face. "Our band name is I'm Not Chun-Li from Street Fighter but I'll Still Fuck You Up."

"You're right," I said. "That's totally better."

We each sat down on a vintage Marshall amp. Wendi reached into a red cooler filled with ice, pulled out a soaking can of Budweiser, and offered it to me. It was emblazoned with stars and stripes, a leftover from the Fourth of July.

"I love this American can, don't you?" Wendi said in her gruff voice and slight Chinese accent. "Don't you feel such freedom drinking from it?"

I cracked it open, causing a small volcano of foam to erupt onto the already sticky floor, and nodded.

Wendi tossed me an open bag of Lay's Classic to go with my beer. "I didn't think you would show."

Neither did I, but now that I had a cold beer and salty chips, I would have stayed forever if she let me.

"I only came to tell you that whatever Lily Madsen told you, it isn't true." I crunched on my chips and avoided Wendi's searing eye contact. "I don't know anything about . . . about anything, really."

"Stop embarrassing yourself," Wendi said, cutting me off. "Have some dignity; don't be a liar."

I went silent and she stared at me hard. "Forget all that for a moment," she said. "First, tell me your story, Tina Fontana."

"My story?"

"You interest me," she said. "The way Lily Madsen the Lean Cuisine Lady interests me."

That could not be a compliment.

"I look at Lily and I know there's a story," Wendi explained. "I want to find out what it is."

"Have you?" I asked.

Wendi shook her pink horns. "It's not so easy getting into her little vacuum-packed world. You're not so different. You have a certain quality, it's difficult to describe. Like a stray cat that you can see is hungry, but if you reach to it, it'll claw your hand off, you know?"

I did, actually.

"Maybe it's those big sad eyes you have." Wendi pulled a soft pack of Marlboros out of her cargo pants pocket. "You have, like, weepy Winona Ryder–from-the-nineties eyes. And she was no cat you could just pick up and take into your lap either." She held the pack of cigarettes out to me. "Smoke?"

"No, thanks."

"Have you ever?" She Zippo'd her cigarette lit.

I shook my head.

"You always been a rule-follower?"

"I guess you can say that."

"You're a first-gen, aren't you? That's typical. Where are your parents from?"

"Sicily and Calabria," I said. "What about you?"

"I was born in Beijing. Came here when I was six."

"Have you always been a rule-breaker?" I asked.

"Did you not hear me? I said I was born in *Beijing*."

She smiled, I think. So I smiled. Then she blew a cloud of smoke into my face. "So how did a rule-follower like you end up as Robert Barlow's assistant?"

"I don't really know."

Wendi glared at me until I said more.

"I was an English major in college, managed a bookstore for a while, worked as a research assistant to a journalist—she's the one who told me Robert was looking for an assistant. She recommended me."

"So did you think you'd become a journalist?" Wendi flicked the ash off the end of her cigarette onto the floor. "By starting out as Robert's assistant?"

"Maybe?" I wiped the potato chip grease from my fingers onto my jeans and went back to my beer. "Honestly, I didn't know what I wanted, but I thought if I could get an in somewhere, my foot in the door . . . becoming a journalist sounded like it could be a solid choice, like an actual job. But now it's six years later and I'm still doing the same thing I was doing when I was twenty-four, with no chance of advancement and . . . I'm rambling."

"You're answering my question," Wendi said. "You're just taking the long way. Tell me about your student loans."

I hesitated, but my hesitation was pointless. Wendi obviously knew everything and she wasn't letting me off the hook.

"It all seems so stupid now," I said, "graduating college with so much debt and no real career plan, but I didn't have a whole lot of guidance. My parents can't even read English. Nobody explained to me what all those numbers meant when I signed for my loans. It all just felt so possible, like I was doing the right thing by investing in myself."

Wendi shocked me by laughing a high-pitched laugh that was one part schoolgirl and two parts hyena. "My parents don't even *speak* English," she said. "But they guided me all right. They guided me through before-and-after-school study sessions, three hours of violin every day, a perfect score on my SATs. They guided me through a nice beating when I missed valedictorian by one-thousandth of a point."

"You were salutatorian of your high school and you still have student-loan debt?"

There was that maniac laugh again. "I would if I went to Harvard like I was supposed to. Six-figure debt, for sure. But instead I rebelled."

Wendi let the word hang in the smoky air between us for a moment. "That was my first broken rule," she said. "I said fuck you to Harvard and went to Queens College instead, for free. My parents haven't spoken to me since. I'm an orphan now, by disownment."

"Wait." I came to fuller attention. "Lily said you have debt. Isn't that why you wanted me to come here?"

"That's what I told her. But the truth is, I wanted to show you something." Wendi nodded her horns at the laptop resting on the floor. "I've been working on a program that I think works well with . . . what you and Emily Johnson have been doing."

"We're not doing it anymore," I said.

Wendi rolled her eyes, stubbed out her cigarette, flicked the filter across the room, and picked up her laptop. "I've created software that would enable you to systemize on a larger scale the base design you and Emily have generated."

"I have no idea what any of those words mean," I said.

"It means I don't want anything from you." Wendi pulled her amp closer to mine. "I'm presenting you with an opportunity. In plain English, I've designed a pay-it-forward network. Let me show you."

She fingered the computer's touchpad mouse with her purple-polished pointer finger. "This program allows you to track all the money you and Emily move around. Checks can go in and checks can go out, and you control it all. So if you wanted to, you could subsidize whoever you approve—me, for example, or some other lowly Titan assistant drowning in student debt—and then allow them to contribute what they can if they choose to. But I see by your glazed eyes that I've lost you."

She'd lost me when she picked up her laptop.

"Look." Wendi snapped her fingers to direct my attention to the screen. "Here's where people can submit their student-loan-debt statements. And here's where you or Emily, or anyone, can submit monetary contributions to the site's account. And here's where you click to send people their e-checks. That's pretty much it, very simple."

"So it's like a charity?" I asked.

"It's not a charity." Wendi reached into the cooler and pulled out another can of red, white, and blue Budweiser. "I like to think of it as a program to aid in the redistribution of wealth. Robert's wealth."

She let that statement float for a few seconds. "For example. I don't have student-loan debt, but I do my boss's expenses. So if I join the network, I can fudge his expense reports just like you and Emily have been doing, but now you can put those funds toward another network member's debt."

"So it's an expense account scheme," I said. "Plain and simple. That's the brilliant idea you're pitching?"

Wendi set her laptop down onto the floor, then put her boots up on the milk crate that served as her coffee table. "It's not a scheme," she said. "Think about the potential here, Tina. We're not only the ninety-nine percent, we're the assistants to the one percent. There's power in that."

I looked around Wendi's cruddy basement apartment. At the cardboard-box bookshelves and repurposed lamps. The cracked claw-foot bathtub that served as a planter for what may or may not have been marijuana.

I had to ask: "Are you proposing this as a way to get rich?"

Wendi squealed with laughter like a poltergeist. "No. I don't want to become rich, because then I would have to despise myself. I'm proposing this to make Robert a little less rich, but not enough that he notices."

I considered this for a moment. To be honest, there was a Robin Hood–esque element to Wendi's idea that I found tempting. My college self would have jumped at it. Actually, that's a lie. My college self would have listened attentively with owl eyes while the more active activists at the Women's Center jumped at this idea. But philosophically I would have totally been on board.

While I was lost in this thought, Wendi tossed me another beer and I reflexively ducked out of its way, letting it drop to the floor.

"Sorry," I said. "Habit." I picked up the beer, opened it without thinking, and it exploded all over the two of us. "Sorry again," I said, but Wendi hadn't even flinched.

"So this program," I said, thinking back to the dream boards currently being constructed in my kitchen. "It would allow me to prevent people from using the money for anything but student-loan debt. Right?"

Wendi nodded gravely. "Not everyone's so honest as you."

"You think I'm honest?"

"I think you're okay, Tina," she said. And from Wendi Chan that was saying a lot.

I RETURNED HOME to find Emily pouting, knees to chest on the kitchen floor, which itself now looked like a haywire linoleum dream board, a sea of discarded, half-crumpled cutouts of luxury goods mottled by smears of glittering paste. Ginger was nowhere to be found.

"You came back!" Emily jumped up and ran to me for a hug. "I was afraid you'd gone for good."

I kept my arms at my sides but allowed her embrace.

"Fine," I said into the skin of her bare shoulder, which smelled like a gardenia—all she was wearing was a lace nightie. "I'm back in. But only if we do this my way."

And my way meant no dream boards, no spending sprees that would land me in a cell.

"Whatever you want." Emily squeezed me tighter. "I'm just so glad you're home."

"We're going to use a computer program," I said.

"I love that."

"I said *computer program*. We're going to use a computer program to pay off Ginger's debt. And I'm in charge of it."

I would control the money. Me and only me. Because if I couldn't stop Emily and Ginger from going ahead with this, I could at least keep them on a leash.

Emily released me and went to the fridge to search for, most likely, a fresh bottle of Asti Spumante.

"Did you hear me?" I said. "I'm going to be in charge. And for fuck's sake, don't tell anyone else! And make sure Ginger doesn't either."

"Okay, okay," Emily said. "I'm just happy you're back."

14

THE NEXT DAY, back at work, it was all I could do to keep from throwing myself down on Robert's $1,200 wingtips and beg for forgiveness. The brief respite I'd felt, the sense that I'd made it to the other side of this mess, had been given over to acute guilt and shame. To make things worse, it was the day of Robert's weekly editorial meeting with his managing editors—for which I was called upon to do the most important task I had all week.

This recurring meeting was the fifteen minutes or so Robert spent deciding Titan's "message of the week," which would then be pounded away at through his various media outlets, resonating throughout the country. (Remember: Even if you haven't heard of Robert, he has influenced you. If you exist in the modern world, he owns all or a portion of the media you consume.) This fact— that one man could have so much influence—enraged many people. To me, all it meant was that it was ten a.m. on a Tuesday.

Today, though, my hand shook as I set down a pitcher of ice water and a stack of cups at the center of the conference room table. Physically, I was falling apart. Someone of my already-anxious constitution was just not designed for a life of crime. If I wasn't careful I thought I might end up giving myself a heart attack, or waking up one day with a head full of gray hair and a face like Keith Richards'.

I stood beside the conference room doorway, waiting, notepad and pen in hand, trying to do yoga breathing, or what I thought yoga breathing was supposed to be.

Dillinger entered the room first, as usual, immediately followed by Cooper, Hayes, and McCready. Then Robert entered, taking his place at the head of the table.

Now I was free to sit, as far away from everyone as possible, which, given the football-field-length nature of the conference table, was actually quite far.

Robert began talking, picking up where he'd left off in some previous statement. "I want our reporters to challenge him," he said. And I began scribbling notes, fortunately (for me) understanding who he meant by "him."

To be clear: the "message of the week" was often a directive to frame (or some might say *spin*) a current piece of news in an unfavorable light for the currently Democratic president. Today, though, Robert changed it up a bit. Today's directive was instead a character assassination on an antitrust activist who'd recently made some public statement that pissed Robert off.

Dillinger and Co. nodded.

"Embarrass him," Robert said. "Humiliate him."

More nodding.

This was how our multiplatform news-media talking points were composed. I wrote down whatever Robert said, while everyone else agreed with him.

"Let's spend a good deal of time discrediting his basic argument," Robert continued. "Anything to disrupt him. Find that information and report it. Got that, Tina?"

I looked down at my chicken-scratched paragraph. It was my turn to nod.

"Good."

Done. Everyone stood up. I returned to my desk, entered the memorandum into an e-mail, and sent it out to the entire staff. God bless freedom of the press.

Character assassination turned out to be the overarching theme of my entire workday, the poignancy of which, in light of my newly renewed role as traitor and embezzler, was not lost on me.

Robert's three o'clock appointment was US Representative Mike Nesbitt, one of Robert's best friends from college. They went to the Cotton Bowl together every January and celebrated opening day of deer-hunting season every November. They even had matching Audemars Piguets. But Nesbitt had dropped the ball on an important favor Robert wanted. Some regulation that Robert needed relaxed (his word). He basically wanted Nesbitt to send the regulation out for a massage, or a colonic. Anyway, news had broken yesterday—a lurid photo of Nesbitt at the W Hotel with a prostitute—so here he was now. The assumption being, of course, that Robert was responsible for the breaking news.

Robert's office door was closed, so I couldn't hear Rep. Nesbitt through the glass, but I could see him yanking on his neatly cut, pomaded brown hair and on the crisp red knot of his necktie. He leaned forward in his chair, pointed his finger into Robert's face, and yelled something along the lines of, *You mother#%!@ing c@#%$ucker!* That was my cue.

As I'd been trained to do any time it appeared like Robert was having difficulty with someone, or they might try to murder him, I picked up my phone and buzzed his line pretending he had an important call. It always amazed me how talented Robert was at this act—he never gave us away by glancing knowingly at me or by not appearing surprised enough. He could have given any Method actor a run for his money the way he refused to break character, except maybe Daniel Day-Lewis, because that guy took pretending to a whole new level of insanity.

At the sound of my first buzz, Robert huffed and held up his hand, cutting Nesbitt off midsentence. He grabbed his phone's receiver like it was the biggest imposition of all time. "This better be important."

"Do you need an out?" I whispered conspiratorially. This was the extent to which Robert's viciousness had, up to this point in my life, been a blood sport I could watch and support and enable from the safety of my cubicle.

"Tell him I'll just have to call him back," Robert barked—which meant he was all good with his fight, that he was winning and maybe even enjoying himself.

He slammed the receiver back down onto its base, like always, except this time he must have knocked some buttons because his phone hadn't hung up properly. Somehow he'd put himself on speakerphone.

"Now, where were we?" I heard him say through my phone's

receiver, with crystal clarity. All I had to do was hang up my phone and it would disconnect us—but then I heard Nesbitt's reply: "We were just discussing what a lowlife rat bastard you are."

Whoa. Not hanging up. This scene had the dramatic potential of a *Dynasty* catfight, circa 1985—my latest Netflix nostalgia binge.

Robert chuckled just like a billionaire on pre-present-day-golden-age television would. Though I'm pretty sure back then the billionaires were only millionaires, since a million dollars was still a lot of money.

"This was too malicious, even for you, Bob," Nesbitt said. (Bob?!) "To turn on me this way, after all we've been through together."

"Who turned on whom?" Robert was cool as a cucumber pickle from Momofuku.

"There was nothing I could do. My hands were tied, you know that."

"Bullshit," Robert said.

I could hear that Nesbitt was about to cry, which would have both disgusted and exhilarated Robert. "You've destroyed my career, Bob, my entire family, for what? Because you're pissed off about not getting an FCC waiver? Are you fucking serious?"

"You betrayed me," Robert said, and the acid from my stomach began boiling up my throat. This was how nasty it got when someone crossed Robert.

"You betrayed me," I heard Robert say yet again, just before I hung up the phone.

I'd heard enough.

Nesbitt betrayed Robert, so Robert ruined him. Simple as that. This was the Robert the public read about in malicious headlines (in the more liberal papers) and cruel blog posts, the one they referred to (like Margie Fischer did) as a bully and a propagandist. A monster. This was the version of Robert that had never applied to me before, that I'd never had to fear—but did now.

THAT NIGHT, we met at Bar Nine. Emily, Ginger, Wendi, Lily, and me. Bar Nine was the only place within walking distance of the Titan building that didn't feel like a Midtown bar. It was a wash of red light and flickering candles, oversize velvet couches and—fortunately for us—a private back room.

The five of us eyed one another from around a too-low wooden table. We'd all come straight from the same place of work, but who could tell? Between Emily's diamonds and Ginger's fuck-me pumps, Wendi's bondage pants, and Lily's cardigan with giraffes on it, we looked like the snapshot of a new Tumblr meme. We may as well have had a neon sign over our heads blinking, *We're a ragtag group up to something no good!* Though a sentence that long would have required a lot of neon, so fluorescents were another option.

Wendi had her laptop out on the table and she was showing us what her computer program could do, which sounded a lot to me like computerstuff computerstuff functionality bitmap vector browser analytics computerstuff computerstuff.

I focused on the clickable pictograms displayed on-screen. They were surprisingly adorable, more than one clearly inspired by a fat cartoon animal. I was finding that Wendi often undermined my expectations this way, reminding me anew each time that beneath all the daggers, skulls, and anarchy symbols was a violin-playing straight-A student who very possibly had a thing for Hello Kitty.

"This here allows Tina to keep track of all the money going in and coming out." Wendi clicked on an icon of a smiling dollar sign with googly eyes and whiskers. "We can subsidize whoever Tina approves and also allow them to contribute what they can."

It went on like this, Wendi clicking and dragging various cartoon personifications, saying stuff the rest of us pretended to understand, until Ginger came to with sudden comprehension.

"Hang on. Wait a minute." She flared her ruby-red nails. "Only Tina gets to decide things?"

"She's the administrator of the site," Wendi said.

"Why is that?" Ginger asked.

"Because that's how I made it," Wendi said.

Emily lingered a few thought steps behind Ginger in recognizing they'd lost the reins of their get-rich-quick scheme. "When you say *subsidize*," she asked Wendi, "what exactly do you mean?"

Wendi appeared perplexed.

"You used the word *subsidize* before," I said in an effort to clear up Wendi's confusion. She wasn't as accustomed as I was to Emily's five-minute delay. "You said we can subsidize whoever I approve."

Lily raised her hand up high, enthused by the opportunity to define something. "A subsidy is a grant or gift of money," she said.

"Right, so, how much will we be subsidized?" Emily asked.

It was time for me to step in. To take control even if it meant having to audaciously imitate one of my toughest role models: Cagney and/or Lacey, Buffy the Vampire Slayer, or Bea Arthur. As far as I was concerned, Dorothy Zbornak from *The Golden Girls* was second only to Robert in toughness overall.

"We'll pay off Ginger's debt using Wendi's website," I said in as Dorothy a tone as I could muster. "Emily, you've already had your debt paid off."

"And then we can take it from there." Wendi tossed a bag of tobacco and some rolling papers onto the table and began constructing a cigarette.

"Take it from there how?" Ginger asked.

"Let's cross that bridge when we come to it," I said.

"I have a few ideas." Wendi carefully rolled her tobacco-filled paper between her thumb and middle fingers. Then she licked the edge of the paper and sealed the cigarette. "Once this groundwork is in place with all of us trickling in funds—"

Lily raised her hand. "Not me though, right? I'm only here for moral support."

Wendi bowed her horns to Lily's concern. "Correct. With the three of us—Tina, Ginger, and me—trickling funds through you, Emily, there is great potential for . . ."

Emily was pitched forward, clutching her diamond necklace. The gear shifts of her calculating mind were spinning.

". . . a redistribution of wealth," Wendi said. "Robert's wealth." She stuck her cigarette behind her ear.

This was just the sort of opportunity Wendi had been waiting for, wasn't it? A foolproof way to get at the evil Robert Barlow. Why else would someone like her want to work for a corporation like Titan in the first place?

Emily and Ginger leaned back, appeased. They returned to their drinks.

It was fine with me that the two of them could mistake such a statement to mean they would be enjoying Robert's wealth. At this point my main concern was that neither of them screech up to the Titan building in a red Ferrari. Now that I effectively ruled the purse strings of *the scheme*, I could keep Emily and Ginger from sabotaging themselves, and me.

Wendi's dreams of a Marxian class war were another story—and an argument for another day. For the moment, that crisis had been averted. I was in control of everything.

"For now though," I added, shooting a look specifically at Wendi, "nobody tell anyone else about this. Okay?"

There was agreement all around—except from Wendi. "What do you mean don't tell anyone? What good is my program if you don't use it to its full potential? We can't build a network in a cone of silence."

Or maybe Wendi's dreams of a Marxian class war were in fact an argument for today.

"I never agreed to build any network," I said as calmly as I could.

Wendi reared back. Her horns stood on end. "I thought we had an understanding."

"I know you did," I said. "But here's what you need to understand. I'm just trying to keep myself out of jail. I'm sorry, but—"

"No." Wendi raised her palm to my face and I braced myself to be hit. "You're better than that. You're better than apologizing after you betray my trust on purpose."

There was betrayal going on all over the place, wasn't there?

"Wendi, what do you want me to say? I'm not an anarchist, or whatever it is you consider yourself. I'm not an activist. I don't even like activists. I think they're annoying and self-righteous, and often smelly."

I looked to Emily and Ginger for support, which they gamely provided.

"Very often smelly," Emily said.

Wendi crossed her arms over the chest of her black hoodie. "Well, what's to stop me from telling people? What can you threaten me with? I can rat the three of you out tomorrow if I choose to."

My eyes must have gone black or something because Emily, Ginger, and Lily drew back, awaiting my reaction.

"Okay, Wendi," I said with a directness that surprised even me. I really wished she hadn't gone there. It forced me to the exact position I didn't want to go to. "Here's how this is going to work. Look around this table, because it ends with us. We'll use your site to pay off Ginger's debt, and everybody wins. You get to screw Robert out of some money, and the rest of us all get to walk away debt-free. And most important, no one goes to jail. On the other hand . . ."

I paused and nobody moved. My apparent composure had befuddled them. I sounded like a boss.

"If you tell anyone else about this, I'm going to come after you. And that goes for everyone here."

My voice was pure intimidation. I was reminding myself a little of Robert.

"Remember this." I leaned back in my chair. "Robert likes me better than any of you. I've been to his ranch. He calls me *Shooter*. So he's way more likely to believe me when I tell him it was all of you—that you all teamed up against me, forced me, blackmailed me, threatened me. Or better yet, that you, Wendi, are single-handedly trying to mastermind an anarchist plot against him."

Silence.

Wendi stared at me hard, pulled her cigarette out from behind her ear, and contemplated it. Then she stood up, shook her horns, muttered something in Chinese, and headed for the door.

The others waited patiently for me to say something.

"Are we all clear?" I asked.

I found myself gripping my tequila too tightly. Robert's drink of choice. Herradura Añejo on the rocks with a little lime. I wondered how many limes I had cut into triangular wedges in the past six years. Eight hundred? Nine hundred? A thousand?

It didn't matter. The lime cutter was officially gone, replaced by this woman sitting here now.

15

THE MOMENT I stepped into the office I knew something was wrong because Robert's door was closed and all his electronic shades were in the down position. *Motherfucker*, I thought. I'd been hoping for a laid-back morning. I had just set my bagel and coffee down silently onto my desk and gently lowered myself into my chair when my phone rang.

It was him.

How in the world . . . ? Could he just sense me through the shades? Were they designed like a one-way surveillance mirror or something?

"Good morning, Robert," I said as normally as possible.

"You're here."

"Yes."

"Can you come into my office?"

Shit.

"Of course," I said.

It was only three steps from my desk to his office door, a five-second walk at most, but in that time I was able to imagine in detail just how I would cover my face with my hands, throw myself down on his feet, and beg for forgiveness. *I was being blackmailed*, I would tell him. *I'm still being blackmailed*, I would lie. *I'll get all the money back for you*, I'd promise impossibly. *I would never intentionally do anything to hurt you, not after all you've done for me.*

It was the longest five-second walk of my life, the aching in my chest and the metallic taste of fear in my mouth assuring me of what I was truly terrified of, more than going to jail—letting Robert down.

He believed in me and I had proved him wrong.

I flashed back to my first week on the job at Titan—me in the backseat of a chauffeured Crown Victoria, returning to the building from an errand: picking up Robert's Derby Day party suit from the Zegna store. I'd just been wined and dined at the store by a staff of salesmen I was sure would have tried to escort me out if I'd been browsing on my own behalf. But since I was there for Robert it was all, "Can we offer you a cup of coffee while you wait, Ms. Fontana? Some Danishes? Complimentary cunnilingus?" They nodded agreeably when I made a breezy suggestion of how they could improve: "You should really start selling androgynous suits for smaller-framed women without many curves." I pointed side to side at my own chest. "No darts here. You know what I mean?" They assured me they would relay my idea to Milan . . . So I was in the backseat of the Crown Victoria on my way back to the office with Robert's suit beside me, and I was feeling utterly abundant. It was such a beautiful day, sunny and cool, and pulling up to the glossy Titan building with its sparkling LEED gold-standard revolving doors, I thought: *I've made it.* Even though I was only fetching a suit that cost more than my monthly rent, for a party I'd never see or even understand (what the hell is Derby Day anyway?), from where I had started, I'd made it so far.

And look at where I was now. Jesus H. Christ. I'd been caught; I could just feel it.

I placed my hand on the leverlike door handle to Robert's office, pushed it open, and stepped inside. Even with all my visualizations, I was in no way prepared for what I saw.

Robert was sitting at his desk wrapped in the throw blanket from his office couch. Only his face was visible, pale as a shriveled white onion.

"I'm so cold," he said.

It was then that I realized how warm he'd made it within the barricade of his glass cube. He must have not only turned the air-conditioning off but turned the heat on.

He was shivering.

Robert was often a frightening man, solid and robust to the untrained eye. But I knew that beneath his broad shoulders and husky bravado, he had the constitution of a sickly Victorian child—allergies, weak lungs, a finicky stomach.

"I think I ate something that didn't agree with me," he said.

The man had the flu. But I knew saying so would only upset him.

"I think you should go home," I whispered.

"I can't!" he shouted in frustration—more at himself than at me. "I have to meet with Wiles in fifteen minutes. And then we've got the board meeting. And today's the day we're going over the new budget. People are expecting me. I can't not be there!" He paused. "Oh god, I'm really not feeling well."

Robert was going to puke. It was plain to see.

I should mention here that the only real relationship I'd ever had (before Kevin) ended over my fear of vomit. It was in college. We'd been together six months—my all-time record—and he caught a stomach bug. "Will you come over and take care of me?" he asked. A self-preserver above all else (the mark of neglected children everywhere), I replied, "Hell no. What good would it do to have us both hurling all over the place?" Truth be told, it's the vulnerability of vomiting I can't handle, the ultimate lack of control, but I didn't need to get into all that. "Suck on an ice cube, to keep from dehydrating," I'd told him. The next day he broke up with me, citing my "selfishness" and "complete and utter lack of heart."

Robert dry-heaved once, twice, and then ran to his bathroom.

I covered my ears, a childish move that thankfully no one could see because of the downed shades.

"Tina!" he cried to me.

Oh god.

"Will you bring me the glass of water on my desk?"

I could have left right then. Made like I was giving him the privacy I thought he'd want. But I couldn't do it. I couldn't abandon the poor man.

I approached his water glass and picked it up, careful to not touch anywhere his mouth may have, and then, holding my breath, I pushed it through the crack in the bathroom doorway. I shuddered when the cold clamminess of Robert's hand brushed against mine.

"Thank you," he said.

A minute later he emerged, no longer white but green.

It was clear that this was only the beginning.

"You're going home," I said, pulling my cell phone from my pocket. "I'm calling your car around." I grabbed his coat from his closet and threw it over his shoulders, then took his sunglasses from his shelf. "Put these on."

He did as I said.

"I'll tell everyone you had an emergency to attend to on the West Coast." I barked instructions into my phone, to have Robert's car pick him up at the building's side exit. "I'll take care of everything." I nudged him toward the door. "You just concentrate on getting better."

He burped and I jumped back.

"I'm really fine," he said. "I just ate something that isn't agreeing with me."

"I know." I helped him get one arm and then the other into his coat. "But no one else needs to know that. It's none of their business."

He smiled. "God bless you. What would I do without you?"

I tried to radiate his affection back at him, but the shame wouldn't let it come. After I got Robert safely out of the building, I went to the restroom to scrub my hands and then douse them with sanitizer.

I allowed myself a breath, but the shame continued to spread.

When I settled back down at my desk, I saw that I had a text message from Kevin: *Can I cook you dinner this weekend?*

And when I hadn't answered right away, he'd sent another: *At my place?*

His place. That meant his apartment. What says "It's about

time we did the deed" more than inviting a girl over to your apartment to cook her dinner?

But it would be a terrible time for me to have sex with Kevin. Especially now that my so-called project had expanded to include his boss's assistant, Ginger Lloyd. Kevin and Ginger worked side by side, which I did not love for a slew of other reasons besides the fear of being caught—mainly, two cantaloupe-size reasons. But that's another story.

Could I really say no to Kevin at this point? *The Oprah Magazine* would argue that it's always a woman's choice to say no. But I wasn't so sure. It was time to *shit or get off the pot,* as Robert would say. (Though in light of that day's circumstances, he may have opted for a less gastrointestinal colloquialism.)

The bottom line was, I had to either break it off with Kevin or stop worrying about how close he was to the truth.

So which was it going to be?

I GOT DRESSED, mentally preparing to not have sex with Kevin at his Upper East Side apartment that night. In fact, I decided I would even ask him for a little space, for just a little while, until things with work and my "project" settled down a bit. It would be better to put off sleeping together until I didn't have so much on my mind. My *Oprah Magazine*–encouraged (OME) five-point plan was simple: Go. Act normal! Eat. No sex! Break up? I visualized its acronym. GAnENsBu.

Upon entering Kevin's apartment, I immediately praised myself for succeeding in the first point in my plan. Acting normal came a little harder on account of Kevin's decorative tastes, which veered toward the mildly suburban: taupe walls adorned with unimaginative prints from the Metropolitan Museum of Art, a Pier 1 Imports sofa, and throw pillows with embroidered hunting dogs on them. I'm not sure what I was expecting. Maybe more of a bachelor pad? Not embroidered hunting dogs—that much I was sure of. In the corner of the room there was an acoustic guitar propped up on a stand, which I deeply hoped was only for show.

If you can learn everything you need to know about a person by scrutinizing their apartment, what new insight was I gleaning here? That Kevin was even softer than I'd originally thought? Guys I'd dated in the past had used old car parts as furniture—the backseat of a 1980 Cutlass Supreme makes for a surprisingly comfortable couch, in case you were wondering—that was the level of comfort and toughness I was accustomed to.

GAnENsBu, I told myself. *GAnENsBu!*

Kevin had cooked us a beautiful meal of lemon chicken and roasted red potatoes. We chewed politely and sipped fine wine over pewter Calvin Klein plates. But our plates were on our laps because his apartment was too small for a proper table.

"You know," I said between forkfuls, "if you were willing to move to Brooklyn, or even below Fourteenth Street, you'd have a lot more space."

The more I considered my surroundings, the less they made sense to me. This prestige neighborhood, this stuffy furniture, the predictable prints on the walls—none of it appeared to be the likely choice of the man I'd regularly watched wolfing down greasy street meat during lunch.

"Are you finished?" Kevin reached for my plate and tossed it along with his into the kitchen sink—barely needing to take two steps away to do so.

"Is it to impress the corporate law guys at Titan?" I asked. "To tell them you live here? Would you be ashamed of Brooklyn?"

"Tina."

"Don't get mad," I said. "I'm only trying to understand."

I craned my neck to get a better look at Kevin's bedroom, separated from the living room by only a bookcase. It appeared tidy and filled with framed photographs. Visible on his dresser was a picture of him and his mom and dad wearing swimsuits. They looked like regular people. The kind of regular people who come preset with the frame from Kodak or whoever, as an example of what you and your family should aspire to.

"It's my parents, okay?" Kevin walked two quick steps to the window and looked out.

I stayed put on the couch. "You live on the Upper East Side to impress your parents?"

"No." When he turned back around to face me I could see the shame he'd been trying to conceal. "This apartment belongs to my parents. They bought it as a sort of pied-à-terre and now I'm living in it." He looked down. "I'm sorry."

I went to him, finally, now that I'd successfully emasculated him. "You don't have to apologize for that," I said. "That makes a whole lot more sense." I rubbed his back half heartedly. "I'm glad you told me."

"You are?" He was so easily pacified. Too easily—especially because I was totally lying. His parents paid for his apartment?

"It's only temporary," he said, leading me the short distance back to the couch. "Until I can buy my own place. But fuck, this is exactly what I wanted to avoid." Kevin was distressed—I could tell by the way his eyebrows were furrowed like two crinkle-cut french fries. "I really like you, Tina. And I don't want you to think less of me just because I come from . . . this. I want to make my own way in the world. To be my own man. I need you to know that."

I think he was expecting me to say, *I do know that*, but when I said nothing, he took my hands into his and squeezed them. "You've got your project with Emily and you're trying to fight inequality, and here I am . . . what? Living in my parents' apartment and working for the Titan Corporation. I wouldn't blame you if you broke up with me right now."

"I'm not going to break up with you," I said. "I'd have to be crazy to break up with you."

Shit. There went the *Bu* in *GAnENsBu*, right out the pied-à-terre window.

Kevin exhaled long and slow. "Well, it's a relief to hear you say that. It's like I've been living with this secret, and it's been terrible, not knowing how you'd react when you found out, if you would lose all respect for me."

"I can imagine," I said.

"I feel so much better, now that it's out in the open."

"Good," I said, longing for such relief.

"Are you still hungry enough for dessert?" Kevin bounced up from the sofa and disappeared to the kitchen nook. He returned carrying a stainless steel electric fondue pot, which he set up upon the floor.

(I hoped the fondue pot also belonged to his parents.)

"So," he said. "What's the latest with your project anyway? How's it going?"

He handed me a skewer and uncovered a plate of bananas and strawberries that he must have spent half the day slicing into equal-size geometric shapes.

I tried to think. What had I last told him? "It's going really well," I said. "We're, um, getting a lot more organized. More focused."

Kevin stirred the pot of chocolate with a wooden spoon, waiting for me to say more.

"We're focusing just on student-loan debt now," I said. "Did I already tell you that?"

"No, you didn't." He paused his stirring. "That's awesome. Can I get in on this? Law school left me about two hundred K in the hole."

"Ha," I said. "No. It's going to be just for women, I think. Women who are underpaid. Assistants, like."

"Oh, that's understandable." He nodded feministically. "You know, my mother would love this idea."

"Please don't mention this to your mother, Kevin. Seriously."

He resumed his stirring of the chocolate. "I won't. I'll wait to let you tell her about it yourself, when you meet her."

I just let that one lie.

"So do you have a website up and running?" Kevin dipped his pinky into the pot for a taste.

"Yes, actually," I said, and then, "No. Not publicly. Not like that you can see."

"Still in the beta stages?" he asked.

"Yup," I said, whatever that meant.

"But you've got a mission statement and everything?"

"Oh yeah, totally. We have a total mission statement."

Kevin let go of his spoon, but he remained kneeling down catcher-style, hovering over the fondue. "Well, when you're ready to take it public," he said, "I've got a few contacts I'd really like to introduce you to. Some friends who work for media companies that are a little more liberal than Titan. They'd be all over this."

I had to put an end to this conversation immediately. The lie was becoming too detailed—but how did I stop it?

I leaned over and kissed him.

He pulled back, surprised. "You like that idea, huh?"

Jesus.

I shoved my tongue into his mouth, harder this time. New five-point plan:

Stop talking, stop talking, stop talking, stop talking, stop talking. (STSTSTSTST.)

I tried to get closer to him, to really go for it. I got down onto the floor, where he was, and wrapped my arms around him—this was going to work like a charm—but that damn fondue pot! It toppled over with a crash, splashing chocolate all over Kevin's parents' CB2 area rug.

"Oh my god," I said.

"It's okay." Kevin tried to take my hands, but they were busy covering my face. "Seriously, Tina, don't worry about it, I hate that fucking rug. Look."

I did look, just as Kevin kicked the remaining setup of fruit he'd so meticulously prepared for our dessert square across the room.

His parents' chocolate-covered rug was now polka-dotted with strawberries. Sliced banana stuck to the sides of their fawn-colored storage ottoman. He kissed me on the mouth before I could laugh.

I grabbed his face and kissed him back, pulling him in closer.

He directed me toward the bedroom, but we'd made it only as far as the bookcase when he pushed me up against the wall. I fiddled with his zipper and he pulled off my shirt. We were naked in seconds.

And that's how good I was at not having sex with Kevin at his Upper East Side apartment that night.

16

I HAVE A CONFESSION to make. No, not that one. It's that my favorite part of sex is after it's over. Which isn't to say I don't enjoy the act itself, because I do, very much—but what I really love is the holding afterward, the lounging, the supreme relaxation of *That went well.*

Sex with Kevin went mind-blowingly well, but it was our post-coital lazing that was the clincher for me. We spent all of Sunday sprawled in his bed in our underwear, laughing, watching videos on his computer, and occasionally having more sex. And the best part: we ordered from Seamless for every meal. Could I ask for anything more?

But before work on Monday morning, some of the anxiety was already creeping its way back in. To combat it, I bought Robert a honey-glazed doughnut from the Peter Pan bakery and placed it on his desk. Robert loved Peter Pan doughnuts. How in the world did Robert Barlow ever eat a hand-rolled doughnut from a tiny Polish bakery in Greenpoint, Brooklyn? you might ask? Because I was stupid enough to bring him one once. I should have known such a mindless act of kindness would lead to weekly text messages at six a.m. and my having to leave my apartment a half hour early to get to Greenpoint before work in order to deliver him this one random doughnut.

Emily once told me a story about how she knew a guy had cheated on her when he surprised her with a pink-frosted cupcake from Crumbs. The Cupcake of Guilt, she called it. I figured now the least I could do was bring my victim a Doughnut of Guilt.

But Robert was having a good day. Something in the islands had gone well, giving him an extra jump to his step, and a political scandal involving a sext had broken overnight, which brought him great joy. This was how I liked Robert best, winning and un-scary, jetting around the office with the energy of a man half his age. (*Faster than a scalded cat. Busy as a hound in flea season.*) Just watching him work, you knew this was a man doing exactly what he was born to do. Robert loved the game. He loved the fight.

His wife called around noon, and even though he was in with Glen Wiles, I knew to interrupt him. The one piece of advice I'd received from Robert's previous assistant, a waif of a woman named Jeannie who lasted only three weeks, was: "Be really nice to Avery and, no matter what, always put her calls through."

Jeannie apparently had not.

"He's in a meeting with Glen, but I'll get him out for you," I told Avery Barlow. "I'm sure he'd rather be talking to you."

She chuckled.

"I heard he took you in three straight sets last time you played," I added.

She chuckled again. "He hasn't stopped bragging about that all week. I'll tell you it was worth it, losing to him so badly, just to have him in such a good mood for a change."

"Hear hear," I said. "Hang on just a moment, I'll get him."

Some days I was so damn good at being an assistant.

Around a quarter to six, I disappeared to the fitness-center bathroom on the fourteenth floor to make the most of the free amenities: toothbrushes, toothpaste, dental floss, mouthwash—basically it was an oral hygienist's dream bathroom. There I encountered Hannah Paley, one of Titan's news desk assistants. We exchanged a nod, then an eye roll when the two women behind the stalls, both producers, began conversing about their fabulous weekends.

"Were you in the Hamptons?" one of them asked the other.

"No, we have a house in Cape Cod."

"Really? I prefer Cape May."

"Oh? Do you have a house there?"

"My parents do. But we have our own summer rental in Amagansett."

Flush.

Flush.

Hannah Paley pretended to gag herself with her complimentary toothbrush.

What sweet validation.

At one time I would have rushed out of the bathroom before those two emerged, to avoid the inevitable questions about my weekend. And if they caught me before I could escape, I would have put on mock airs, claiming that I needed this weekend to "just relax and do nothing for a change." Like nothing was the new something. Or I would just make up something vague, like "I'm going to this great farmer's market in Williamsburg." There's always a great farmer's market in Williamsburg to fall back on.

What was that about, anyway? Was I lying to allay *their* guilt? To make *them* not feel bad about the fact that I couldn't go away every summer Friday, that I could barely afford my Netflix subscription? Or was it to trick them into believing that I was someone better than I was, someone more like them?

"They don't have a fucking clue," Hannah Paley said under her breath. Then she scooped up all the remaining boxes of sample-size Crest Whitestrips from the counter and dumped them into her bag.

It was a good day.

So I was caught completely off guard when I returned to my desk to find Robert waiting for me, skulking around my files.

"Do you need something, Robert?" I asked.

"Sit down," he said.

I sat.

He brought one of his brogues up on top of my drawer stand and leaned in. This gesture made all the men in the office extremely uncomfortable since it effectively brought his ball sac in line with his subject's chin, but as a woman I was accustomed to this compromising position.

"You know how I feel about you, don't you, Tina?"

"I think so."

"I've always felt comfortable with you. Since the first time you walked through that door, I felt I could trust you. That's why I hired you."

I heard myself gulp.

"Now, let me ask you something. Are you familiar with Margie Fischer from Accounting?"

I hesitated.

"Big lady," he said. "Talks too loud."

"Yes," I said. "I know who you mean."

"Has she been bullying you in any way?"

"Bullying me?" I swallowed down the acid making its way up my throat. "No."

"No?"

"Uh-uh." I shook my head like a toddler. "I hardly have any contact with her at all." Though the Titan security-camera feed from the previous weeks would have reported otherwise.

"Good," Robert said. "If she does start bothering you at all, asking you questions, anything like that . . ." Robert stared deep into my eyes, still with his leg up. "Because you know there are a lot of people out there who would like to see me hurt, so I can only surround myself with people I can trust."

"I don't want anything to do with Margie Fischer," I said. "I'll come to you immediately if she—"

"Good." Robert stepped back and took his balls out of my face. "That's all I wanted to hear. Now go on home." He turned toward his office.

Finally, I exhaled. What the hell was that about? I shut down my computer and prepared my escape from the building. At least it wasn't Emily he was asking about—or anything I'd done. But, still, whatever had prompted that could not be good for any of us.

I checked for my keys, wallet, phone; glanced one last time at Robert, whose eyes were glued to the many flashing flat-screens in his office; and headed for the elevators—and by the time I reached them, an idea had formed: Could I pin all this on Margie Fischer and get out unscathed? And even if I could . . . *could* I?

It was me and Dillinger heading down in elevator C, but all we did was nod at each other and then stare dead-eyed ahead. How much would I allow this situation to change me? I wondered. It seemed to have changed me already, but in many positive ways. I was becoming more assertive, figuring out how to be in charge of stuff—but was there a point of diminishing returns? Was I about to cross over into being a truly hardened criminal, a Tony Soprano, a Walter White, a Martha Stewart, willing to take out anyone in order to save myself?

The elevator door opened and Dillinger let me exit first. No man who worked for Robert would ever exit an elevator before a woman. It was both gallant and totally annoying.

No. I came into this a halfway-decent person, and that's how I'd leave it. Margie Fischer didn't mean much to me, and she did harass Emily and me that day at Michael's, and she'd told Lily about us, and there was that one time she scolded me for sniffing the cafeteria half-and-half, but I couldn't just throw her to the dogs. She was doing the best she could, like everyone else. She meant well, just like me. I meant well, didn't I?

On the way down the escalator to the main doors, I tried to calculate how many more weeks we had before I'd shut everything down. A complicated equation filled my mind: 3 of us contributing (me + Ginger + Wendi) + 1 signing/approving (Emily) + 2 who it was safe to assume would keep their mouths shut from here on out (Margie + Lily) = X.

The sun and heat of the outside struck my face.

X = Approximately four weeks. Also known as one month.

One month, thirty days, the amount of time it takes for the moon to complete its lunar cycle; for rent to be due again; to form a new habit (according to *The Oprah Magazine*). But I wouldn't let it be enough time to turn me into a sociopathic, amoral misfit. I had no interest in becoming an antihero—or a villain, for that matter. Even if Martha Stewart had somehow managed to find her way back.

17

SOMEHOW, SUMMER FINALLY began giving itself over to the fall. A drop in the temperature, oranges and browns where there had been green, a light jacket added to my V-neck sweater and button-down. I'd never made it to the beach, I realized, probably because I was too busy worrying all the time—I'd worried Ginger's debt all the way down to four figures, which as far as I was concerned was way better than ending the summer with a suntan and a brag-worthy vitamin D count. Sure, Kevin had tried for a trip out to Southampton, and then Montauk, and then Fire Island, but on account of not owning a bathing suit that wasn't part T-shirt, I always talked him into al fresco tacos and frozen margaritas instead.

Today, Kevin had big plans for us that would not be deterred by any talk of guacamole. In the full spirit of the change in season, he'd thrown on a shawl-collared sweater, rented a car, and driven us an hour upstate to an apple orchard.

"It's McIntosh season," he explained as we waited in line to purchase empty plastic satchels and pay the entry fee. "The quint-essential New York apple. Later we can bake a pie."

Is this what Kennedy-like families did to ring in autumn? They picked apples and baked pies instead of taking down air condition-ers and installing storm windows?

I'd never been apple picking before. It was unclear to me how we would reach the apples. Weren't trees tall? Would we have to climb? But I kept quiet, and soon we were riding on the back of a flatbed truck out to the fields. We were surrounded by children—a group of fourth- or fifth-graders on a school trip—at least half of whom were shorter than I am, so I assumed some system for reaching the apples had been worked out in advance.

When the truck came to a halt, Kevin and I jumped down and made an effort to move in the opposite direction of the children. The dirt beneath the rubber soles of my Converse felt soft, almost powdery. And the fruit on the trees hung low. The air smelled sweet, like a lollipop. (*Sweet as stolen honey*, Robert would have said.) We were only about sixty miles out of Manhattan, but we may as well have been in . . . what state was known for its apples? Washington? Or was New York known for its apples? Is that why we were the Big Apple? I always thought that was a nickname that had something to do with prostitution.

Kevin unfolded the two plastic satchels he'd bought when we arrived. "Let's hit the trees," he said with such gusto I feared that at any moment he might embark on a monologue from Dr. Seuss's *The Lorax*.

"So all of these trees have the same kind of apple?" I asked.

"McIntosh," he said.

Right, right, the quintessential New York apple, I remembered. So, basically, I could fill this bag in about two minutes and be done with it, head home with a satchel full of McIntoshes, and cue up Netflix, but I observed that's not how it worked.

Kevin inched toward one tree like he was sneaking up on it. He felt and rejected two or three identical McIntoshes before plucking one from its branch.

I did as he did. The subtle, almost meditative nature of this process reminded me a little bit of how people talked about yoga. Yoga is pretty much just a lot of standing around in dumb poses if you're not focused on your form, right? The nearly imperceptible details? Apple picking contained the same mystery for me.

"Look at this one." Kevin held what he considered to be the perfect specimen in the palm of his hand.

"That's a good apple," I said.

"I want you to have it." He held it out to me with both hands.

This must have been what Adam felt like in Eden.

"Thank you. I'll cherish it," I said, adding it to the pile in my bag.

"Hey." Kevin got a funny look on his face. "Let's go sit on that wooden bench over there."

I followed him toward the bench, diminutive and rickety-looking as it was, like something a gnome might have built in woodworking class—but before we could reach it, a small herd of screaming kids piled onto it like it was a jungle gym.

"On second thought," I said, turning around, "let's continue standing."

Kevin set his plastic satchel down carefully at his feet and wiped the dust off his hands. He was still wearing his funny face, and for a split second I was overcome by a wave of panic. Was he going to drop onto a knee and propose to me right here in the apple orchard? I hadn't even put on eyeliner today.

"Don't be mad," he said. "I know you hate surprises, but I sort of have a surprise for you."

"Okay." I fully prepared to become enraged at whatever this surprise was. I figured if it were an engagement ring, he wouldn't have prefaced the moment with a request for me not to get angry, so I really had no idea what was coming.

"Last week," he said, "when I was hanging out with my friend Tim, I mentioned your project. And he totally flipped out over the idea."

Tim was an editor at BuzzFeed.

"He just so happened to be working on this list of young New Yorkers who are trying to make the world better, and he was short on names and running out of time, so when I told him about you and your website . . ."

I couldn't move and it wasn't because the bag of apples in my left hand was cutting off the circulation to my fingers. That pain was far more manageable than the horror that was now running through my mind.

"You look mad," Kevin said. "I didn't mean to do it. But I was bragging about you, and then it just slipped out. I know how private you are about it, but I just couldn't help it—I knew you'd be perfect for Tim's list."

"You shouldn't have said anything." I let my bag of apples drop to the ground.

Kevin's eyes shot to where they fell, seemingly concerned for their structural dignity.

"You'll have to tell Tim to forget it," I said. "I can't be a part of any buzz list."

"Tina." Kevin reached for me. "Don't you think you're overreacting just a bit?"

"No, I don't." I pulled back to avoid Kevin's touch, just as my phone got a text.

"I'm really sorry you feel that way." Kevin searched his pockets for his phone.

I immediately got another text, which apparently Kevin thought was his phone going off, because he was still searching for his phone, which made the same text sound as mine, neither of us willing to be the one to change what was obviously the most appropriate sound to indicate a text message.

"It's fine," I said, retrieving my phone from my pocket. "Just undo it."

"No, I mean I'm really sorry Tina, but Tim already—"

Another text.

"Jesus, what the hell?" I looked at my phone. I had three messages from Emily, two from Wendi, and one from Ginger.

Kevin was thumbing furiously at his phone and then turned it around to show me its face. "You should read this," he said.

"*Twenty-Five Dog Selfies That Changed the World?* Why are you showing this to me?"

"Oh wait, hang on." Kevin thumbed at his phone some more and then turned it around again.

The headline read: *Twenty-Five New Yorkers Who Are Doing Something About It.*

Ohmygod.

Kevin kicked at a rotten apple at his feet. "I thought you'd be happy, once you saw it."

Ohmygod. I frantically scrolled down the list to number twenty-five, *"Tina Fontana's New Nonprofit Will Take on Student Debt,"* hardly able to believe what I was reading. The short paragraph referred to a "rumored, yet-to-launch website" and employed the terms *inequality* and *consciousness raising*, which tipped me off that Kevin must have had a hand in writing some of the content himself. It didn't contain much detail because how could it? It was framed more like a leak—a sort of *we heard about this cool thing before anyone else and even though we don't know anything useful about it, here we are with the scoop!* But it did state in no uncertain terms that my mission was to help underpaid women pay off their student-loan debt.

Mission. I bet Kevin chose that exact word. I remembered how over fondue he'd asked me that specifically, if we had a mission statement. And like an idiot I was all, *oh yeah, totally, a mission statement.*

"I don't really understand why you're so upset," Kevin said, hands stuffed deep into his jeans pockets now.

I checked myself then. More than anything, I wanted to peg Kevin dodgeball style with an overripe McIntosh to the mouth, but I needed to chill the fuck out.

I forced myself to take a breath. "I'm just a little shocked, that's all," I said. "I wasn't ready for this. This kind of exposure."

Kevin blinked his big brown eyes at me. "I really thought I was doing a good thing. I thought it was just the little push you needed to take the site to the next level."

Yeah. I'd say this was definitely a whole new level.

"I appreciate the sentiment." I silenced my phone and forced an unnatural calm into my voice. "And you're probably right." I picked up my bag of apples. "Come on, it's a beautiful day. Let's enjoy it and forget about all this for now."

"Are you sure?" Kevin picked up his satchel hesitantly, hopefully. "You're not mad at me?"

Of course I was mad at him. He'd outed me! Now I understood how George Michael felt, how Queen Latifah felt, how Ryan Seacrest felt—he is out, right? Regardless, there is no going back in once you are out, so what the hell was I going to do?

"I'm not mad at you," I said, taking Kevin by the hand.

With my free hand, I sent a text to Emily, Wendi, and Ginger: *Don't worry, I'll handle it.*

Now all I had to do was figure out how.

18

EARLY THE NEXT MORNING was Titan's workplace sexual harassment prevention seminar—the two hours every year when all mid-to-lower-level female staff had to gather in the building's auditorium (which was actually a state-of-the-art theater) to be reminded how disenfranchised they were. Male and upper-level staff had a seminar, too, but theirs was conveniently conducted entirely online. Ours was all, *We're gathered here today, ovaries-to-ovaries, just us girls, in this safe space to air any and all grievances.* I thought my period would come just sitting there.

I chose a seat in the last row and searched the crowd for Emily. It wasn't easy picking out her long blond hair from all the other long blond hair in the room. I had to locate Ginger's ginger first and then hone in on Emily beside her. Wendi and Lily were also sitting next to each other, but on the opposite side of the room. The four of them had all seen the piece on BuzzFeed, as evidenced by yesterday's series of exclamatory text messages, but aside from my misleadingly confident *Don't worry, I'll handle it* text, there had been no further discussion. Mostly because I'd turned off my phone and spent the night at Kevin's, so I hadn't even had the chance to see Emily before coming to work.

Needless to say, I hadn't yet tackled *handling it* thus far, at this point in time, etc., etc.

A woman onstage wearing a gray pantsuit tapped her microphone three times. She looked either old for twenty-five or young for thirty-five—it was hard to tell from a seat practically in the lobby. She told us her name was Carolyn and that she worked in HR.

She wasn't the head of HR, obviously, or she wouldn't have been stuck leading this seminar. The same woman never led these things more than once, so it was very possible she was an assistant.

"Today we're going to go over what constitutes harassment under federal and state law," Carolyn said, too close to the microphone. "We'll explore Titan's anti-harassment policy, activities that violate the anti-harassment policy, as well as some practical examples and interactive scenarios."

I zoned out then to gaze at the audience. There must have been about two hundred women in the theater, which meant there were two hundred phones throughout the building going unanswered, and twice as many unreturned e-mails. At this very moment there were two hundred angry men who needed packages couriered, documents scanned, car services requested—with no fucking clue how to do it.

"How do we recognize and respond to harassment?" Carolyn asked us. "Do you know how to report incidents of harassment?"

She seemed to have more questions for us than answers.

Someone from the audience who was way better at verbalizing her thoughts than I was called out: "Today I had to sop up the coffee my boss spilled all over himself, while he just stood there."

Carolyn looked up from her notes and adjusted her microphone. "Well, technically that's not harassment, I don't think, unless it was sexual in nature, the sopping."

I was not the only one to chuckle.

"Last week my boss called me at six a.m.," someone else from the audience yelled out, "to tell me he needed a PowerPoint by nine."

A wave of knowing groans swept across the auditorium.

Poor Carolyn had lost control of the room. Nowhere in her introduction had she indicated this was a call-and-response sort of thing. "Perhaps I should continue going over what constitutes harassment before we address individual questions," she said.

"You think that's bad?" A Latina woman with hair that was brown on top and blond at the bottom stood up and addressed the crowd. "Last night my boss drunk-texted me at three a.m. to ask where he'd left his car keys."

This bullshit seminar was turning into real entertainment. A woman near me in the back row, who was wearing too-big glasses, shouted out, "My boss lies down on his office floor and has me walk on his back before he leaves to play tennis."

Then the woman sitting next to her, who was wearing even bigger too-big glasses, chimed in, "My boss makes me taste his sandwiches for him to make sure there are no hidden onions inside."

"Okay, okay." Carolyn waved her skinny arms behind her lectern. "Some of these may or may not qualify as workplace harassment, but it sounds more to me like—"

"You said we could air our grievances." Ginger stood up in her Kelly-green skirt suit and with one swift motion tore off her silk neck scarf and used it to tie back her fiery red hair. "These are our grievances."

This from the woman who had to deal with Glen Wiles day in and day out.

A few people began to applaud for Ginger.

"You know what? Let's take a break." Carolyn looked at her watch. "We weren't supposed to break until the end of the first hour, but let's do it now. There's coffee and refreshments in the lobby."

I was the first one to the snack table thanks to my strategic seat location. I had a steaming, eco-friendly paper cup of coffee in hand before anyone else had even made it to the samovar.

Suckers, I thought—but as I turned around, I found myself surrounded.

There were three of them: two blondes, one brunette, all dressed like they'd just raided the sale rack at Zara.

"I heard about your nonprofit," the brunette said.

"When's it going to launch?" one of the blondes asked.

"Ohmygod, ohmygod, Tina." A woman whose name I could never remember, who always wore monochromatic outfits with one brightly colored accent accessory, bulldozed through the Zara girls. "I need to get in on this website of yours. How do I get my loans paid off?"

"What's it called anyway?" the other blond Zara girl asked from behind Accent Accessory. "And can I give you my name now so I can be at the top of the list?"

They were a fierce bunch. I may not have known their names, but I recognized them from around the Titan building, lugging bags that weren't their own, lunches not for them, hauling their bosses' crap up the escalator wearing six-inch heels, sweating through a dry-clean-only dress. I never imagined any of them having student-loan debt because they were all so well put together, so much better put together than me anyway.

But now that I was really looking at them, I could see how beneath all the lacquer these girls were hungry, like they ate Top Ramen for dinner every night, and I'd bet at least one of them had at one time or another considered selling her eggs to make rent.

"When's the site going to launch?" one of the blondes asked again.

It was clear to me all of a sudden how many of us had taken to heart the dicey, New Yorkian advice to "fake it till you make it." The worst part was that we were the ones who had already made it, over a number of astounding hurdles. And look at us. Look at them—circling me like overdressed vultures.

That was when it occurred to me, what I had to do.

"Soon," I said. "The site will launch very soon."

I would launch it. Make it real, legitimate.

"Where are you getting your funding?" someone called out.

I swallowed hard. "Well . . ."

"It's going to be crowdfunded," a brusque voice that wasn't mine replied. Wendi stepped through the group and positioned herself at my side. "When the site launches, anyone will be able to make donations."

"*You're* involved in this?" brunette Zara asked.

"I'm only assisting with the technical aspects," Wendi said, and then stared the girl to silence.

"But I am." Emily came up behind me. "I'm totally involved in this. I'm Tina's business partner."

Ginger appeared on the other side of Emily, smiling for a camera that wasn't there. "So am I," she said. "And we're having a huge launch party. Right, Tina?"

I had no words.

Wendi's jumping in I could understand—she was a veritable genius and quick to catch on to things. Not to mention, this was what she'd wanted all along, for her site to grow and expand. But Emily and Ginger were simply so swept away by their desire for attention that they just gave themselves up as part of this. Or whatever this was becoming.

Accent Accessory tugged excitedly at her chunky neon-yellow necklace. "When's the party going to be?"

"TBA," Emily said.

"It's a fund-raiser," Ginger added. "There will be an announcement when tickets go on sale."

"So wait," brunette Zara chimed back in. "What's the site called?"

Emily and Ginger turned to me with vacant faces.

Right. It needed a name.

I ran circles around my brain, trying to think of something

amazing on the spot, like Peggy Olson would have done in a *Mad Men* pitch meeting, but I was coming up blank.

"It's called," I mumbled, "it's called . . . the Assistants?"

"What?" brunette Zara asked.

"The Assistance," Accent Accessory said.

"Can you spell it?" one of the blond Zaras asked.

"The Assistance," Accent repeated, annoyed now. "A-s-s-i-s-t-a-n-c-e. As in, the act of assisting."

I formed an expression that said, *Duh, that's what I said.*

Wendi gave me a nod of her pink horns and pulled out her phone, presumably to buy the domain name immediately.

"All right, everyone," Carolyn called to us from the auditorium doors. "Finish up. Have you all had a chance to relax a little bit?"

Not a moment too soon, we were directed back into the seminar.

19

IN THE HOURS that passed between the haywire harassment seminar and my and Kevin's after-work fall-foliage stroll through Central Park, my plan solidified.

I would make good on this. I would make like the purpose-seeking millennial I almost was by transforming this obstacle into opportunity. *If life gives you lemons* . . . What would Robert say? Make a lemon cake? A lemon-drop martini?

This wasn't the worst thing that could have happened. The worst thing that could have happened was the truth being outed—not this nonsense about a crowdfunded nonprofit. But now that a crowdfunded nonprofit was what we were dealing with, well, lemon-meringue pie, anyone?

Kevin and I entered the park near Columbus Circle, drifting past a pickup string band and multiple dudes trying to sell us a rickshaw ride.

"I'm sorry I had such a strong reaction yesterday," I said, "to you leaking the info about the site. I just got scared." I paused momentarily in front of a pop-up shop hawking Banksy spray-paint-art knockoffs (or were they?).

Kevin nudged us along. "You were right, I should have asked you first. Though I did have Tim specifically say it was 'rumored' and 'yet to launch,' just to be safe. Did you catch that?"

I had. But rumors spread way faster than fact. Everyone knows that.

"How about you buy me a hot dog," I said as we conveniently confronted a street truck, "and we kiss and make up?"

He kissed me first, and then bought us dogs with mustard and sauerkraut. We ate them while we ambled farther into the park.

The funny thing was, this whole mess was sort of turning into Wendi's original plan—a pay-it-forward network. Taking money from the haves and distributing it to the have-nots. Except without our stealing to fund it. (An essential distinction.) It really wasn't such a bad plan after all.

"We're going to have a big fancy party," I said. "To launch the site. Will you be my date?"

Kevin stopped in his tracks and wiped his mouth with his mustardy napkin. "Do you even have to ask?"

"But I'm going to be the host," I said. "So you can't get mad if I don't pay enough attention to you."

"I'll make sure you pay attention to me." He wrapped his free arm around my torso and pulled me in closer.

We kept walking that way even though it was totally awkward and uncomfortable and kind of lame.

At this point, I will make like Zack Morris from *Saved by the Bell* and call a time-out, because I noticed something about this little scene in the park as it was happening. How I took the initiative in asking Kevin to be my date. How I was being uncharacteristically playful and flirtatious by not shrugging out of his affectionate-while-walking hold. In fact, I noticed that nothing about this scene said Tina Fontana.

Was I actually becoming a girl who threw parties? A woman in charge of a *real thing*? What could be next—would I start accessorizing?

"You look happy," Kevin said. He took a prideful bite of his hot dog.

Happy, not so much. Determined, yes. Because the best way to get away with a lie was to convince yourself of its truth.

"I like seeing you this happy." Kevin rubbed his hand in gentle circles over the small of my back, finally convinced he had in fact done the right thing by outing my project, just like he thought.

The truth, I told myself, was that (maybe) I could actually do something with the site once it was out there. (Maybe) I could really help people. Like the forearm tattoo of that girl Brutus from the NYU Women's Center said, maybe I could be the change I wanted to see in the world.

I laughed at myself, and then groaned.

Kevin crumpled the checkered cardboard boat that had previously housed his hot dog into a ball and tossed it into a trash can. "Aren't you hungry?" He pointed at my dog with only one measly nibble missing. "Usually with you and me it's a race to the finish."

"I'm fine." I smiled and sunk my teeth in for a hearty portion to prove it.

I guess the new Tina Fontana had less of an appetite than the old one.

"Coming up behind you, coming up behind you!"

A red Adidas tracksuit on Rollerblades sped past us, knocking me into Kevin and my hot dog onto the ground.

"Oh, hey." Margie Fischer spun around to face us, surprisingly adept on wheels.

Her tracksuit was just like the one Run DMC used to wear, except she paired it with a protective skating helmet, knee and elbow guards, and fingerless racing gloves.

"Are you two an item?" she asked, wagging her half-gloved finger between us.

"No," I said, as Kevin said, "Yes."

Margie laughed with gusto. "Sounds like you need to get your story straight."

What a thing to say. What did she mean by that?

"So what's this I hear about a party you're having, Tina?" Margie said. "For your *non-profit* website." She drew out the *non* and *profit* for special emphasis.

Dear god, I thought, *please don't let her say anything incriminating in front of Kevin.* And I remembered just then how Robert had asked me about Margie that day in the office, how he stared deep into my eyes all creepy like. *If she does start bothering you at all, asking you questions, anything like that . . . Because you know there are a lot of people out there who would like to see me hurt.* Robert had wanted to know if Margie was trying to bully me in any way. I wondered if this counted. She had knocked my hot dog out of my hands, after all.

"Do you want to come to our launch party, Margie?" I asked. "I think you'd agree with our site's mission."

Kevin grinned at my usage of the word.

Margie lifted her eyebrows all the way up to the brim of her helmet. "My, haven't you come a long way?" she said. "You're a regular Norma Rae now, aren't you?"

I wasn't sure what that meant, so I neither nodded nor shook my head.

"I don't like parties." Margie scratched at an itch beneath one of her elbow pads. "But we should talk, you and me. I am interested in your site's mission, as you put it. And how much does this one know?"

Kevin looked to me, a confused and slightly terrified retriever pup.

Again I neither nodded nor shook my head.

"Yeah." Margie smacked the top of her helmet with both hands. "That's what I figured." Then she spun around and peeled off, leaving us in her gravel dust.

I made an attempt to continue walking forward, but Kevin stayed put. "What was that about?" he asked.

"Nothing." I took his hand in mine and gave his arm a rub, as this situation called for an emergency public display of affection. "Margie's always messing with me. All because I once accidentally told her she should switch to skim milk."

Kevin tilted his head at me.

"Don't worry about it," I said, pulling him forward, and thankfully he followed along.

Back at my apartment, I inadvertently stepped foot into launch-party planning headquarters. Emily and Ginger, still in their work clothes, each with a phone to her ear, glanced up from their laptops.

"It needs to be someone big," Ginger declared into her cell. "I mean really big. Do you still have a relationship with Don Julio? How about Patrón? Or even Captain Morgan?"

Presumably, she was not referring to some excellently named male strippers she wanted to hire for the launch.

Emily ended her call and gestured for me to take a seat in the empty chair at the table, but I stayed put. Then she began waving her manicure in front of Ginger's face while loud-whispering, "Don't forget to ask about swag bags."

I bolted for my bedroom while her attention was diverted. God bless the two of them for being the exact sort of girls who were my polar opposite, because I'd never pull this off without them. They took to this abrupt change in plan *like white on rice*, as Robert would say. They were built for this shit—party planning, attention getting, convincing people to give them money.

I changed into my pajamas even though it was only eight thirty at night and took out my contact lenses, enjoying the soft, comforting blur the world became when I could no longer see it. I plopped down onto my bed and stared up at the ceiling bubble. It had lost a little weight on account of the recent dry spell. *Who knows*, I thought, *if the current drought continues, the ceiling bubble might dehydrate into the ceiling dried apricot. Then who would I tell my problems to?*

I glanced at my bedroom door to make sure it was tightly shut but I could still hear Ginger on her phone. "Remember that time you accidentally forgot to book your boss a hotel room, and he was stranded in LA, and I managed to call in a favor to get him the penthouse suite even though it was already booked? And he never even knew how badly you messed up? Do you remember that? Because here's what I need from you now . . ."

I listened to one call after the next, one favor traded for another.

"If you can get Brooklyn Brewery to sponsor us, I can get you a reservation for the best table at Per Se."

"If you score us Cipriani, I'll score you press tickets to Katy Perry at the Garden."

"I can get you on the list at Provocateur if you can hook us up with a DJ."

It was like listening to a podcast on high-end bartering. Access as currency, access in lieu of currency, because I knew for a fact that neither Ginger nor Emily, nor any of the assistants on the other end of the phone lines, had two dimes to rub together. After all, that's what got us into this mess in the first place.

As Robert Barlow's assistant, I understood the value of being in close proximity to power. Of being power's gatekeeper. Everyone who was anyone owed me a favor, and if they didn't owe me a favor they were dying to. But I never *called in* any of them, so to speak, because I never cared about any of that crap. Restaurants, nightclubs, hotels. I was much more of a Seamless-in-bed type.

But Emily and Ginger . . .

"You slept with my boyfriend while I was right in the next room. The least you can do is design our logo for free."

. . . were masters of leverage.

I wondered what Robert would think if he heard about our launch party, or when he heard about it, because Robert heard everything. Would he be proud of me, say, *Good job, shooter*? Would he become suspicious? And once the website went live, would it alter the way Robert looked at me? Would it force him to see something he hadn't seen before? Maybe he would sit me down for a drink in his office, and someone else would cut the limes. Imagine that. Maybe he would trust me a little less but respect me a little more. That was a trade-off worth making.

Ginger was on the phone with someone new. "You want a meeting with him? I'll put you on his calendar for this Wednesday morning, right after his massage so he'll be in a good mood, but only if you can deliver us no less than five donors. And I'm talking significant donors, like the Rockefeller kids, or the offspring to some oil mogul, or a Russian metals tycoon."

"What about George Clooney? Can't we get him involved somehow?"

I had the urge to go to the kitchen to remind Emily of that one altercation Robert and Clooney had on a Long Island golf course, the one where Robert made Clooney rerake his dune dirt or whatever—but I resisted. Perhaps Clooney's assistant would want to bury the hatchet, or the rake, as it were, and help us out.

My lord, this was blowing up fast. *Fast as small-town gossip. Faster than a prairie fire with a tailwind.*

How much money could we raise from real donors? I hadn't truly considered the possibilities, but all of a sudden it seemed like there was so much money all around us.

"Fontana!" Emily shouted in the direction of my bedroom

door. "What are your measurements? I want to call you in a proper dress for the party."

I turned off my lamp and threw my covers over my head.

Maybe there was such a thing as too much money. Imagine that, ceiling rain bubble, imagine that.

20

It was pretty crazy, how everyone hopped on the Tina Fontana train. How there was a Tina Fontana train. Emily and I (and sometimes Ginger, Wendi, and Lily, too) started going to Bar Nine after work, taking over the back room to make plans, talk things over. And each night that we went, more Titan assistants showed up. They'd linger for a while near our table before making a move, but then it would be: *Hi, I'm so-and-so, assistant to so-and-so. Hi, Tina! You probably don't know me, but I'm so-and-so's assistant. Hey there, my name is so-and-so and I assist so-and-so.*

I need help, each of them said.

These were the assistants to some of the most influential men in the world. They ran their boss's high-powered lives with formidable efficiency. And so, so many of them wept.

I've been perma-lance with no health insurance for four years, and he

*spends my year's salary on a jaunt into Prada on the way back from
lunch.*

*I live with two roommates in a one-bedroom just to get by, while my
boss takes a cab to the Hamptons every weekend. Do you know how much
a cab to the Hamptons costs?*

Most of them addressed me, not Emily, even though she was
prettier. I had a hunch it was because I was the Big Boss's assistant,
so by proxy I was the big boss of whatever this was. We were all
defined by whom we assisted. On e-mail chains among us with
bosses of the same name it was: *My Jeremy can do Tuesday at ten a.m.
Does that work for your Jeremy?* But Robert was always just Robert. I
was queen bee assistant.

All of the women who came to us had their own story, but
it was the same story, and not so different from Emily's or mine.
Student-loan debt coupled with shit pay had driven them all to
desperation—okay, *desperation* might be an overstatement. We
were assistants, not coal miners, not janitors at a nuclear power
plant—but I'm talking serious frustration here.

After two straight weeks of this, I finally took Emily aside in a
quiet corner of the room, pushed a fresh mojito into her hands to
keep her calm, and said, "What the hell is going on? Why are all of
our lives so utterly fucked up? We're college-educated white
women, for fuck's sake."

She didn't have a ready answer, for once. She only suckled her
mojito.

"Do you even realize what this has become?" I gestured toward
the flock of women converged at our table, awaiting our return.
"This started as a means to an end, but it's not anymore. We should
be preparing."

Emily got serious then. "You're right, we should get facials. And you definitely need to get your teeth whitened. They do it with a glow-light now, it only takes an hour." She moved past me to return to our table, but I caught her by her bracelet.

"We might have to make a statement," I said. "Like publicly. These girls are already looking to us for—"

"They're looking to us for money, Fontana. That's it." Emily freed her wrist from my grasp and rubbed at it dramatically. "Don't flatter yourself."

I took a pause. Was I flattering myself? Was I putting myself at the center of this, egocentrically?

I thought back to my years at NYU's Women's Center. *Egocentrically* was a term used ad nauseam there, along with *gaze* (e.g., "the male gaze") and *voice*. *Voice* was huge. There was one girl who sang to herself all the time—like, constantly—and if anyone asked her to please be quiet, we're trying to plan a Take Back the Night rally here, she would scream out, "Don't try to silence me! This is my voice!" And the room would concur, because the Women's Center, if nothing else, was a place where everyone had a right to their voice no matter how annoying and disruptive it may have been. Was that me now? Flattering myself into thinking I could sing and should be singing aloud when other people were present, and believing I had anything worth singing about?

"Can I go back to the table now?" Emily asked.

"We're probably going to have to do an interview," I said. "What are you going to answer when a reporter asks how we got here?"

Emily aligned her posture and locked her jaw. "I'll simply tell the truth. That I didn't always know what I wanted to do, but I always knew the woman I wanted to be." She tipped her drink toward me. "Diane von Furstenberg said that. I think she was talking about how she invented the wrap dress, but it applies here, too."

I gave up then and let Emily return to our table. At least she had a role model whose quotes she could bootleg, which was more than I could say for myself. I shuffled my One Stars upon the distressed wooden floor and watched Emily reclaim her seat, maintaining her perfect posture. Only Emily, Ginger, Wendi, and Lily were sitting. Everyone else fluttered around them. *Like moths to a bug light.*

I disagreed with Emily. These girls were looking to us for something more than just money. But I wasn't sure that we could actually give it to them. I wanted to, I really did. I wanted the Tina Fontana train to be real.

IT WAS the Friday morning before our launch party when Robert snuck up behind me. "I hear you're hosting some kind of charity shindig."

I jumped at the sound of his voice before the literal threat of his statement could set in.

"Did you?" I swiveled my chair around.

"I'm surprised you didn't come to me," he said.

Pause.

"We are the media, you know." He was polite enough not to say "*I* am the media," but that's what he meant.

"Oh, it's just a little thing," I said. "Something I got roped into helping out with."

"It doesn't sound little."

I started to sweat.

Instead of heading into his office like I'd hoped he would, Robert brought one of his brogues up on top of my drawer stand and leaned in.

"I never knew you were such an activist," he said.

"I'm not." I laughed nervously. "I'm really not."

Robert stared deep into my eyes, still with his leg up. "I wish you would have come to me, Tina. Before you went ahead with all this. You're a representation of this company, you know. And of me."

"Oh," I said. "I'm sorry, I didn't realize." I looked around aimlessly—at the silent screens flashing today's news in Robert's office, at a quartet of fresh-faced interns being trained on the coffeemaker, at Dillinger across the way trying to listen in on our conversation.

Robert leaned in closer. "If you're unhappy here, or with your salary . . . Or if you think things are unfair . . ."

"I'm not. It's not. It isn't even about me."

"But you started it," Robert said in a tone reminiscent of a sandbox argument. He shot a forbidding glance around the office to divert anyone from staring.

It occurred to me just then—Robert's tone. It wasn't challenging or aggressive or even belligerent. He was making this out to be about the company's image, or his reputation, but that wasn't it at all. It was far simpler than that: I'd hurt his feelings.

If there was one thing I understood about Robert, it was how important it was to him that you mind your manners. *Think before you speak,* he'd always say. *Think before you do. And if you make a mistake, be a man and own up to it. Make it right.*

I didn't think about how it would make Robert feel to hear about the launch from some website or, worse, one of his employees—but I should have. It was a matter of pride and a matter of respect.

I should have told him first.

So I adjusted my tone accordingly. "Shoot," I said. "I really screwed up. I didn't intend for this whole thing to become what it has, you've got to believe that. Other people got involved, and—"

"It'll be fine." Robert waved his hand dismissively. He stepped back and took his balls out of my face. "I just wish you would have come to me and talked to me about it. After all we've been through together."

After all we've been through together. I could literally feel my heart breaking.

I stood up then, which was a massive gesture on my behalf.

"Robert." I shocked us both by taking his hand. "What can I do to fix this? Tell me. I'll do anything."

"Forget it." He tugged his hand away, embarrassed—I'd gone too far.

"But I'm sorry," I said, and I truly was. "I'll do everything I can, to make sure this doesn't . . ."

What? Get any *more* out of hand? Who was I kidding?

"Good." Robert's dark eyebrows settled. And it seemed like he was about to say more when Glen Wiles arrived like a whirlwind for their daily meeting.

"Tina," Wiles said. "I hear you're the mastermind behind this new socialist website that's about to launch. That true?"

"Leave her alone," Robert said, protective in a fatherly way that made me silently swear an oath to somehow, someday, pay him back every cent. "When you have a free moment, Tina, would you fix us a cocktail?" Robert led Wiles into his office and closed the door.

In the meantime, I'd do the only thing I could do—fix him the best tequila with lime this side of Texas.

21

THE NIGHT BEFORE the launch party felt to me like what I imagined most girls feel the night before their wedding: terrorizing helplessness. There's nothing more to do, nothing more that can be done but go to sleep knowing the very next time you lay your head down, all this crazy shit will have already happened. So you can't stop imagining exactly how it'll all go, the getting from here to there, what will go wrong. There's also, of course, the enduring dread that this whole thing might turn out to be the biggest mistake of your life. It was enough to give a girl dry heaves, if that girl was me.

So I decided to drink, and Emily helped.

One glass of wine, two glasses of wine, and then Emily said, "We should probably go over your speech one more time."

It had been decided a week prior (by Ginger and Wendi) that I should be the one to give the speech at our launch party because I was supposedly "more real" than Emily was. "Emily's the face and Tina's the brains," were Ginger's exact words. Even I knew this was a stretch. Perhaps I did read as "real," which was often just code people used to describe a woman who was willing to eat a hamburger in public, but I would never really pass for a brain. If I were a character from *Alvin and the Chipmunks*, there's not a chance in hell I would be Simon. I would be Dave, the quick-tempered, insecure songwriter whose only companions were anthropomorphic rodents.

"Now?" I said to Emily. I was just about to curl up with my laptop and call it a night.

"Let's go over it one last time for good luck." Emily reached for the stack of frayed and food-stained index cards on my nightstand and handed them to me.

"I didn't even study for my SATs this hard," I said, taking the cards from Emily. Then I cleared my throat and began the speech that Wendi and Lily had helped me write—most of which we lifted verbatim from a pile of library books and a couple of Elizabeth Warren YouTube videos.

Emily reclined against my bed pillows and waited for me to begin.

"Here are the facts," I said. "Money buys less than it did a generation ago, while at the same time paychecks have dwindled."

"Stand up," Emily said.

"Are you serious? Come on." But I stood even as I protested because I really did want to do a good job when I gave this speech. It's a well-known fact that public speaking is ranked up there with the death of a spouse, divorce, and Christmas when it comes to the detrimental stress it can cause, so I was willing to stand the hell up if Emily really thought it would help my performance.

"Here are the facts," I said again. "Money buys less than it did a generation ago, while at the same time paychecks have—"

"Project your voice!" Emily shouted. "Pretend like you're confident!"

"Paychecks have dwindled!" I yelled back at her.

"Stop." Emily scowled like the head cheerleader at bitch-squad practice. "Take a breath and try again, better this time."

I started my speech yet again from the beginning, striving this time to exude a no-nonsense confidence, which somehow, coupled with the wine I'd ingested, resulted in my Bronx undertones rising to the surface.

"Here aw the facts," I said with my hands. "Money buys less than it did a generation ago, while at da same time paychecks have dwindled."

Emily muffled a laugh.

"Screw this." I chucked the index cards onto the floor and flopped back down on my bed beside Emily. "What I don't know by now, I'll never know." I took my wineglass back in hand, and Emily let me, both of us understanding that all there was really left to do was nothing.

THE FRONT OF CIPRIANI looked like the Parthenon, with Greek-style monolithic columns and decorative sculptures missing limbs. Inside the ballroom were glittering lights, shimmering cocktail dresses, suits and ties—all of which were to be expected. Unexpected was the multitude of electronic cigarette tips fireflying around the room. Why were these ridiculous things actually taking off?

The crowd was a handsome mix of new-media enthusiasts and the young philanthropists who appeared every Sunday in the *Times* fashion pages—the new generation of wealthy liberals who attended parties each weekend to give away their parents' money. These venerable future donors to the Metropolitan Opera, the New York Public Library, and the Museum of Modern Art appeared at ease in their fancy clothes and trendy haircuts, and they all seemed to already know one another.

"There he is," Emily said, referring to Kevin, who was standing at the bar.

Emily was wearing vintage Valentino (that some ex-boyfriend must have bought her) in silvery pearl. My dress was basic black with thin shoulder straps, nothing to come in your pants over, but Kevin opened his arms and dropped his jaw at the sight of me like I was Belle from *Beauty and the Beast* (the only Disney princess, mind you, who loved to read, and also the only one whose name literally meant *beauty*). He went in for a kiss that I swore made even the chandelier overhead blush.

Kevin had been the model supportive boyfriend since the announcement of the site. Partly, no doubt, because he still felt a little guilty for being the reason we had to prematurely announce it, but also because what Kevin had so Freudianly declared on our first date at Nougatine proved to be true: he was used to having a strong woman around telling him what to do. And I, against all odds, in the course of a few months, had become a strong woman who was telling a lot of people what to do. Kevin loved it. So the guy had mommy issues. Big deal. At least he'd finally stopped asking so many questions.

An hour of mingling passed, most of which involved Ginger

leering over me, with her breasts about to break free from their low-cut scoop neck, and removing alcoholic beverages from my hands. "Pace yourself," she'd say. "You have a speech to give." And then she'd down the drink herself.

By the time Emily appeared onstage to thank the crowd for coming, for their generous donations and their encouraging support, I'd managed to sneak just enough sips of booze to keep myself from throwing up in my mouth.

Emily was a presence onstage, confident, attractive, poised. All those years of acting training were finally paying off. She called my name with perfect elocution.

Kevin squeezed my hand once, twice, three times, and everyone else was clapping, so I knew it was time to drag my trembling ass to the stage.

I tried to breathe, but my heart was a bird that had just swallowed an Alka-Seltzer. I tried to remain calm, but the ruffled feathers of said bird had clogged all my airways. There were so many heads trained on me, each with a set of hopeful, expectant eyes.

The Titan assistants I'd gotten to know from our nights in the back room at Bar Nine stood out from the rest of the crowd. They were the ones whose dresses hung a little more cheaply, who hadn't just sat for professional blowouts, who weren't dripping with Harry Winston diamonds. They were the ones who'd volunteered to help out with the party planning in return for attendance. I still didn't know most of their names, but they all knew mine. The group of them stood together at the center of the floor: the Latina woman with hair that was brown on top and blond at the bottom; the women wearing too-big and bigger glasses; the blond and brunette Zara girls.

The one I referred to as Accent Accessory was holding her cell phone up in the air like a lighter at a Coldplay concert, videotaping me. "Yeah, Tina!" she called out, which I understood meant I was taking too long to begin.

"Thank you," I said, and forced a smile. I decided to focus on the chandelier hanging serenely above us, without falling down. How I wished to be that chandelier, or any inanimate object, really.

"Here are the facts," I said, and then paused. "Money buys less than it did a generation ago, while at the same time paychecks have dwindled."

These words, when I'd practiced them, had made me uneasy. (Who was I to be saying them, really? What did I know about any of this?) But hearing them now, amplified across this beautiful ballroom into the ears of all these flawless people, it felt like . . . well, honestly, it felt like singing.

"Add student-loan debt to the mix . . ." Pause. Eye contact with the audience. "The cost of a college degree in the United States has increased twelvefold in the past thirty years. That's one thousand, one hundred twenty percent."

Pause. Take a breath.

"Forty million Americans currently have outstanding student loans. Seven in ten college seniors will graduate with student debt. And forget about the six-figure graduate-school or law-school tuition debt so many of us take on in addition to our undergrad loans, as we race to super-educate ourselves, collecting more and more diplomas . . ." Pause. "For what?" Look up. "It's honorable that today's students think they'll be able to rise above all this, that they accept the skyrocketing cost of a college education without question. That they refuse to give up on their dreams in spite of these debilitating obstacles. But as the years pass, they struggle to pay down their loans, while striving to find decent work at a fair wage, while fantasizing about one day buying a home or starting a family . . . and they are just buried. And do you know who they blame? Themselves. They wonder: *Why can't I get it together?"*

The audience began to applaud. A few people whooped and hollered. This hadn't happened when I'd rehearsed alone in my bedroom.

I had to raise my voice to speak over them. "Our country is failing to live up to its promise of opportunity and fairness. It used to be true that if you went to college and worked hard, you could count on having a decent middle-class life—but that's just not true anymore. Economic and political changes that have occurred over the past three decades have made the middle-class American dream for today's twenty- and thirtysomethings far less possible than it was for their parents' generation. It's not that we're lazy, that we have no work ethic, or that we have outrageous spending habits. It's that we've been screwed."

The room roared. I felt it in my chest. In my loins, wherever they may be. Unintentionally, I smiled.

"So we're taking things into our own hands. Our goal is to help all the women out there who've tried so hard to do everything right but still can't get ahead. And maybe, just maybe, the people in power will take notice of what we're doing here. What we're trying to do. And then we can really spark some change."

I stepped back from the microphone and flashbulbs exploded.

Kevin's was the first face I saw, once I could see again. By the way he was beaming at me, smacking his hands together hard and high in the air, I knew I'd done a good job. Against all odds, I'd rallied this crowd. They better than liked me.

Emily joined me onstage, carrying a remote control. She adjusted the microphone to her height and pointed the controller at a giant screen behind us.

"And now the moment we've all been waiting for," she announced as the screen came to life.

It was the website. Our website. Wendi had fiddled with it since I'd last seen it. She'd made it cleaner, sharper, less wordy, and she'd added two scrolling tickers across its top.

"We are live," Emily said.

The ticker on the left was labeled *Members*. It started at two. Emily and me, I guessed.

The ticker on the right was labeled *Money Raised*. It started at $250,000. The amount taken in from tonight's tickets, I supposed.

And then it happened. The numbers started rolling.

The site reached fifty-two members in less than sixty seconds.

"Look at 'er go," Emily said, reluctant to step away from the microphone. "Your donations made this possible. Thank you."

The *Members* ticker rolled like it was on molly. We reached 102 members in less than another minute.

"But if you're feeling a little extra generous," Emily said, "after all the delicious beverages you've enjoyed tonight, provided by Patrón and the Brooklyn Brewery . . ."

She smiled. Sponsorship shout-outs, check.

". . . our diligent volunteers are coming around with iPads . . ."

Out came Wendi and Lily, each carrying an eye-high stack of iPads. They were both wearing T-shirts featuring our logo. Our logo was just the words *The Assistance* in a cool-looking font, but this "design" was garnering lots of attention because the designer was some kind of art star. "I could have done that," I whispered to Emily when I first saw it, and I'll say it again here. Design is a career that baffles me, along with consulting and hedge fund management, and waving the flag at a construction site. But I digress.

Lily's T-shirt was pale pink; Wendi's was black and she'd torn off the sleeves, so it was more of a muscle shirt. The iPads were unknowingly on loan from the Titan digital supply closet.

"Feel free to pick up an iPad," Emily said, "and donate a dollar, or ten dollars, or ten thousand dollars, just to see the ticker here on the big screen change."

What a bunch of fools. Would you believe they actually fell for this? Half the crowd scrambled for an iPad and began tapping away at it while watching the big screen.

The *Money Raised* ticker started to flip as quickly as the *Members* ticker.

I figured it was safe for me to leave the stage at this point. My work for the night was done, at last.

Kevin appeared the moment I stepped down and handed me a glass of wine. "I'm so proud of you," he said.

I gratefully accepted the wine, as well as his praise. "Thank you so much for coming," I replied, which was a throwaway comment, but I followed it up with, "I'm really glad you're here." And the moment I said it, I realized just how much I wasn't bullshitting him. I actually *was* glad he was there. I would rather have had him there with me than anyone else in the world. Which may not sound like much—but I'd never been able to say that about anyone before.

Kevin put his hands on my bare arms, and they felt so warm. He slid them up to my shoulders, then back down to my elbows, and pulled me in toward him. He kissed my cheek, then my neck, and then whispered into my ear, "I love you so much."

Love, he said. *Love*. For the first time.

He reached for my face and kissed me with a passion that brought even the tickers to a stunned halt. If a photo of the moment hadn't been Instagrammed, I would have been sure I'd imagined it. I would have been sure I'd imagined the entire night.

22

I AWOKE the morning after the launch party to the sounds of hipsters gossiping their way to Sunday brunch, which told me I'd slept till at least eleven. My alarm clock verified this and Emily arrived shortly after, still wearing last night's dress.

"Walk of shame?" I asked.

"I didn't walk." Emily reached for my coffee cup and finished what was inside. "The young gentleman I went home with last night was the most generous lover I've ever known. I think his father is some sort of Russian metals tycoon? He bought me a thirty-dollar breakfast." She unzipped the back of her dress. "Eggs Benedict."

"Congratulations," I said, reaching for an Oreo from the stack on my nightstand.

Emily waddled into the kitchen on bare feet, her dress wide open in the back. She returned with a fresh cup of coffee for herself and resumed her striptease, ceremoniously stepping out of her dress and then wrapping herself in a silk kimono robe that my mother surely would have described as Oriental.

"Have you looked at the website?" she asked. "How much money did we raise last night?"

"I don't know," I said with my mouth full. "I haven't checked."

"Are you kidding me? You're just lying there eating cookies and didn't even think to turn on your computer?"

"Why didn't *you* check?" I shot back in the vicious manner of voice I usually reserved for the a-holes who worked at the South Williamsburg post office.

"My phone is dead or I would have. What the hell is your problem?"

"Kevin told me he loved me last night."

"Whaaat?" Emily pulled her silk kimono tighter and took a seat on the edge of my bed. "And what did you say?"

"Nothing."

"Nothing?"

"I guess I panicked. I was so caught up in the moment." I knew what Emily was going to say: that I was socially inept, emotionally stunted. And she was right. I was basically the Holden Caulfield of adult dating.

I sat up to shoo away the cookie crumbs that had gathered on my chest just as the apartment's buzzer rang out.

"Oh my god." I locked eyes with Emily. "I bet it's Kevin. He's been doing this supposedly romantic thing lately called 'surprising' me."

"Or he just wants to hear you say *I love you* back, you idiot." Emily glanced out the window and then back at me. "You can't let him see you this way. You're a goddamn mess. You have Oreo all over your mouth."

"What do I do?"

"Go hide in the bathroom and run the showerhead. Quick!"

I did as she said. I could have probably used an actual shower, but instead I put my ear to the bathroom door, trying to hear the action over the whooshing water.

The apartment door opened with a squeak, followed by heavy footsteps.

A gruff voice penetrated the quickly rising steam, nothing like Kevin's consistently agreeable baritone. "You're not who I came to see."

Emily called out to me. "False alarm!"

I skulked out of the bathroom to find Wendi sitting down at our kitchen table. She eyed Emily from head to toe. "This robe you're wearing," she said. "It's bordering on racist."

Emily swept her hands down the front of her robe's silky, cherry-blossomed surface. "It's not like I taped my eyes back or something."

"I will let that one slide because today is such a happy day." Wendi reached across the table for Emily's laptop, pecked it to life, and tapped at a few keys, bringing up the Assistance website.

"Holy cannoli!" I said, sounding like the Italian version of the chick from *Fifty Shades of Grey*. "Look at all the money!"

The *Money Raised* ticker had hit $406,813.54.

"This happened overnight?" Emily scrambled for the chair closest to Wendi. "While we were asleep? Do you think people were drunk-donating?"

"Still counts." Wendi scrolled through the thousands—thousands!—of members who'd already submitted their debt statements to the site.

"I've got to hand it to you, Tina," Wendi said. "This was not my original vision for my program, but it's working out pretty nicely."

"This wasn't my original vision for becoming a millionaire either." Emily's face shone with the radiance of her laptop screen. "But it *is* working out nicely. It's like, who even remembers anymore what we took from Titan?"

For a moment, I feared Wendi might gore Emily with her horns.

"It's okay." I cautiously touched the elbow of Wendi's hoodie. "She knows not to talk like that outside of this apartment."

Wendi contorted her face into a sneer and then shifted the laptop away from Emily and closer to me. "Let me show you how the new site works." She continued scrolling through our many members. "Until we can make this a more perfect science, I suggest just picking a winner at random, like a lottery. Watch me now."

She double-clicked to open a debt statement for $81,101 that belonged to a twenty-nine-year-old woman in Chicago.

One click, two clicks, three clicks, and an e-check for $81,101 was sent to the woman's account. The ticker labeled *Money Donated* flipped accordingly.

"That's all there is to it," Wendi said. "The only tricky part is to pace yourself with the money." She turned the laptop toward me. "Your turn."

It was so idiotically simple a Gen X monkey with no computer training could have done it. I clicked on a debt statement for $108,023 that belonged to a twenty-six-year-old woman in Portland, Oregon.

One click, two clicks, three clicks, and an e-check for $108,023 was sent to her account.

The *Money Donated* ticker flipped to $189,124. It made me lightheaded, like my first adolescent drag of a cigarette, which by the way was not electronic.

"This could get addictive," I said.

"Let me do one." Emily slid the laptop back toward herself.

"Just a moment, Memoir of a Geisha." Wendi placed a bullying hand on Emily's silken shoulder. "You have to be careful to limit the amount you give out each day. It has to be a ratio, so people recognize there's a direct correlation to the giving and receiving. Like supply and demand, understand?"

Emily glanced up from the screen. "Do you honestly think there'll ever be a supply to meet this much demand? That's absurd."

Wendi erupted in inexplicable high-pitched laugher. "You've got a better head for business than one would think. You're correct, this site is the technological equivalent of throwing a bunch of money onto the street. There's not going to be any left over when you walk away." She turned to me. "But the more money we take in with time, the more we can distribute. For now, send out five checks a day. No more, no less. This'll make people excited about it, like a contest or a sweepstakes. Try to mix it up, some small debts with some large ones each day. But obviously you can't exceed the amount we've got in the *Money Raised* bank at any time."

"That's it?" I'd already snatched the laptop back from Emily and was scrolling through the statements, searching for our next winner. "Only five a day?"

I felt like God, or what I sometimes imagined God to feel like when he was blowing off steam: scrolling through people's lives on his iPad like an old lady at a Vegas slot machine. Cherries-orange-apple—you'll get hit by a car today. Lemon-grapes-banana—sorry, that's cancer. Triple sevens—jackpot; someone just paid off all your student-loan debt.

It felt good, playing the Almighty. Because like the Tibetan Buddhists who don't even believe in Him claim (and who, by the way, threw awesome concerts with the Beastie Boys in the late nineties), real happiness just might come from putting others first.

Though the Buddhists would probably insist that the "real happiness" also be egoless—and this was definitely not that. No, this was a way more Americana type of happiness, steeped in pride and self-regard. *Happy as a pig in shit,* Robert might have called it. Or maybe that's what I'm calling it, I don't know. Because something about it was sort of shitty. Yeah, I was happy I was helping others. And I was happy I'd struck upon something I was good at, and even got applauded for. And I was happy to really feel like somebody for the first time in my life. But more than all that, I was happy that we'd gotten away with it.

Emily was right. It was like, who even remembered anymore what we took from Titan? But I remembered. And somehow seeing how all this was turning out—how at times I'd catch myself being genuinely excited and hopeful and optimistic about my future, and then remember—it was making me realize the person I could have become if only I hadn't . . .

. . . what?

If only I hadn't stolen? Broken? Made a bad choice? Made a dozen bad choices? But we'd gotten away with it, and I have to admit that I was really fucking happy about that.

23

Arriving at work on Monday morning, I was struck by how similar it felt to my first day at Titan. The tingling in my belly, the good nerves mingling with bad, the way I was thinking as I rode the escalator up to the elevator bank, *Do I have time to run and grab a bagel at the café?*

But unlike my first day, today there were people greeting me and smiling at me. Both in front of and behind me on the escalator there were girls craning their necks to catch my eye and wave. On the escalator parallel to mine, Gwendolyn Clark, a producer who was a known starfucker, paused midsentence in her conversation with one of Titan's most celebrated newscasters to acknowledge *me*. I'm not gonna lie, it felt pretty good, because attention, even the whorish kind, can seriously boost one's endorphins.

In the elevator—elevator B—there were women who I was pretty sure had been instructed by the central kiosk to proceed to elevator A or C but filed into mine anyway. I didn't even know what to do with all these women batting their extra-long eyelashes at me. Should I be aloof and check my phone? Pretend to look for something in my bag? And then it hit me: This was why people walked around wearing giant headphones all the time. Because when you're popular, it's the easiest way to ignore everyone who wants you to notice them. It wasn't about the music at all, was it?

When I reached the fortieth floor, it was pretty much business as usual, but Robert wasn't in yet. Which meant I could have totally run to the café for a bagel after all.

I settled in at my desk, logged on to everything I had to log on to, checked the phone messages, and then got to the real business of the day: opening the Assistance page and allocating the day's checks to our five lucky winners.

When Robert walked up behind me, he didn't make a sound.

"Tina."

I jumped an inch from my chair.

"Robert!" I shouted.

"What's that you're looking at?"

"Nothing." I X'd out every window on my screen like a game of computer Whack-A-Mole.

Robert took off his suit jacket and draped it over his arm. "Will you come into my office, please?"

I reached for my pen and notepad and didn't feel the least bit nervous.

For months now, every time Robert had asked to speak to me I'd nearly lost control of my bowels. But not this time. This time I gave Robert the usual three-step head start, watched the carpet into his office, and closed the door behind me, thinking the whole time about getting back to my desk to send out those checks.

"Please sit," he said.

I sat, anticipating great praise. Maybe a good ol' boy's smack on the back for a job well done. Perhaps a *Man oh man, your site took off like a greased sow.* Or a *You're as smart as a hooty owl, aren't you?*

Instead he leaned on his elbows with his hands enfolded in front of him. "Is there anything you feel you need to say to me?" he asked.

I was a master at deciphering Robert's tone, but whatever it was I was hearing now was entirely new. It didn't strike me as the falling timbre of disappointment. More the enfeebling tonic of sadness.

"No," I said.

We sat staring at each other for a moment. From the outside, any stranger could have mistaken us for lovers, or, more appropriately, father and daughter when the daughter has done something wrong, but she isn't sure which wrong thing the father knows about.

What did he want from me? Did I do something at the launch party that rubbed him the wrong way? Robert could be so impossible when it came to how much he relied on my knowing what he was thinking without his having to tell me.

Fine. I would have to be the one to speak first.

"Have I done something to upset you?" I asked.

He broke eye contact then, which I didn't know what to make of. Breaking eye contact was something Robert did not do. Ever.

He looked down at his desk, and then at his shoes, which had remained securely on the floor. When he returned his eyes to me, he said, "It's been great working with you, Tina."

I said, "What?"

"Really. I'm going to miss you."

"Wait. You're firing me?"

"No, no," he said. "But you can take a few minutes to clear out your desk and all that." He tossed an envelope at me. "This is a generous severance package. It'll keep you afloat for a while."

So he wasn't firing me, but he was?

His words, the envelope, the room, all swirled around me in slow motion. I was afraid if I tried to talk it would come out sounding like stroke-speak, all loose lipped and tongue addled.

"Don't look so unhappy," he said. "I'm kicking you out of the nest because I know you'll never leave on your own. And it's time." He stood up and extended his hand for a firm shake. "You're welcome," he said. "Now go on."

Everything was spinning.

Had I been caught or hadn't I? I honestly wasn't sure.

Lurking at my desk were two jar-headed Titan security guards. Robert gave them a nod and I knew that was my cue to get up and leave quietly and immediately, with my dignity intact. They had already placed an empty cardboard box on my chair to speed up the process. These guys knew what they were doing.

I scanned the office as I collected my belongings. Dillinger had his headphones hanging sideways off his head and his mouth was a speechless O. All the guys on the floor appeared equally flabbergasted. Nobody made a sound.

One security guard flanked me on either side to escort me into the elevator and down to the lobby. "Titan policy," they told me. "Legal reasons."

"I don't have a gun," I joked.

They didn't laugh.

The elevator dropped and its doors slid open to a small crowd of inquisitive eyes. I clutched my cardboard box of stuff to my chest—an image that would hit Twitter and the like within minutes—and watched the textured floor tile, step by step, to the top of the escalator.

It was incredible how quickly word had spread, via IM most likely, from a few nosy, gossip-hungry coworkers on my floor (Jason Dillinger, I'm looking at you) to all corners of the Titan building.

I could hear Kevin pleading with my security guards. "What's going on here?" he asked, louder each time he repeated it. "Roberto," he said. "Sal. What's up?"

A few cell-phone cameras documented it all. One followed me in a diagonal parallel down the opposite escalator.

Another cluster of onlookers lingered around the front doors. I searched for Emily or Ginger, or Wendi or Lily—or even Margie Fischer—but there was no sign of any of them.

Lobby security dispersed the boldest looky-loos blocking my exit and escorted me out of the building, to the curb, where a black sedan waited with its door ajar.

Roberto and Sal guided me into the backseat, careful not to bump my head, and shut the door behind me. Those who made it out to the sidewalk watched me get driven away through their LCD screens.

"I'm going to Williamsburg," I said to the driver.

He nodded. "I know where you're going."

Twenty minutes later I was inside my apartment, sitting at my kitchen table, staring at my cardboard box of stuff, which wasn't much stuff at all really. My cell phone was blowing up, but I was too catatonic to answer. Kevin, Ginger, Wendi, Lily—they all left voice mails I didn't bother to listen to.

Since the day I deposited that first check, I'd created dozens of different renditions of what it would look and feel like for Robert to sit me down and fire me. Sometimes the police were involved. Sometimes Glen Wiles was involved. Usually I cried. A few times Robert cried. But things never turn out how you picture them, do they? I never imagined it would end so vaguely.

Or had it still not ended? Was there more to come? What if this was only the beginning of the end, or in the way of a too-long Scorsese film, only the end of the beginning?

My front door swung open then, and Emily stormed in looking like she had an approximate blood pressure of heart attack.

"Are you okay?" I asked.

"What the hell do you think?" She tossed her purse into the bedroom.

Emily wasn't carrying a cardboard box, which indicated to me that she, at least, hadn't also been fired. She sat down across from me at the kitchen table, too upset to even think of first fixing herself a drink.

"What happened?" she asked. "What did Robert say to you?"

I felt my cheeks go hot. "He said he was letting me go because he knew I would never quit on my own."

"He didn't mention anything about . . ."

"No," I said.

"Well don't let that trick you into a false sense of security. You're likely to be wearing an orange jumpsuit by next week."

"But he gave me a severance package," I said. "Would he have done that if he—"

"Fontana, if you want to pull that cardboard *Just Fired!* box over your head and leave it there, be my guest. But we're caught. There's no other explanation."

Emily unlatched her necklace, unclasped her bracelet, and slid off her rings. "You know I hate having to get real with you this way," she said, speaking to me in her lower-class accent now. "But we've got to figure out our next move before it's too late. You get me?"

I nodded.

"So the only remaining question," she said, "is what do you think of Mexico?"

I stared at the pile of gold and jewels on the table. "Are you asking me to Thelma and Louise it with you?"

"The alternate version, where the car lands safely over the border?" Emily said. "Yes, I am."

I tried to imagine what that would be like. Emily and me living the south-of-the-border fugitive life. Would it be all Coronas and avocados? Or would it be more like Montezuma's revenge? And, from this point on, would I always frame my questions-to-self in the style of a Carrie Bradshaw column?

Emily pulled her hair back into a ponytail, which she tied in place using only the hair itself.

"There's about four hundred fifty K on the site right now." She watched my reaction closely. "We can take it and run. It's enough to start a new life, and then we can, like, open a fruit stand or sell handmade bracelets or something."

"You're serious," I said.

"*Sí*," Emily answered. "*Mucho.*"

"I don't know," I said. "I'm so pale, and I've never been good at crafts. I need to think."

"Well think fast, Fontana. Because we're just about out of time."

I shut myself into my bedroom to do just that: think. If thinking mostly consisted of crying out to the ceiling rain bubble, "How did this happen? What am I supposed to do now?!" I'd never been great when it came to tragedy or decision-making, and this was both. This was like having your dog hit by a car and having to choose a paint color for your vestibule at the same time. I tried going over my options. Run away? Stay and confess? Take a Xanax and a long nap and hope for the best?

Later that night, I met Kevin at Diner in South Williamsburg because I refused to leave Brooklyn and he insisted on taking me out to dinner so we could "talk." My true intention was to do as little talking as possible. Really I was only buying time till I figured out what to do next, and I figured I might as well have a decent meal in the interim.

Diner is in no way a diner. I want that to be clear. Like all things Williamsburg, it's ironic and expensive and you're either in on the joke or you're not. After a forty-minute wait, we were finally seated.

"I still don't understand," Kevin said, squeezing into our tight booth.

"Neither do I. Why is this stupid place so crowded?"

"I was talking about Barlow firing you."

"Oh." I made a quick scan of the knitted hats and scruffy beards on either side of us to be sure no one was hiding a tape recorder. Then I remembered tape recorders were rendered obsolete in 1991, and with a minimum of two iPhones on each tabletop, my caution was pointless.

"Has anyone ever understood why Robert Barlow does the things he does?" I said.

"I thought you did," Kevin said.

Suddenly, our waiter squeezed into our booth beside me, to tell us about the menu. There aren't any menus at Diner because their food options are seasonal. If you insist on seeing a menu, or pretend to be deaf, they'll belligerently scribble down the names of a few food items onto your paper tablecloth. This is intended to be authentic. Authentic what, I don't know.

We had a short chat with our abundantly tattooed waiter about how organic and grass-fed everything was, and then he asked us what we wanted and I realized I hadn't been listening to him at all. I'd completely zoned out on our verbal menu options.

Kevin ordered some kind of fish. He actually just said, "I'll have the fish," which signaled to me that he'd also zoned out and taken a shot in the dark.

"Soup?" I said.

"Soup's out of season," the waiter replied.

"Burger," I said.

"And some beer," Kevin added. "Whatever you recommend."

This date was swiftly turning into the blooper reel of a Food

Network reality show. Our craft beers arrived, and I immediately knocked mine over. Another thing about Diner is the tables aren't level. Diner's too artisanal for unslanted surfaces.

Our waiter dutifully brought me a new beer and I sipped it carefully with both hands.

"Do you think Robert fired you because of your website? Because he disagrees with it politically?" Kevin rubbed at the condensation on his glass. "You might have legal standing, if you think that's the reason."

I gazed around the restaurant's interior, which resembled the inside of a zeppelin airship. "I spy three separate girls wearing tights for pants," I said. "Can you find them?"

This effectively made it impossible for Kevin to rest his puppy eyes on mine. I couldn't deal with puppy anything right now. My intestines ached and I felt like crying. All I really wanted was to go home and be by myself.

But Kevin persisted. "Tina, I can't help you if you don't let me into what you're feeling right now."

Jesus.

"I don't know what I'm feeling," I said as honestly as I could. "Robert didn't fire me exactly. It's more like he gave me a nudge out of the nest."

"I don't know what that means," Kevin said. "Was it your decision to leave?"

"Ultimately, yes," I lied. "I got a generous severance package, and now I can focus all my attention on the site."

"But the way you were escorted out, he made it look like you were some sort of criminal—"

I nearly spilled my second beer at the word. "That's what they do when people who are close to Robert leave the company," I said, which sounded plausible even to me. "It wouldn't have been such a big deal if a crowd hadn't formed to see me out."

"So you quit." Kevin's puppy brows were crinkled in that way that suggested he didn't fully believe me. "But everyone's saying you were fired."

"I didn't want to be an assistant anymore," I said. "Is that so hard for you to understand?"

Kevin drew back like I'd spit in his face. I hadn't spit, I don't think. I was pretty sure it was his sensitivity that made him draw back like that. It was a constant struggle for me to keep my Bronx in check and not steamroll over Kevin's gentleness at any given moment.

"I'm sorry," I said. "I didn't mean to snap at you. The truth is, I'm feeling a lot of different things right now. This is a big change for me, and I'm not great with change."

I impressed even myself with this one.

Our food came, finally, and Kevin, recalibrated to his former balance, held a perfect forkful of his entrée up to my mouth. "Do you want to try this? I think it might be trout. Possibly in truffle oil?"

"I hate truffle oil," I said.

"Yeah, fuck truffle oil." He threw his fork down onto his plate, smiling wide.

He was trying so hard to be a good sport.

But I was barely keeping it together.

There were suddenly so many variables, everything that felt like a given only yesterday now had to be called into question. Even my relationship with Kevin. If Robert had caught on to anything, or if my being fired wasn't the end of this, or if I was going to Thelma and Louise it with Emily before the week was through, I should maybe, like, give Kevin a clue that things weren't kosher. That everything wasn't coming up roses. Or whatever other idiomatic cliché existed as shorthand for saying things had in fact become totally fucked. What would such a clue be? I didn't know, but blatant avoidance of meaningful conversation and random tantrum throwing appeared to be my current course of action till I came up with something better.

When dessert came, the flourless chocolate cake we ordered had walnuts hidden inside it. I wasn't allergic—but, come on, walnuts?

"The flourless chocolate cake is a classic," I shouted, loud enough for the entire airship to hear. "Why do this?"

Maybe our waiter had mentioned the walnuts during our chat and we'd missed it, but still.

Kevin called for the check.

We didn't talk the entire walk back to my apartment, which was only about twelve minutes, yet a lot of time for silence. And when we reached my front door, I didn't invite him inside. Instead I just stood there like a moron.

"Listen, Kevin," I started to say—fully prepared to let him off the hook and break up with him right there—before he leaned in and kissed me.

I drifted backward, momentarily dazed. In spite of my hysteria, of behaving suspiciously and dodgily all night, of refusing to eat my dessert on principle—he still wanted to kiss me good night.

"Don't worry," he said. "Everything's going to be okay." And he kissed me again.

The sensation of his lips on mine made the taut muscles of my jaw relax. My shoulders settled and the knot in my gut loosened just so. But I knew I had to go inside alone.

You're likely to be wearing an orange jumpsuit by next week, Emily had said. What if she turned out to be right? And what if starting over in Mexico with a new identity, subsisting on empanadas or whatever, was better than finding out?

"Thank you for dinner." I closed the door in Kevin's sweet face, and it felt like I was closing the door on my entire life.

If you love someone set them free, I told myself. *Before they're brought in on accessory charges.*

24

THE NEXT DAY, I didn't have a job to go to. When was the last time I was just hanging around my apartment alone on a Tuesday morning? Couldn't tell you. I might have immediately lapsed into boredom, ambling around, opening the fridge, closing it, opening it again—had the future of my entire adult life not been pushed to the edge of a cliff the day before. So I made coffee and checked the website.

Overnight, Wendi had apparently gone into full-on fixer mode (à la Olivia Pope from *Scandal*). Wendi was a gladiator when it came to manipulating the Internet. She'd somehow managed to turn a clear negative (me, fired) into a positive (me, class hero). Wendi posted photos of me being hauled out of the Titan building onto the *"News"* section of our website, beneath buzz-worthy headlines like: *Tina Fontana Quits Titan Corp., Escorted Out.* And:

Fontana to Barlow: I Quit! The subtext here, if you hadn't caught it, was that I left my job of my own accord.

Thankfully, no one had yet struck upon the terms *embezzlement, forgery,* or *grand larceny.*

For now, Wendi's posts and the resulting online chatter only gained traction for the site. Our donations spiked. Such is the justice of the digital age.

Robert understood this sort of justice better than anyone—he'd been its master for years, using his vast media empire to control the layman's chatter. How many times had I sat in the conference room, taking the editorial-meeting minutes, and jotted down a variation on the same statement: *We don't have to win this argument. We only have to muddy this argument enough so they don't win.* Robert may as well have had those words tattooed across his bare chest (which, to be clear, I had never seen). So it was surprising—and perhaps fitting?—that this was exactly what we accomplished in the hours following my firing. Wendi stirred up enough mud to make a clear winner impossible to decipher.

Only yesterday Emily had wanted to run away, and I was on the brink of setting Kevin free into the wilderness, the way John Lithgow and the Henderson family had to do back in the eighties with their beloved bigfoot, Harry. But as far as I was concerned, that plan was officially off the table. How could I run away from this? Google *Tina Fontana* now, and it was me who came up first, not those other Italians and Spaniards of lesser notoriety who shared my name. Such success came with responsibility, didn't it? I couldn't just bolt.

Besides, in the light of a new morning, with a fresh pot of

coffee in front of me, I reevaluated my situation more favorably. If Robert had actually figured anything out, wouldn't he have pressed charges immediately? He could have had me airlifted straight to Guantánamo if he wanted to. So maybe he really was just kicking me out of the nest. Because deep down he loved me like a daughter (maybe even more than he loved his one daughter who wrecked his Mercedes that one time). And maybe it finally occurred to him, like it had only recently occurred to me—and to these total strangers on the Internet—that I was capable of doing more with my life than just filing papers, keeping a calendar, and mixing drinks.

So I brought my coffee and my laptop into bed with me, to more comfortably explore all the new features Wendi had added to the site—and there were many. She'd created tabs where people could submit short essays, so they could tell us how they would pay it forward if we paid off their debt. And she'd added a place for users who'd just had their debt paid off to tell us how their lives had already changed for the better.

She'd added a few banners, too. One read: *Did paying off your student-loan debt free you up to get married? Buy your first home? Start a family? We want to see photos!*

There were links to my speech from the launch party. And, of course, user comments: *The problem is that nobody talks about what they make. It's shame disguised as humility. Screw that. I'm a thirty-two-year-old assistant and I make $30,000 a year.*

I clicked around some more and discovered a place where users could upload videos.

Great, I thought. This was all we needed. DIY porno and homemade cat movies. But when I began scrolling through the thumbnails, I quickly got sucked in. First I chose a video posted by Lisa in

Detroit (former debt: $78 K). Then one from Su-Yung in Philadelphia (former debt: $103 K). Then one from Joanna in New Orleans (former debt: $91 K). All the women looked to be somewhere around my age. *Thank you,* each of them said. *This changes everything for me.*

I let my head fall back onto my pillow and allowed my eyes to go soft on the ceiling rain bubble. Robert had tie clips that cost as much as those debts. One man's private-jet ride to Key West was another woman's second chance at life. I know, this isn't news to anyone—and it sure as hell wasn't news to me.

What can you do?

Gratitude is so much more dignified than ungratefulness, than speaking out about a subject as frowned-upon as an "unlevel playing field," so these women simply said thank you. They promised to pay it forward. They went back to their jobs as office assistants and teachers and X-ray technicians and worked extra hard. I got it. That's just the way it was. But if one wasn't careful, it was enough to turn a girl like me into a girl like Wendi Chan, at least in the privacy of her own collapsing, overpriced bedroom.

That's where I was, and what I was thinking, when I received Kevin's text.

KEVIN ASKED ME to come over, to meet him at his apartment after he got home from work, which should have been my first clue that something was amiss. In spite of what New Yorky television shows have misled non–New Yorkers to believe, city dwellers, especially those who reside in different boroughs, never just say *come over*. In truth, we usually don't meet face-to-face without scheduling a week ahead of time and confirming the day of. Our LA counterparts who come to visit and want to hang out may be frustrated by this, but they just have to learn to deal. We're busy here. Also, when we do meet, it will probably be at a bar, coffee shop, or restaurant located halfway between our starting points, because unless you're very rich or lucky enough to have a dead grandmother who left you her rent-controlled mansion, you live in a cramped one-bedroom.

Yet I refused to question Kevin's ominous text requesting that I take the forty-five-minute subway ride from my apartment in Williamsburg to his on the Upper East Side. Nope, nothing weird about that at all.

Like attracts like, I told myself on the way there, which was obviously something I'd read in *The Oprah Magazine*. It was a New Agey way of saying: *Think positive, dear one, because if you think bad thoughts, really fucking awful things will happen to you and it'll be your own goddamn fault.* But in spite of this positive self-talk, my heart began to race while I rode the train to Kevin's apartment and then waited on his doorstep to be buzzed in. The blue-black night sky took on an eerie prescient glow, the way the light changes in a movie flashback, or when you've had too much Red Bull and vodka.

Kevin opened his apartment door and I went right for him, wrapping my arms around his torso, burying my face into his neck. "I missed you today," I said.

He held himself rigid, then carefully detached me and took a step back. He was wearing a Hanes T-shirt and loose jeans. I wasn't used to seeing him dressed so casually, and the first thought to run through my mind was, *This is what he'd look like around the house all the time if we got married.* Clearly I was not feeling like myself.

"Can we sit down for a minute?" Kevin said. "I want to talk to you."

I followed him across his minuscule apartment, to the couch, with an impending doom coagulating in my gut.

"I had a meeting today," he said. "With Glen Wiles."

I stared down at the area rug, which was still vaguely discolored with chocolate and strawberry stains.

"Tina, can you look at me?"

I did, though it took effort, and I noticed then that Kevin's wholesome eyes were tinged with red. His mop of dark hair looked Beethoven wild, as though he'd been tugging on it nervously.

"There were some very important people at this meeting, Tina. Lawyers, and they were talking about your website. Specifically, how it's funded."

It's interesting, how long I'd dreaded exactly this, the hours of night sweats I'd devoted to foreseeing my reaction, the first-thing-in-the-morning anxiety attacks I'd offered up to foretelling my response—but now that it had actually happened, now that the words had been spoken, all I could do was not hear them. I wasn't pretending. I literally did not hear the words because how could I, when I wasn't even there in that room? When I wasn't even present in mind or body within the suffocating confines of that coffin-size apartment?

"Why is the Titan legal department looking into the funding of your website?" Kevin asked.

I swallowed hard, willing myself to pass out or succumb to an attack of angina, anything that would keep me from having to give him an explanation. I returned my attention to the area rug, wishing to collapse onto its hand-tufted surface, to roll myself up into a New Zealand–wool burrito.

"Tina."

The funny thing was, technically all of the official website's funding was legitimate. But if they started digging, they would probably uncover how Emily and I got it started.

"What exactly were the lawyers saying?" I asked.

"So it's true," Kevin said.

"What is?"

"Tina, is there a part of this nonprofit thing that you're not telling me? I'm giving you a chance here, to come clean. To trust me. With the truth."

"The truth," I said, "is . . . complicated."

"I don't believe this." Kevin brought his fingers up to his temples. "Why did Robert really fire you, Tina?"

"I don't know. I swear."

He ran his hands through his maniac hair. "I hope you realize that I'm associated with you now."

"You're *associated* with me?"

"I'm just saying I'm part of this whole thing, so if there's something illegal going on, I need to know about it."

I had no idea what to tell him, or what to leave out. I felt like I needed a lawyer present, but he was the only lawyer I knew.

"Tina, do you understand I don't want to be—"

"Disbarred," I said.

Kevin closed his eyes and his head dropped. "Heartbroken. I don't want to be heartbroken, but maybe it's already too late." He stood up and went to the window to look out, at anything. "You should have told me."

"Told you what?"

"You haven't actually denied anything, do you realize that? You haven't said, I have no idea what you're talking about, Kevin, nothing illegal's going on, I never stole any money from the Titan Corporation."

"Kevin." I joined him at the window. "Nothing illegal's going on." Beat. "Anymore."

"I don't believe this." He stormed to the other side of his tiny living room. "I don't believe this!"

"Please, don't freak out on me." I followed after him. "I'm sorry I didn't tell you, but I was only trying to protect you."

"No. No, you don't get to rationalize any part of this. I put up with a lot, but you stole money from Robert Barlow?"

"It wasn't stealing exactly."

"And Emily, too?"

"It's kind of all her fault."

"Oh my god. What were you two thinking?"

"Kevin, listen to me . . ." My mind raced in such a way that I experienced every trauma to come in sped-up form: the getting kicked to the curb, the being left there to die, alone, forever and ever.

But I had nothing to say for myself. I had no valid excuses. What we did was wrong, it was so wrong! So I did the only thing I could do. I grabbed Kevin by the collar and shoved my tongue into his mouth.

He hurled me off him like I was a ravenous zombie. "You're insane," he said. "And I think you need to go."

"You can't kick me out," I cried. "I love you!"

"Now? Now you decide to say that?"

I grabbed at him again. "But it's true. It isn't any less true just because I waited till now to tell you. Please, Kevin."

He steered me toward the door.

"Please don't," I said. "I need you."

"Tina, it's over." He opened the door and shuffled me out. "I'm done."

25

Of course on my way back home from Kevin's, I got caught in a heavy, melodramatic rain that left me drenched by the time I dropped like a felled tree onto my bed. I closed my eyes and listened to the storm pounding at my windows, thinking about how my life was over. Which was something I'd thought a number of times before, to an embarrassing degree, but this time it had to be true. Because what else did I have to lose?

What else could possibly go wrong?

It was a masochist's favorite question, and intuitively one knows the asking is a dare. It's: *Go on, nothing can bring me any lower; I have nothing left to care about.*

And so the impossible and inevitable happened while I was just lying there feeling sorry for myself. I never even saw it coming.

It was a break, a cascade. Not the clean trickle of baptism, more the membrane-addled gush of the womb. Plaster. Paint chips. Crumbly gray cement. When the ceiling rain bubble finally burst, it erupted ninety years' worth of spackle matter all over my head.

My sheets were muddled to charcoal black and brown, soaked through to the mattress. My hair, stuck wet to my face, smelled inexplicably of ashes.

I looked up and was surprised to find an opening no bigger than the circumference of a quarter—surrounded by a flailing popped balloon.

Amazing, I thought. *Drop by drop, how much it grew, how much matter it collected over time.*

I plugged the anticlimactic hole with a plastic *I-heart-NY* bag and some masking tape. I tossed my sheets into the trash. I didn't have any clean sheets to replace them with, but I hadn't thought that part through.

I took a shower.

Only then did I begin to cry, because, in truth, there is nothing more self-satisfying than sobbing in a steaming shower.

That's how Emily found me, sodden and pruned, curled up on the shower floor. We didn't have a bathtub, mind you, so it was a stand-up shower I was lying down in, no easy feat for a full-grown adult. Luckily I only ever got to be half-grown. Still, my thigh or elbow must have been blocking the drain because I'd managed to flood the room.

Emily was standing ankle-deep in water. "What happened?" she asked.

"The rain bubble popped," I said.

"And it made this big of a mess?"

I shook my head. "Kevin broke up with me."

Emily's perfectly symmetrical Anglo-Saxon features did a thing I'd never seen them do before. They warped hideously with grief. She knelt down and lifted me up from my puddle. "Why?"

"Because I'm me," I said. "He finally figured it out."

To Emily's credit she didn't kick me while I was down, literally or metaphorically. She also didn't try to say anything to make me feel better. She barely spoke at all. But she got me dried off, and dressed, and into bed.

As previously stated, I didn't own a second set of sheets, so Emily made up the bed with a checkered tablecloth and a few bath towels. She fed me Girl Scout cookies from the freezer and glass after glass of Jameson. When she opened up my laptop, the Assistance site appeared.

"Let's not worry about this now." She clicked off the page and opened up Netflix instead. "How about something with Channing Tatum . . . ," she said. "Or Ryan Gosling."

"No." I curled into the fetal position beside her. "I only want to watch ugly people tonight."

"All right, well, that shouldn't be too hard." She scrolled through the new releases. "In what category would you place Jeff Goldblum? He's sort of got an ugly-sexy thing going, don't you think?"

"Emily?" I slurred into my pillow. "There's something else."

I wasn't looking at her, but I could tell she'd stopped scrolling. "What?" she asked.

I took a deep breath to calm myself—a profound, bottomless inhale of fresh air, followed by a stanky, whiskeyed exhale.

"Before Kevin kicked me to the curb," I said. "He told me something . . ."

I could feel Emily bracing for the worst, tightening her jaw and sphincter muscles as if that would help to make what I was about to say less awful.

"What did he tell you?" She tried and failed to sound composed.

I couldn't utter the words out loud, because then it would all be too real, how bad this was, how serious it was, the trouble we were in.

"Fontana!" Emily was yelling now. "What did Kevin tell you?"

"He told me that he got called into a meeting at work," I said. "And they were talking about our website."

Emily was quiet for a moment. The plastic *I-heart-NY* bag that I'd masking-taped to the ceiling crackled from the wind outside.

"The Titan legal department," I clarified, because I wasn't sure if the words drooling from the side of my mouth were puddling onto my dishcloth-covered pillow in coherent sentences. "Glen Wiles and the rest, they're looking into our funding."

"I knew it. I knew when you got fired." Emily shut her eyes and let out her breath in this defeated way that got me sobbing again.

"Oh no, don't do that." Her eyes shot back open. "Don't start crying again, we just dried you off."

She reached for my glass of Jameson and waved it beneath my nose, but I batted it away. She tried a Girl Scout cookie next with the same result.

"What are we going to do?" I bawled.

"Listen to me." Emily wrapped her arms around my shuddering torso. "We're in this together, okay? Till the end. And I'm not going to jail, so neither are you. Do you understand?"

She squeezed me with a brute strength I never knew she had.

It was impressive, her ability to rise up and be strong this way now that I had totally fallen to pieces. "Whatever we have to do," she said, "we'll do it. I promise you, okay?"

It was a question, I realized, that I was supposed to answer. "Okay," I said.

"Do you believe me?"

"I believe you," I said.

"Do you trust me?"

In this case I did. Because if anyone could figure out a way out of this it was Emily, even if it meant our having to run away and forge new identities. Reinvention was Emily's specialty.

"I trust you," I said.

"Good." She let me out of her hold and stared straight ahead for a moment, calculating something invisible. "Our site really ticked them off. They're probably just looking for a way to discredit us."

"But the site's funding is legitimate," I said. "We haven't faked an expense report in weeks. Do you think—?"

Emily began shaking her head. "Now that they're on a hunt? No. And if Glen Wiles is already involved, forget it, it's only a matter of time. We were safe before because no one had a reason to take a second look at anything, but now they do."

"Yeah, that's what I think, too." I sat up to retrieve my drink. "Does this mean we should pack a go-bag? I don't own any actual luggage, but I do have one of those giant blue IKEA sacks."

Emily glanced at the window. It had finally stopped raining. "How drunk are you right now?" she asked. "Too drunk to—"

"I don't think I'm sober enough to drive anywhere," I said. "But I could definitely fly a plane."

Emily blinked her eyelashes at me a few times. "Okay. For now let's just get you through the night."

She returned to my laptop's keyboard. "You said you wanted ugly. How about something with Michael Cera? Or Steve Buscemi?"

"Emily, I fucking love you." My eyes welled, but I fought off another sob. "I'm sorry I've never told you that before."

"I love you, too, Fontana," she said. "I really fucking do. And that's why I think we should leave first thing in the morning."

26

IT WAS FIRST THING early the next morning when they came. One man cop, one woman cop, wearing regular-people clothes. Business wear. Neither wielded a gun but they each probably had one.

"Tina Fontana?" the woman said when I opened the door.

"Yes."

She was polite and she did all the talking. A black woman with auburn corkscrew curls. Past the doorway were a few squad cars, uniformed cops.

Emily was at my side. We were both in sweatpants, what Emily called *house clothes*, which for her meant pajamas that actually covered her body and provided warmth.

"Are you Emily Johnson?" the woman asked.

"Yes."

The man cop pulled out handcuffs then, shoved me aside, not

roughly, but assertively. He began reciting the rights, just like out of a TV show where the antihero finally gets what's coming to him.

The man cop had his olive-skinned palm on the back of Emily's T-shirt. He'd gone around behind her and secured her wrists.

I held my wrists out to the woman, waiting.

"Please step aside, Ms. Fontana," she said.

Emily's blue doll-eyes pooled, but she remained silent. Not because she had the right to, but because her shrieking was coming out without sound in a silent scream.

"You have the right to an attorney," and all that, the man cop was explaining to her.

"What's going on?" I asked. "Why are you only taking her?"

They guided Emily to the door and she finally eked out a sound. "Tina?"

"I don't know," I said. "I don't understand, but listen to me, I'm going to figure out what's happening."

Yet even as I said it, I knew. Robert had spared me. Emily was going down for the both of us.

"I'll take care of it," I said. "I'm going to get you out, I promise."

Makeup-free tears streamed down Emily's face. She hadn't even had a chance to put eyeliner on—that was the thought that ultimately broke me up. I knew how much Emily would be pained by sitting in a cell wearing her house clothes and no foundation. It would feel to her like they'd stripped her naked.

I followed after them, out to the street, where the cool autumn morning air stung my cheeks.

"Step aside, Ms. Fontana," the woman cop ordered me.

"Can I come with you?"

"Ms. Fontana, please step aside."

They stuffed Emily into the back of their black sedan. She locked her eyes on mine through the window.

"I'm going to get help," I screamed at the glass. "Don't be scared."

Then they drove her away. The uniformed cops got in their squad cars and peeled off in sporadic directions until everyone was gone but me.

I stupidly never asked where they were taking her. When I turned around to go back into my apartment, throw on some sneakers, and call a cab, I realized I had no idea where to have the cab take me.

I took my computer into the kitchen and tried a few searches, but Google was failing me. I needed Kevin, but I couldn't ask him for help now. Wendi, Lily, and Ginger would all be at work by now, and there was no sense terrorizing them with this unexpected turn of events any sooner than necessary. It would only transform the next few hours into a cacophony of opinions and scolding, finger pointing and self-reproach—and I needed to think!

What would Emily do, I wondered, if I'd been the one taken? There was an acronym that would never find its way onto a rubber bracelet. What Would Emily Do? But she would do everything in her power to help me, wouldn't she? She wouldn't run, right? Just last night she'd professed that we were in this together, that she wasn't going to jail, so neither was I. And I promised her the same just now when she had her hands up against the glass of that cop-car window like a new breed of Pound Puppy. So I couldn't just pack my blue IKEA sack and go—I had to do the right thing. I had to preserve what was left of the goodness in my soul. But for the record, this was exactly why I never wanted to have friends.

So much for being an island.

Thanks to the Legal Aid website, I eventually figured out that Emily had most likely been taken to the local precinct, and the best I could do for now was wait for a phone call. I couldn't even bring her some clothes. Some moisturizer. Her hand lotion, so she could at least smell like herself while she was there.

I moved back into the bedroom, sat down in the middle of my bed, upon the checkered tablecloth and bath towels Emily had laid out the night before. I pulled my knees into my chest, observing a circumference of spilled-whiskey stains and cookie crumbs, and I shuddered at the thought—it was all up to me now.

BY THE TIME evening drew near, I'd stared my entire day away and not come up with any ideas of what to do next. Emily hadn't called. And I needed to leave the apartment. I needed to speak to another human being, so I texted Ginger, Wendi, and Lily.

It was shocking news to deliver over a table of drinks at Bar Nine—that early this morning one of us had been put into a cage. But their initial reactions, across the board, weren't what I had expected. I thought Ginger would immediately insist that she actually had nothing to do with any of this. I thought Wendi might smash a glass against the wall or break someone's neck. And I thought Lily would just pass out. Instead, they all went still.

I'd never seen such stillness over our table at Bar Nine. The only positive element I could glean from their sincere surprise and terror was that business at Titan today had obviously gone ahead as usual. Only Emily had been taken out, and it had been kept black-ops quiet.

"How many hours has it been since they carted her away?" Ginger asked after a solid sixty seconds of no one saying anything.

"I got the runaround all day," I said. "They wouldn't let me talk to her and she's not allowed visitors."

We all stared at my taciturn cell phone on the tabletop.

"How can they not even allow her a phone call?" Lily said, her voice cracking.

"Probably because Robert has everyone in his pocket," I said. "Everyone answers to Robert. Anything he wants." I could hear my own paranoia regarding Robert's superpowers, which made them no less real. Even that big book of mental disorders used by psychiatrists worldwide to call crazy as they see it stated that you could be paranoid and also be right. I'd read that in an issue of *The New Yorker* at my dentist's office, mistaking it for an article on the season finale of *Homeland*—but it still applied here.

"I hate to be the one to ask this"—Ginger's usually sharp eyes had dulled to cloudy sea glass—"but should the rest of us be preparing for the police to yank us out of our apartments next?"

"Is that all you can think about right now?" I fired back at Ginger. "Yourself?"

"I hate to be the one to agree with Ginger about anything ever," Wendi said, nervously flipping her Zippo lighter on and off. "But she's right."

If I knew Robert—and I did know Robert—he'd taken out Emily to make a statement so loud and clear that he wouldn't have to be bothered going after everyone else. "I don't think you should be worried," I said. "Emily's the one he chose to sacrifice. That's how Robert operates."

Ginger took a sip of her vodka gimlet, a sure sign she was beginning to feel better. "I guess it makes sense that Robert would want this to end quietly. It would only make him look bad if what we accomplished got out to the public."

Wendi nodded her sad horns, which had faded to near invisibility. "This way he still wins. I suppose we should consider ourselves lucky. But I don't feel lucky; I feel like I want him to lose." She flipped her Zippo on and off, then threw it onto the table with a force that nearly scared Lily off her chair.

"We have to get Emily out of there," I said. "That's what we should be focusing on."

"We will." Lily gripped the edge of her chair with both hands. "As soon as they actually charge her with something and set her bail."

"If," I said, because, again, I was afraid of what Robert was capable of. "If they set her bail."

"Son of a bitch," Wendi said.

"Emily's screwed," Ginger said.

"Oh aah well," Lily said.

I was just about to give up on trying to find comfort in human contact and head home when my cell phone rang. I bumbled it to my ear. "Hello? Hello?"

All I could hear was measured sociopathic breathing on the other end.

"Emily?"

"We need to meet," a brusque voice answered. "In an hour."

"Who is this?" I took a few steps away from our table.

"Central Park, near the statue of the giant sled dog."

I continued farther away from our table, holding my non-phone ear closed with my pointer finger. "Margie? Margie Fischer? Is that you?"

"Be there." She hung up.

I slipped my phone into my jeans pocket and looked around. Ginger, Wendi, and Lily were waiting for me to return to the table, perched halfway out of their seats.

"Was that Emily?" Ginger asked when I reached them.

"No." I grabbed my jacket and messenger bag from the back of my chair without sitting back down. "Wrong number."

"Then where are you going?" Wendi squinted at me like she wasn't buying it.

"I just can't sit here anymore." I threw my bag over my body like a sash. "I need some fresh air. I need to be alone."

They believed me, because it was a very Tina Fontana reaction to have to the scalding disappointment of a wrong number when waiting for an important call. Still, I made sure none of them tried to follow me out of the bar.

27

I went to meet Margie because there's just no negotiating with a mouth-breather, and because Margie Fischer was partly responsible for this mess to begin with. If she hadn't blackmailed us into helping Lily, Emily and I would have stopped (I'm pretty sure we most likely would have probably stopped) fudging expenses before anyone noticed a thing.

Anyway, finding the statue of the giant sled dog took longer than I'd anticipated, but when I did, I wasn't sure how I could have missed it. Margie was sitting on top of the heroic bronze husky, straddling it like a horse.

She disembarked at the sight of me. "I'm getting a windburn out here," she said. "Where the heck have you been?"

"I'm sorry, I got lost. I'm sorry." I apologized more than necessary considering Central Park was literally a maze. We sat on the rock landing beneath the statue.

"Emily got arrested," I said.

"Did you think me asking you here had nothing to do with that?" Margie was sweating gratuitously in spite of the cool evening air. Her short legs didn't reach the ground from the landing, so they just hung suspended, like two khaki'd hams.

I let my eyes wander in the direction of the prehistoric boulder where Kevin and I used to have lunch and I imagined I could still see us there now, laughing and eating, and him not hating my guts.

Margie tried to follow my line of vision, like she suspected I might have been followed, and it struck me how amusing it was, that this Humpty Dumpty of a woman was one of the few people on the planet Robert Barlow actually feared.

I'd managed to avoid her since our last, Rollerblade-themed encounter—she'd said she wanted to talk about the site, and I did not want to talk about the site—yet now here we were back in Central Park, together again, talking.

"I'll get right to the point." Margie smacked her palms together in a way that startled me. "I asked you here to give you something. Something that'll save your pretty little asses from this pickle you've gotten yourselves into."

She heaved herself back up to a standing position, wiped the dirt off the seat of her khakis, and reached for a knapsack she'd stuffed behind the bronze dog's posterior. It was the kind of knapsack you see high school kids wearing, JanSport or whatever, and there was a button pinned to its front that read *If You're Not Outraged You're Not Paying Attention*. Beside that was another button, a close-up of Dolly Parton's face from her *Best Little Whorehouse in Texas* era, or maybe *Nine to Five*.

Margie unzipped her fantastic knapsack and pulled out a thick manila envelope, which she tossed onto the landing beside me.

"There you have it," she said. "The answer to your problems, right there in black and white."

"You'll forgive me if I find that hard to believe," I said, ignoring the envelope.

"You don't even know what's in there."

"Whatever it is, I'm pretty sure it's not going to solve all my problems."

"Right, I forgot. You've been brainwashed like all the men in that sausage-fest of an office into thinking Robert's the second coming. That he's just smarter than everyone else. What a load of BS." Margie wiped her forehead sweat back onto her slicked pony-tail and scanned the area for anyone in earshot, then lowered herself back down to a sitting position beside me on the landing.

"You're probably too young to remember this," she said. "But twenty years back or so there was a major dustup when this big Swiss bank entered into a deferred prosecution agreement—" She paused. "Do you know what that means, *deferred prosecution agreement*? Of course you don't. Basically, this bank was charged with conspiring to defraud the United States by impeding the IRS. They were helping people open accounts using sham identities."

"Um," I said, raising my hand Lily Madsen style, "what?"

"Okay, try to stay with me here, buttercup." Margie slowed her explanation down to a *Junior Scholastic* classroom-magazine comprehension level. "This Swiss bank was helping businessmen avoid paying their taxes. Then they got caught. So to save themselves, they made a deal to give up the identities of their shadiest clients—

the ones with undeclared accounts, doing cross-border business. You see where I'm going with this?"

I did, but I stopped Margie there. Didn't we already have this conversation on day one at Michael's?

"It's no secret that Robert has offshore accounts," I said. "But they're all perfectly legal. He has an army of people making sure of that, starting with Glen Wiles."

"Yes," Margie said. "He does. Now. Because of this." She nudged the envelope closer to me. "This was an early-career slipup, a rookie mistake, and that's what makes it so special."

Margie scanned the surrounding area again. "When this bank got in trouble, they threw client confidentiality right out the window. They handed over a list to the US government and all the documentation needed to prove that these individuals had crossed that fine line of legality, of tax evasion versus tax avoidance. Do you understand what I'm telling you, Tina? It was beyond a shadow of doubt that the people on this list had filed false tax returns that omitted the income earned on their Swiss bank accounts, that they failed to disclose the existence of those accounts to the IRS. There were records, Tina, records." She picked up the envelope, shook it at me, and threw it back down. "This might not sound like much to you, but at the time it was a milestone. The newspaper headlines were practically written in lights, because the good people of America needed this so badly back then. Hardworking, law-abiding taxpayers who always paid their fair share needed to know that those who didn't would pay the price. So the slimeballs on that list? They all got indicted; many of them went to prison. But here's the kicker. Guess whose name wasn't on the list?"

I looked down at the incriminating envelope, then back at Margie, and nodded.

"No," Margie said. "I want to hear you guess, Tina."

Now I was the one checking the surrounding area for anyone within earshot.

"Robert's?" I whispered.

"Robert's." Margie folded her thick hands in her lap and smiled. "Because even among the slimeballs, Robert is the slimiest. His name and account information was surprisingly—shockingly!—not on that list. But it should have been. And right here is the proof."

I remained dubious.

Margie crossed her arms over her chest and leaned slightly backward to better gauge my response. "What? You think I'm BS-ing you?"

"No, but—"

"But what then?"

I wanted to believe what Margie was telling me, but could Robert really have messed up so badly? He was Robert.

I shrugged. "This was twenty years ago. Does it even matter anymore?"

"Oh, it matters," Margie snapped back. "Do you know how many people have devoted their careers to trying to nail Robert Barlow on tax evasion? There are men and women in the SEC and the DOJ who would sacrifice their firstborn sons for these documents."

"Then why haven't you done anything with them before?"

"Because there's a reason no one's ever been able to catch Robert, Tina, come on!" The volume of Margie's voice increased exponentially with her frustration. "You know how he owns everyone. I was scared it would blow up in my face if I went after him. Besides, I was waiting for the right moment. And it just arrived. Slow and steady wins the race, Tina. It always does."

She pulled a thumb drive from deep inside her khaki pants pocket and tossed it on top of the envelope. "Digital or hard copy, take your pick. Either way, Emily is as good as free."

I stared down at both but still wouldn't touch either. "So you want me to blackmail him?"

"You catch on real quick."

"I can't blackmail Robert."

"Why the hell not?"

"How do you even have all that?" I pointed accusingly at the forbidden hard- and soft-copy evidence sitting between us.

"I'm glad you asked, because you of all people can appreciate this." Margie elbowed me in the arm. "I was only an assistant at the time; nobody was paying any attention to anything I was doing. They assumed I didn't understand anything."

I could certainly appreciate that. So could Emily.

"Mind you, I wouldn't hand this off to just anyone," Margie said. "But to be honest, I feel a little guilty for what happened to you girls. I feel a little responsible."

"It wasn't your fault," I said. "Things got out of hand."

Margie chuckled and shook her head. "Yeah. You can say that again. Even I wouldn't have taken it this far. That took serious guts, man, I'm talking real cojones." Her face had a sweetness to it that I'd refused to acknowledge earlier. "*Cojones*," she said. "That's urban slang for 'big balls.'"

"Yes," I said. "I know."

She chuckled again. Margie had the body build of a linebacker and the social skills of a construction worker, but underneath all that was a big soft sweetie pie. A heavy-beating heart.

"No hard feelings?" she said.

"None." Finally, I picked up the envelope and thumb drive, and held them both in my lap. It was weird to realize it, but I really didn't have any ill will toward Margie. I was sort of glad she'd threatened and scared the hell out of Emily and me that day at Michael's. If she hadn't, there'd have been no website—and that was real. It was honest.

If someone had told me a year ago that I'd be sitting in Central Park with Margie Fischer thinking these thoughts, not feeling entirely sorry for what we'd done, I would have been sure they'd consumed ayahuasca. But it was the truth. What we'd accomplished with the site meant that much to me.

"Now, remember," Margie said, "Robert has a lot more to lose than you do. And for what he's done, he could go to jail for a long time, maybe even longer than Emily. He'd have to be crazy not to cut you a deal."

I shoved the envelope and thumb drive into my messenger bag. "I appreciate this," I said. "But I'm still not sure if I could bring myself to blackmail Robert. He did spare me, you know?"

"Your daddy issues baffle me." Margie checked her black Casio calculator watch from 1989 and climbed up to a standing position. "But I suppose it's your call."

She wiggled each of her arms into the straps of her now-empty knapsack. "I will say one thing, though. I'm proud of you girls. I was so pleasantly wrong about you."

She nuzzled the underside of the bronze husky's snout before leaving me alone with him.

BACK HOME, I ordered delivery from Pies 'n' Thighs because, frankly, I needed all the comfort a greasy fried-chicken dinner could provide.

I used to be so good at eating alone—truly, it was perhaps my best skill. But tonight the apartment felt mortally empty, and it was really getting to me. Gone were Emily's shrouded insults and sarcastic jibes at my every fashion choice and facial feature, gone were her Jimmy Choos left in the middle of the floor for me to trip over and the drawers she left open for me to slam into. I missed her. I had to dip my chicken leg into my macaroni and cheese just to keep myself from crying into it.

I asked myself: could I blackmail Robert to rescue Emily?

This was *Robert*. He was the first man to give me a shot, to take a chance on me. There were worse jobs out there than a full-time position at the Titan Corporation. It wasn't his fault I didn't have the drive to angle my way into a better job title in six years. Robert had treated me with nothing but respect for all the years I'd worked for him; he'd never said an unkind word to me. Which was more than most assistants could say about their bosses. The man taught me how to shoot a gun, for heaven's sake. Plus, I just liked him, plain and simple. *And you can't beat that with a stick.*

But Emily was Emily. Sure, she could be a real pain, and if anyone actually deserved to go to jail for what had occurred, it was probably her. But truthfully, when you looked at the big picture, the amount of money Titan lost to us was so minuscule compared to what it had—to what Robert had.

And this new development was no minor detail. Robert was technically, beyond the shadow of a doubt, guilty of criminal activity. Just like Emily was. Just like I was.

Pot calling the kettle black? Maybe. We were all blackened with guilt.

28

It was nine a.m. the next day, Thursday, and Emily could have been anywhere. She could have been carted off to Rikers Island or the Tombs; I had no idea. But I knew exactly where to find Robert. Like I said, it was nine a.m. on a Thursday morning—he was at the rich people's gym on East Fifty-Fifth.

So that's where I went.

Luckily, the desk clerk at the rich people's gym and I had a three-year-long phone relationship—scheduling workouts for Robert, canceling training sessions for Robert, reserving machines for Robert. Her name was Kimberly and she looked exactly like she sounded. Effervescent, always. Tan. Blond. Pretty, if you like that kind of thing.

I marched right up to her and introduced myself.

"We finally meet in person!" she said with the overzealousness of someone required to sit in one place all day while other people got exercise.

She could have passed for nineteen, but I'd have put money on her already having a bachelor's degree in one of the fine arts.

"I need to speak to Robert right away," I said. "It's a private matter. An emergency."

She didn't hesitate. "You go on in, honey. I hope it's nothing too serious!"

That's how easy it was to cross the threshold of the gym Madonna sometimes twerked out at.

I'd always wondered what the inside of this gym might look like. Would the equipment be constructed of pure gold? Would the air not contain that sweaty-foot undertone of other gyms? Would there be a selection of muscular Oompa Loompas you could hire to do the actual exercising while you enjoyed a manicure and sipped an organic vegetable juice?

I scanned the beautifully sunlit space, noticing how cushiony the matted floor was beneath my rubber-soled Converse One Stars. The gym was mostly empty—only a handful of people in the whole city could afford a membership there—so I had no problem locating Robert. He was climbing in place on an elliptical machine like it was Machu Picchu, wearing gray sweats, a black T-shirt, and pristine white sneakers.

It sort of melted my heart to see him this way. Sweatpants could deteriorate a man's dignity like that. It was like seeing someone with their fly open or a fleck of spinach in their teeth—it somehow raised your affection for them alongside your pity.

I held Margie's envelope close to my hip, concealed securely in my messenger bag, but seeing Robert in the flesh only confirmed what I already knew: I couldn't use the documents against him. I wouldn't expect anyone to understand this. Unless you've been the assistant to a great man—or even a man who's not so great, but was great to you—it's difficult to comprehend the sacred relationship between bosses and assistants.

Robert had only fired me, while Emily ended up behind bars—this was the sacredness of our relationship at work. So I couldn't turn up now and blackmail him. There was etiquette to be observed, and Robert was big on etiquette.

If he would just hear me out, allow me to explain, I knew we could work out a compromise. Robert was a pragmatist above all else. He didn't want to deal with the messy public fallout of a rogue Titan employee. The negative PR alone made it worth his while to end this briskly and quietly. And he never even needed to know the documents in my bag existed.

I padded across the cushiony matted floor toward him, but he was so focused on the window, on a distant point on the horizon, that he didn't notice me.

Rather than startle him, I mounted the unused elliptical beside his and started climbing.

I waited a few seconds and then said, "Hi, Robert."

He turned to me with a neutral expression at first, and then he looked aghast. "How did you get in here?"

He stopped climbing, looked left, then right.

"I wanted to say thank you," I said, knowing that would calm him and keep him from calling out for security. "In person. For sparing me."

Robert turned his head forward, pretending I was no longer there, and resumed climbing.

"And I wanted to explain a few things," I said.

This was the hardest thing I'd ever had to do. I stood still on my climber to conserve my energy.

"Emily doesn't deserve to be in jail," I said. "She really doesn't. I take full responsibility for what happened, even though I swear to you it was all sort of an accident."

Robert refused to acknowledge me. I watched a sweat tear run down from his dark and sopping sideburn.

"What happened wasn't Emily's fault," I continued. "She shouldn't be the one who gets punished."

"You want me to send you to prison instead of her?" He still wouldn't look at me, but at least I'd gotten him talking.

"Well, no, not particularly," I said. "Not if we can avoid that as a resolution."

Robert's silhouette smirked.

"Tina." There. He finally turned to face me. He paused his climbing and gripped the elliptical's handlebars tight. "You couldn't have been responsible for that scheme. I know that. She's the one who signed every one of those false expense reports. I don't know why you're trying to cover for her. Maybe you like her a little too much? If that's it, I don't want to hear about it."

He reached for the towel draped over the machine's frame and dried off his face. "I know you well enough to know you don't have it in you to be the mastermind behind anything. I can only imagine how she bullied you."

This surprised me.

"So wait," I said. "You went after Emily and not me because you think she's smarter than I am?"

Robert squinted his eyes to avoid responding right away.

I could see that's what he meant but he didn't want to be insulting.

"I've seen her," he said. "I'm aware of who she is. She went to Harvard, you know."

Sweet Jesus.

"She can be very persuasive," he went on. "You're not the only one she's managed to trick."

Robert was explaining what an excellent con artist Emily was, but more than that, he was explaining how ineffectual *I* was, how incapable. How lost and aimless.

He hadn't seen me in action these past months, being the boss and, when necessary, being the bitch. He didn't know that I used to be Tina Fontana, a thirty-year-old assistant making forty thousand dollars a year with zero options of upward mobility—but that I wasn't anymore.

I dismounted my elliptical. "So you think I'm just some gullible girl who got exploited by the sneaky Harvard grad?"

I could feel the girth of Margie's fat envelope in my messenger bag.

Robert laughed. He *laughed*. The bastard.

And then the words just came out. "How do you know I didn't come here to threaten you?" I said. "To blackmail you?"

"Tina, I recognize you've been through a lot, so I'm going to excuse you your tone, but I'm beginning to lose my patience, so I suggest you move along now."

Little girl. He didn't say, *Move along now, little girl*, but that's what he meant.

"Well, I hate to break it to you, Robert." I put my hands on my hips. "But I came here to tell you that I've got it all on paper. And on disk. Hard copy or digital, which do you think the Feds would prefer?"

Robert stepped off his machine and we stood face-to-face—well, as close as we could get to face-to-face considering our height difference. "Now what in the hell are you talking about?"

"I'm talking about the dustup twenty years ago, when that big Swiss bank entered into a deferred prosecution agreement—" I paused, astonished by myself and my recall ability. "You remember that, don't you? That list of tax evaders you were supposed to be on? I've got the proof you should have been on that list."

Robert was unsuccessfully trying to hide his panting. This man whose daily prescription medications I knew by heart, whose daughters' birthday presents I always picked out, whose salads I laced with quinoa because of its phytonutrient benefits.

"I know," I said. "You were younger back then, less wise. Maybe it was the first and only time you screwed up, made a bad decision, drifted just slightly over the line. Believe me, I get it."

Robert put his hands on his hips, like I had mine, and bored his eyes into my eyes. He brought his body in so close that I thought he might literally be sniffing me out, like a lion would do before pouncing.

I stood very still. There was no way I was going to be the first to break eye contact this time.

"You don't have shit," he said finally.

I was impressed by how he said it. His tone. He was no longer speaking to me as his assistant, or even as a woman. But as an unexpected adversary.

"I promise you, Robert, I am not bluffing. Let Emily go and you won't have to find out for sure."

He remained stunned for a few seconds and then laughed again. "You have got to be kidding me."

"I am not kidding you," I said, and turned to go, praying my shaky legs wouldn't give out on me.

"Who do you think you are," he said to my back, "coming in here and making demands like this?"

Who did I think I was?

I stopped, considered turning back around, but then thought better of it. Let him think I was bluffing.

"Go ahead and underestimate me some more," I said while walking away. "I dare you."

29

I WAS STILL SHAKING when I turned the key to my apartment door. I dropped my messenger bag on the kitchen floor and fell onto my bed with my sneakers and jacket still on.

That so didn't go according to plan.

I hadn't intended to walk in there and threaten Robert, but I also hadn't intended to be so insulted by his total lack of belief that I could—what? Steal from him? Shouldn't I have been glad he found it hard to believe I'd be capable of that?

But that wasn't it. It was the way he doubted my intelligence and my drive. My ability to manifest (as *The Oprah Magazine* would say). Somewhere along the line I'd started believing in myself and I wanted Robert to believe in me, too.

Walking out of the rich people's gym the way I did, I didn't know if Robert would call my bluff or not—even though it wasn't actually a bluff. I did have in my possession enough documentation to send him to prison. But I didn't want to manifest him into a cell, or even one of those country-club prisons they made special for wealthy white men, where they get to wear chinos and play shuffleboard and then write a memoir about it that gets made into a movie after they get out. I just wanted Emily to come home.

I checked my phone to be sure Emily hadn't called. She had not, but I did have a text from Wendi: *We're coming over.*

Jesus, what now?

I brought my laptop onto my bed with me and checked the latest news about the site. I Googled *the Assistance* and what I found was inevitable, I guess—word of Emily's arrest had finally reached the Internet.

Assistance Cofounder (the Hot One) Hauled Away in Cuffs, said BKmag.com.

Girl Who Founded the Assistance May Be a Thief, said Gothamist.

The first commenter asked the question on everyone's mind: "The hot one? Or the other one?"

We weren't looking good in the public eye, with my getting fired and now Emily in a cell. All the posts I read mentioned that Emily hadn't been charged with anything yet, but this seemed to only stir more curiosity. A lot of people were asking questions, and if there was one thing I understood about the Internet, it was that multiple questions posed in all caps were basically the same as answers.

Then I began typing my own name into Google. T-i-n-a-f-o-n-t-a—and Google tried to help by finishing my search for me:

Tina Fontana fired, it suggested.

Tina Fontana thief.

Tina Fontana lesbian.

My buzzer buzzed just in time.

On my doorstep, Wendi, Lily, and Ginger were waiting to be let in.

"What, do you guys travel in a pack now?"

They'd come from the office and were dressed accordingly. Ginger in a cobalt-blue skirt suit, Wendi in a black hoodie, and Lily in her favorite pink cardigan with cartoon giraffes on it. Someone should really start enforcing a dress code upon the entry-level staff at Titan.

I led them to the kitchen table and brought my computer out from the bedroom. "Have you seen the Internet in the last few hours?"

"That's what I'm talking about." Ginger flared her manicure at Wendi. "She needs to do something. Make a statement or something."

"This she you speak of is me, I assume?" I took a seat next to Wendi.

"No she shouldn't," Wendi said. They seemed to be continuing an argument that had begun on their way over.

Wendi took control of my laptop and opened up the Assistance page. "Have you looked at how much donation money's come in?"

It was a shitload of money, actually. Twenty thousand more than last time I'd checked only a few hours ago.

"Wow." Lily's eyes got big behind her glasses. "Where did all those donations come from?"

"There is no such thing as bad publicity," Wendi said as an explanation.

Ginger leaned forward, offering the table a beguiling view of her cleavage. "But there are rumors flying around that Tina and Emily stole from Titan. People are calling them thieves."

Wendi pulled back in her chair to offset Ginger's onslaught. "And for every person calling them thieves, someone else is calling them heroes."

This got me thinking.

Wendi was right. It didn't matter so much what people were saying as long as they were saying something. Wasn't this the golden rule of the new millennium? Had we been taught nothing by Her Imperial Majesty Miley Cyrus, Emperor of the World Wide Web?

What was happening now wasn't really so different from when I got fired and Wendi used the Internet rumor mill in our favor. This was worse, but all that meant was that we had to go bigger.

"Shouldn't Tina at least defend herself?" Ginger said. "And what about Emily? Has the girl even gotten a phone call yet? For all we know, she might have a face tattoo by now."

"No," I said. "I'm not going on the defensive."

They all turned to me like it had just now occurred to them that I was sitting there at all.

"What?" Ginger said.

"I know what we need to do," I said.

My voice hardly sounded like my own. It came out sounding deeper than usual, more sure of itself. "I want to put a call out to the network. Everyone who owes us a favor, all those assistants, the ones with the too-big glasses, and the Zara girls, and Accent Accessory. Everyone."

I sounded calm and confident.

"I want them to float a news piece for us. A fluff piece. It doesn't need to be based in any fact . . ."

It occurred to me that I sounded a lot like Robert. A *helluva lot* like him.

"And this news piece needs to state that some say Robert's a tax evader. That he has a long history of hiding a bunch of his money in illegal offshore accounts. That's it. We're not saying it, per se, but some people are."

Ginger, Wendi, and Lily were all staring at me like I'd just spoken in tongues or that snake-speak Harry Potter came out with on occasion.

I should explain where this idea came from: Basically, it was Robert's idea. Or at least he popularized it.

Titan's twenty-four-hour news channel was known for many things, but thanks to a documentary some liberal folks made a few years back—whose mission was to criticize Titan's not-so-objective methods of reporting the news—this little tactical nugget was brought to the attention of a discerning public: *Some say. Some people say. Some would say.*

These were magic words that, when uttered before anything— anything—served as an automatic disclaimer, a get-out-of-jail-free card. Hopefully, in this instance, literally.

"Huh." Wendi was the first to respond. "That's so Titan."

For a split second I thought Wendi might tip my kitchen table onto its side and screech out some sort of "the beast is us" statement, or claim that she could no longer distinguish which of us card players were pigs and which were human beings—but that was all in my literature-heavy mind.

In fact, Wendi smiled at the idea, I think.

"I love it," she said.

"I don't get it," Ginger said.

By the looks of Lily's suspicious scowl, she didn't get it either.

"We just need to put the words out there," I said. "Get people asking questions about what Robert's done instead of what we've done. He's smart enough to catch on that we're willing to play dirty, and then he'll back off."

"Oh aah well, are you sure this is wise?" Lily's suspicion had evolved to full-face incredulity. "Making public accusations like this, especially ones that are false?"

She uttered the word *false* in such a way that made me wonder if she knew exactly how not false these accusations were. She was Margie Fischer's assistant after all. It was possible Margie had hinted at the existence of her stockpiled documents. But with Lily, who could tell? You'd have better luck getting an emotional read on Siri.

Either way, I wasn't ready to make those incriminating documents public. Which meant first and foremost keeping them a secret from Wendi and Ginger.

"I'm only trying to scare Robert into doing the right thing," I said. "We're not accusing him of anything new. It is true that some people say Robert's a tax evader. People have been saying that for years. No one's ever been able to prove anything, and no new evidence has come to light, but we're not claiming it has. We're only bringing the subject back up."

"I guess it's now or never." Ginger undid the knot on her fuchsia neck scarf. "Legally, I'm pretty sure they can only hold Emily till tomorrow—then they either have to charge her with something or let her go."

"See?" Wendi said. "And you thought law school was a total waste of time and money."

Ginger gave Wendi the finger.

"What are we waiting for then?" I reached for my phone. "Let's start making calls."

BY TEN P.M., my bedroom looked like ground zero of an eighth-grader's slumber party. Pizzas had been ordered, a candy run had been made, and we all had our eyes attached to some form of electronic screen.

Earlier, I'd bitten the bullet and called Tim, Kevin's friend from BuzzFeed. Fortunately, he hadn't yet heard that Kevin had dumped me and was therefore eager to be of assistance. Using me as an anonymous source, he lobbed the first softball-size piece of clickbait into the airwaves—*Is Robert Barlow About to Be Ruined for Life?*—abruptly followed in kind by the rest of the Internet-beast feeders.

Our "news" story got coverage on sites big and small, indie and corporate: Slate, the Hairpin, the Huffington Post, the Daily Beast Cheat Sheet, *New York* magazine's Daily Intelligencer, even the YouTube channel of that girl who got famous for putting on makeup.

It wasn't hard to envision all those e-mail chains: the under- or unpaid blogger at HuffPo calling in a favor owed to her by the politics editor; the intern at the Daily Beast who craved the bragging rights that would come with aiding and abetting us; even the trust-funded freelancer at the Daily Intelligencer who wanted to contribute to our efforts in order to appease her own class guilt.

All their articles pretty much said the same thing—nothing. But that was good, that's what we wanted.

I sat at my desk in front of my computer, hitting *refresh* over and over again, announcing every time a new version of the story appeared someplace new.

Robert Barlow Guilty of Tax Evasion? Some Say Yes.

Crime, Corruption, and the Caymans: Is It Time for Robert Barlow to Come Clean?

Barlow a Fraud? Some People Say, Uh Duh.

"Yes!" I called out. "We just scored Upworthy."

Ginger had been hovering over my shoulder, but she finally stepped away to make herself comfortable on my bed. Careful not to flash us as she tucked her knees beneath her cobalt-blue skirt suit, she flashed us anyway. "Well, if getting Robert's attention is what you wanted, Tina, I think you might have done it." She reached for a Whirly Pop from our candy stash. "You really think all this is going to scare him into backing off?"

Lily was on the bed beside Ginger, picking her way through a sack of Jujubes, choosing only the green ones. "Oh aah well, it would if we had any actual evidence that Robert's done something wrong."

I let that one go unanswered.

"How many page views is our site up to?" Ginger asked as she peeled the clear wrapper from her lolli. "I bet all this chatter is only improving our traffic."

I clicked onto our site and hit *refresh*. "We're almost at a million views."

"Wow," Lily said, with her mouth full of Jujubes. "That's a lot of people."

Wendi was lying across Emily's air mattress with her boots propped up against the wall, gnawing on a stick of red licorice. She had her iPad on her lap. "No it's not. That video of the cat that plays the piano has, like, twenty million views."

Lily blinked at us obviously behind her thick glasses. "But that's a cat that plays the piano."

"You're not considered a welebrity," Ginger said, between licks of her Whirly Pop, "until you hit at least five million."

"Tina's not trying to become a welebrity." Wendi threw a stick of licorice at Ginger's face. "She's trying to get Emily out of jail."

Ginger reached for the nearest gummy ring and chucked it at Wendi, nailing her square in the horns.

Lily ducked for cover, probably fearing for the giraffes on her cardigan, as Wendi retaliated with a handful of Swedish Fish.

"Stop throwing the candy!" I yelled. "It's more teasing than the rats in the walls can handle."

Wendi agreed to a truce and returned to her lying-down position, further scuffing my walls with her boots. "If I knew you'd be this good at bluffing, Tina, I would have entered you into the World Series of Poker."

I laughed like I thought I should.

Let everyone think it was a bluff. I didn't trust Wendi to not go ahead and leak the documents if she found out about them—and then what? There would be no undoing that once it happened. I'd probably get subpoenaed, sworn to an oath to tell the truth and nothing but the truth, and what the hell was the truth anyway? None of that mattered. I only needed one person to believe I had those documents, and that was Robert.

30

I woke first, dry-mouthed and momentarily confused as to why there were other people's limbs draped across my chest. Then I remembered how the night had turned into a sleepover, all candy and pizza and late-night stomachache. There had even been an impromptu hairbrush sing-along to Aretha Franklin's "Respect" when our page views reached one million—which in retrospect made little if any literal sense, but it felt right at the moment. I know, girls singing into hairbrushes, right? But would you believe I'd never done that before? I mean, not when I wasn't by myself, alone, doing my own backup vocals. It was different in a group—louder, for sure. My upstairs neighbor had to bang on the floor with a broom handle to quiet us down. But now all was silent.

I reached across Ginger's rack to grab my cell phone from my nightstand. She stirred but didn't wake. Lily was curled up at our feet like a house cat, and Wendi was sprawled out on Emily's air mattress. We'd all fallen asleep in our clothes. I found it impressive how Wendi managed to snooze comfortably in pants with chains on them.

"Oh shit," I said aloud, but no one heard me. It was later than I thought, already almost nine a.m., and there had been no call from Emily.

Robert didn't take the bait.

"Oh shit," I said again. Why wasn't anyone waking the heck up?

Emily was probably being charged right now. What was I doing just sitting here? I had to do something. Anything. Call a lawyer, cry for help, check on Margie's envelope maybe—the documents I'd hidden in the freezer beneath the ice trays, camouflaged behind a forest of frozen vodka bottles.

I hurdled over Ginger and Lily to stand upright—and then stopped. I'd caught sight of myself in the mirror above my dresser.

Sometimes in an instant you realize everything.

I know that sounds like the tag line to a Taster's Choice commercial, but I swear that's how this was. All at once I knew I had to turn myself in. Not only for Emily, but for that crazed woman in the mirror.

She wasn't who I wanted to be. Cowardly, rationalizing, passing off blame. Where was my integrity? Had I not once been a wide-eyed NYU student underlining her *Norton Anthology* raw, elated by the words of Emerson and Thoreau?

Nothing is at last sacred but the integrity of your own mind.

What you are comes to you.

Be true to your work, your word, and your friend.

Real integrity is doing the right thing, knowing that nobody's going to know whether you did it or not.

That last quote may have been Oprah piggybacking on Emerson, but you get my point. I couldn't let this go on this way. So I took a breath and went to her, that crazed woman in the mirror, and pulled a hairbrush through her frazzled hair—a hairbrush that had just last night been a microphone. Then I tugged on my shoes and threw on my coat, all the while allowing the decision to settle over me.

They say people who decide to kill themselves experience a profound tranquillity once the deliberation is over, the ending decided. I was feeling something like that, with a bit more gastrointestinal bustle.

I popped two TUMS into my mouth and bade Ginger, Wendi, and Lily a silent good-bye. They stayed sleeping like they'd been roofied, or whatever kids were using to drug one another's drinks those days. I let them sleep. They'd figure it out when they woke up and found me gone; they'd understand without my having to tell them.

A hero is no braver than an ordinary woman, but she is brave five minutes longer. (That's me piggybacking on Emerson.)

Slinging my messenger bag across my shoulder—empty except for my phone, keys, wallet, and photo ID, because I wouldn't need anything else—I reached for the doorknob, just as the door swung open, smacking me in the face.

I cried out, covering my face with my hands, and fell backward, then removed my hands, looked up, and there she was.

"Emily?"

She was disheveled, wearing the same "house clothes" she'd had on when they took her away, and her hair was pulled back in a frizzy ponytail, but it was her, in the flesh, Emily fucking Johnson.

"They let me go," she said.

I hobbled up to standing, disregarding my aching and probably broken nose.

I couldn't believe it. She was home.

"I was just on my way down there," I said, letting my messenger bag slide from my shoulder onto the floor.

Emily surveyed the kitchen, the empty pizza boxes and candy wrappers. "I see you've been eating your pain," she said. "Because you missed me."

That blond-haired, blue-eyed bitch from Connecticut. She was home!

"I did miss you," I said. "I missed you so much."

The others, finally, had woken up from all the commotion and were out of the bedroom—Wendi with creases on her face, Ginger with her hair wild as a house fire, and Lily struggling to get her glasses on fast enough.

"You're all here?" Emily said. "For me?" Her voice cracked and she lapsed, unconsciously perhaps, into her natural lower-class accent. "I thought for sure you all were just going to let me . . ." She broke off, her neck and cheeks reddened, her eyes filled with tears. She covered her face with her hands.

"Never," I said, going to her. "I was just on my way to turn myself in." I folded my arms around her, squeezing so hard I thought for sure she'd complain, but she didn't.

Wendi, Ginger, and Lily huddled around us, clinging, howling, crying. My upstairs neighbors might have thought someone had died, because when you get right down to it, there's such an indistinguishable line between crying out for dear life and crying out for dear death.

I always wondered what the sensation was like, to win. The lottery, the Super Bowl, a gold medal—to win anything, really. To want something so much, and to get it. Now I knew.

Beneath all the tears, I was saying thank you, thankyouthankyouthankyou, to God, the Universe, Buddha, Oprah, anyone and everyone who'd helped out with this in any way. And then I made a silent promise to pay my good fortune forward, because suddenly I had something to pay forward. I was supposed to be an island, and hell might be other people, but what I had there at that moment in my overfull kitchen—well, it was something.

LATER THAT NIGHT, Emily and I drank champagne in our pajamas. Me in my leisurely stripes, she in her lace two-piece. It was just the two of us again, lounging on my bed. Ginger, Wendi, and Lily had gone home; the news that Emily was free had quieted the chatter on the Internet, and we could take a deep breath and relax back into our old selves—or, the newly updated versions of our old selves.

"So, how exactly did you manage to get me out of jail?" Emily asked while uncorking our second bottle of Asti Spumante.

"Long story. I sort of had Robert by the balls." I held out my glass to be refilled. "The cojones."

Emily set the bottle onto my nightstand and scrolled through a few new messages on her phone. She was already being bombarded with calls and e-mails. Everyone wanted to know what had happened. Why was she held in custody? Why wasn't she charged with anything? People wanted answers. Emily didn't have any of those answers, but she was still enjoying the attention nonetheless.

"You're going to have to be a little more specific," she said. "I have to have a good story to tell my fans; that's what they want from me now." As she was scrolling, her phone chimed again.

I checked my own phone, not for messages—which was good because there weren't any—but for the time.

It was only a little after eight p.m. Not so late as to make it entirely insane for me to forgo my champagne flute, lift myself from the bed, throw on some clothes, and make my way uptown. Kevin had to have heard the news by now that Emily and I had come out okay. I liked to imagine that he'd been closely monitoring my situation on the sly since we broke up; I pictured him peeping around Titan corners, eavesdropping on conversations, worrying over Emily's arrest, and even cheering on the snowballing success of our website from his too-small couch in his too-small apartment.

Of course I understood that in real life Kevin was still angry. And that even now, my being exonerated didn't un-betray him. I'd still lied to him over the course of many days and nights and hamburgers—and that was unforgivable. But I wanted to go to him, tonight, immediately, unforgivable or not.

"I'm running out of battery." Emily poked at her phone without looking up. "Have you seen my charger?"

I wheeled around to the side of my bed, put my feet on the floor, and stood up. By the time Emily realized I wasn't searching the room for her phone charger, I was already pulling my pea coat out of the closet.

"What the hell are you doing?" she asked, suddenly aware of me. "Where are you going? Out to sea?"

I buttoned my pea coat closed. "I won't be gone long."

"Where could you possibly have to go? I just got out of prison, I'm an ex-con, the least you could do is drink with me all night."

I leaned over her and gave her a kiss on the forehead just as her phone chimed again—but this time she ignored it.

"Hey," she said, making her eyes big. "Fontana. I know where you're going."

Heating up quickly in my heavy wool sailor's coat, I vacillated between dashing out the door and disrobing.

"Good for you," Emily said, full of pride. "Go to him."

"Fuck off," I said to sabotage the moment, and then left the apartment before the vulnerability and my wooly sweat could really seep in.

Go to him.

Who did Emily think I was, pre-op Meg Ryan?

You know what Robert would say to that? *Hogwash. What a buncha hokum. Grow a set.*

Once outside I became acutely aware of my light-headedness, the wobbliness in my knees. In a split-second decision I called a cab. And, no, it wasn't because I was going to start living like a spoiled rich girl who took cars everywhere now that I was all out of debt and not a criminal. It was that it was post–rush hour—the trains would take forever and traffic would be light. I also wanted to give myself the least opportunity to change my mind and turn back. The investment of a $30 cab ride was as good a deterrent as I could think of.

Plus, cab rides are awesome. Except for the slight carsickness and occasional fear for your life, there is nothing like zipping through nighttime New York in a foul-smelling automobile. To get to the Upper East Side from Williamsburg, you have to go over the Williamsburg Bridge, which isn't quite the Brooklyn Bridge, but it's no scrub either. Crossing it, the view of the Manhattan skyline always made my chest feel too full, like my heart had suddenly swelled in the way of the Grinch who stole Christmas the moment he went soft. I was a real sucker for shiny lights and tall buildings. Tonight the sky was so black and clear, the skyscrapers looked Photoshopped against it—it was truly beautiful, and I thought to myself, *This is going to be horrible, what I'm about to do.* This was going to make me feel like I wanted to die, but once it was over, I could move on. I'd continue with my life knowing that at least I tried. At least I fought for him. That Tina Fontana—island unto herself—was willing to do everything in her power to keep someone in her life.

My cabdriver carried on a conversation in a foreign tongue as he negotiated the FDR Drive and it dawned on me gradually: this would make two people now that I didn't just wave off with a *see ya* before closing the door and plopping down in bed with Netflix and some cookies.

"*Ana baneek omak!*" my driver shouted, but he was addressing someone else.

When we finally turned onto Kevin's block, it was the strangest thing—Kevin was right there, trudging alongside us up the sidewalk, with his hands dug deep into his coat pockets. It was a moment I recognized from a thousand movies, starring Meg Ryan and her contemporaries. Kevin was on his way to find me just as I was on my way to find him.

"Stop the car!" I yelled to my driver. "Pull over. I want to get out here."

He did so without hesitation or a blip in his earpiece conversation. Kevin, possibly alarmed he was about to be clipped gangster style, jumped back.

I stepped out of the cab, slammed the door, and looked at him. "Where you headed?" I asked, trying to make light of the fear in his eyes.

I was on my way to find you, I was sure he was going to say.

"I was on my way to get a slice of pizza," he actually said.

"Oh."

Then my driver palmed his horn and cussed at me from inside the car. I needed to pay him.

So I took care of all that and once he peeled away, I returned my attention to Kevin. It was just cold enough for condensation to blow from our mouths. He didn't move. So I went to him.

"I won't keep you," I said, forcing myself to look at him, not down at the sidewalk. "I just wanted to tell you in person how sorry I am. For everything."

Kevin exhaled a deep breath that made it look like he'd been smoking an invisible cigarette. Then he knelt down and took a seat right there on the curb.

I didn't wait for an invitation to sit beside him. "If you're willing to hear me out—" I began, and then broke off.

Were there even words?

Tears welled in my eyes, so I closed them, but that only made the streams form faster down my face.

"I'm just so sorry," I said, because it was all I could say. I reached for Kevin's hand and he didn't pull it away from me. Instead he wrapped his arm around my torso and drew me in.

He smelled like himself. And his shoulder was both soft and hard all at once. How I'd missed his shoulders.

"I shouldn't have run out on you like that," he said. "When you needed me most." He hugged me tighter. "I won't do that again, I promise."

I let myself lean into him. There was so much I needed to say, but unlike the inappropriate moment I had chosen to blurt out that I loved him, I recognized now wasn't the time. "Does this mean you're willing to give me another chance?" I asked.

He kept holding me, letting his authoritative grasp speak for him. It said: a man of such decency and intelligence would never clutch so tightly to anything without value.

"If you'll give me another chance," he said.

I really let loose then with the crying. I couldn't help it. I was a girl sobbing into her boyfriend's sleeve on a public street. But only for like a minute, and then I got my shit together.

"I'll explain the whole story from the beginning," I said, wiping my face dry. "But please believe me when I tell you, I never intended to do anything so incredibly illegal."

Kevin exhaled another long smoky breath. "I think I understand why you did what you did," he said. "Don't forget, I know what goes on at Titan and what Robert's like. You think I haven't had any revenge fantasies of my own?"

"No. I don't."

"Well don't be so sure. I'm not as wholesome as you think."

"Yes you are, and that's what I love best about you." I moved in for a kiss, but he pulled back.

"That is so *not* what you love best about me."

"It is." I placed my hands on both sides of his handsome face. "It just took losing you to make me realize it."

Then he let me kiss him, kissing me back tenderly enough for my whole body to loosen.

After a moment, he paused and said, "I have something to tell you."

Immediately my mind went to: *He slept with some other girl while we were broken up*. Already I was deliberating whether I was going to be okay with it, or if I was only going to pretend to be okay with it. Before I could decide, he said, "I quit my job today."

"What? You quit Titan?"

He nodded. "I think I'm ready to move into public service. The nonprofit sector. Maybe I can come work for you, if you're hiring."

I loved this man, I truly did. And he loved me, all of me, the real me.

There was a December chill in the air, but I felt warm. Look at where I was. Look at who I'd become.

I rested my forehead on Kevin's. "Funny enough," I said, "I am looking for an assistant."

afterword

It's been about six months now and people are still talking about the Assistance. The site has more followers than Taylor Swift's Twitter feed, and we've given away nearly three million dollars in donations. Three million dollars of student-loan debt, obliterated. We did that.

Our humble DUMBO office space is small, but it does have hardwood floors and one exposed-brick wall. It's no Titan building, but it's ours, and I even have an office with a view. The Realtor referred to it as an "urban view"—it's basically just a bunch of decrepit buildings and what I'm pretty sure is a water tower, but who needs to stare at the Brooklyn Bridge all day anyway?

Our staff is where we really excel.

Kevin oversees all things legal. He still wears a necktie to work every day, but only because that's how he's comfortable. And, yes, we did do it in my office one day after everyone else had gone home and that is totally in accordance with our sexual harassment policy.

Lily manages our accounting. She's chilled out a bit. Sometimes she even forgoes her Lean Cuisine meals and joins the rest of us for lunch at AlMar or Superfine. Her cardigan with giraffes on it is still in common rotation and that is totally in accordance with our dress code.

Wendi is in charge of digital everything and anything that has to do with a computer. A video of her band's most recent single, "Kiss Your Stock Options Good-bye, I'm Going to Set You on Fire Now," has developed a cult following among a newly forming anarchist subset of Assistance members, a fierce and loyal superfan group who call themselves the WendiChanimals. You can recognize them by the two pink horns dyed into their bangs.

Ginger runs PR, which suits her much better than being a legal assistant pursued on the regular by an in-heat Glen Wiles. It's incredible how no longer having to worry about getting your ass grabbed can really free up a girl's mind. Ginger transformed herself into a self-taught public relations maven faster than you can say *end-user deliverables*. She regularly lectures the rest of us on the importance of our horizontals and verticals (insert sex joke here) and our target media. I used to think Ginger was just a mean girl all grown up; now I know it for a fact—but mean girls make excellent publicists, especially when they're smarter and more determined than any mean man you've ever met.

Emily has done everything possible to milk her five minutes of fame. She has finally (like Diane von Furstenberg) become the woman she always knew she wanted to be. Her main responsibility is coordinating the nonprofit's fund-raising (i.e., asking rich people for money, which she naturally rocks at). But she's also turned herself into a much-sought-after public speaker. At the moment, she's preparing her talk for a TEDx event, which she's hoping to parlay into a guest spot on the *Ellen* show, which she's hoping to parlay into her own show—a reboot of *Lifestyles of the Rich and Famous* called *Emily Johnson's Champagne Wishes and Caviar Dreams*. What sort of accent she would put on for such a show is still up for debate.

I mostly keep quiet, running the less glamorous behind-the-scenes aspects of the nonprofit. Holding meetings, making decisions. And I'm surprisingly *good* at it. After the long and complicated route to getting here, I've finally arrived at a place disarmingly simple: I'm happy. Because it feels good to do something positive with my days.

My assistant is a brilliant, fresh-faced young woman just out of college. After a year of her dedicated service (not to mention keeping us up-to-date on the coolest new apps, the latest bands we've never heard of, and the correct pronunciation of words like *GIF*), we'll pay off her $72,000 student-loan debt, in full. Then we'll promote her.

Yesterday, she buzzed me while I was going over a spreadsheet and staring out my window at the water tower.

"There's someone here to see you," she said. "It's . . ." Her voice dropped off.

Fearing she'd passed out, or suddenly come down with a nasty bout of narcolepsy, I went to the doorway.

She was fine. But standing across from her, with his hands on her desk, was—I understood why her voice had dropped off.

"Robert." His name caught in my throat, too.

"Tina," he said. "Or should I call you Ms. Fontana now?" He pointed at the doorway I'd emerged from. "That your office?" He marched toward it.

"Yes." I followed him inside and closed the door behind me. "Please, have a seat," I said in the freakiest role reversal of my entire life.

I sat at my desk.

Robert was dressed in a gray Armani suit, white dress shirt, and navy-blue knit necktie—which I recognized as his uniform for when he had a meeting with the board or a public appearance. Did he put on his best clothes just to come see me?

"It's been some time," he said, stretching his legs out in front of him and crossing his ankles above his freshly shined shoes.

I brought my voice down to a whisper. "If you're here about the documents, you don't have to worry."

"No, no I'm not," he said.

"Because if I were going to—"

"I know."

He shifted in his chair, loosened his necktie. "You've done really well for yourself, Tina. It's good, it's good. I'm proud of you."

A knot formed in my throat. As if the one he loosened from his neck had passed directly into mine.

"I never meant to hurt you," I blurted out.

He leaned in, hands on his knees, and I became terrified in an old and familiar way.

"I'm not much of an admirer of in-your-face attitudes," he said. "But I have to concede that y'all put a pistol ball in me. I've got a certain amount of respect for that." He leaned back in his chair again.

I could tell that he was yearning to put his leg up on the desk. But he couldn't, because it was my desk.

"Anyhow, I'd call us even. What do you say?" He extended his hand for a shake.

I took his hand firmly in mine. "*Even* I'm not sure about," I said. "But you've got yourself a truce."

"Well aren't you just tough as a boiled owl!" Robert tugged hard on my hand, like he didn't want to let it go so easily. "Is that a bottle of Herradura Añejo I'm looking at back there?" He nodded at the shelf behind me.

"It is," I said, without having to turn around. "But it's strictly for after five p.m."

"Fair enough, fair enough." He laughed and then stood up. "I suppose I should get going."

The knot in my throat dropped with a pang to my heart. I didn't want him to leave.

"I guess I could make an exception," I said. "This one time."

He smiled the way he used to whenever he got his way and sat back down.

I felt better. I felt calm, calmer than I'd ever felt in my life. I reached for the bottle. "But you're slicing the lime," I said.

acknowledgments

Thank you to my agent, Kerry Sparks, who boarded an airplane with the first ten chapters of *The Assistants* in her carry-on luggage and landed a few hours later ready to take a chance on me, and to everyone at Levine Greenberg Rostan, especially Tim Wojcik and Lindsay Edgecombe.

Thank you to my editor, Kerri Kolen, who is everything I could ask for in a collaborator and partner in crime (her proficiency in the late-'80s oeuvre of Shelley Long is just a bonus), and to Ivan Held, Alexis Welby, and the entire Putnam publicity team.

Thank you to Amy Einhorn, who saw the potential in an early version of *The Assistants* when no one else did. And to Dana Spector at Paradigm, who believed very early on that this book could make a fun movie.

Thank you to David Granger for pretty much every good thing that's happened to me in the past five years. I will be forever grateful to you, David. And to Tyler Cabot, who wishes he could be a jerk but is one of the best guys I've ever known. Thank you also to Joanna Coles and all of my talented coworkers at *Cosmopolitan* for their support and encouragement.

For being the sole reader of countless drafts of this manuscript and my trusted confidant, I'd like to thank Victoria Comella. I'd also like to thank Summer Smith for her advice and guidance. Courtney Gillette and Emily Moore, you've helped me become a better writer and a better person.

For their friendship (and patience when I disappear from the face of the earth for days, weeks, and sometimes months at a time), I'd like to thank Shellie Citron, Tiana Peterson, Mary Barbour, Elyssa Kilman, Ana Saldamando, Laura Lampton Scott, Joanna Greenberg, Penny Citrola, Amy Badagliacca, Lisa Jusino, Natalia Chiemi, and Alison O'Connell.

Thank you to all of my friends and former coworkers at the East Meadow Public Library and the Great Neck Library, especially Susan Newson, Harriet Edwards, and Frances Jackson. Thank you to my former teachers Priscilla Gray and Cynthia Eagle. Thank you, Richard Strauss, for saving my life on a weekly basis.

Thank you to everyone at the Blue Stove, especially Jackie Zebrowski—you make my every day better. R.I.P Verb Café—you'll live on in my heart forever.

To Helen Pennock . . . Helen, I could not have done this without you. Thank you for helping me through the hardest times and for making the good times even better. I love you so much.

And finally, to my family: my father, Frank Perri, and sisters, Francine Azzariti and Maria Balsamo, and in loving memory of my mother, Angela Perri, who always told me I should write a book someday.

the assistants

Camille Perri

Discussion Guide

A Conversation with Camille Perri

BOOK
ENDS

Discussion Guide

1. Why do you think Tina is still an assistant at thirty years old? Do you think her past has shaped her present in any way? How might Tina be different if she grew up with more money? Is she a victim of societal structure, or is she stuck where she is because of her personality and her choices?

2. Do you believe Tina's decision to use Titan's reimbursement check to pay off her student loan debt is justified? What about Emily's actions? How do their respective life circumstances and goals influence your view of their moral character? Should we hold a disadvantaged person to different moral standards than we hold a person of privilege?

3. Discuss the roles of income inequality and gender in this novel. Did the novel change your opinions and ideas about those issues? How do you feel constrained (or empowered) by your own economic status or gender?

4. Do you think this is a political book? Discuss the interplay between the story and the corporate politics. What makes a good (or bad) political book?

5. Do you view Robert as a villain? Do you think Tina sees him as such? How might your perceptions of Robert and Tina be different if there was a more objective narrator, or no first-person narrator?

6. What role does friendship play in this story? Why do you think Tina and Emily become so close even though they're seemingly so different?

7. Discuss how Tina changes throughout the novel. What does she learn about herself?

8. How is Tina and Kevin's relationship affected by her involvement with the Assistance? How does her view of Kevin change as the scheme evolves?

9. How important do you think setting is to this novel? Would Tina's predicament have been the same or different if she lived someplace else?

10. Was the ending of the novel satisfying? Did anything about the ending surprise you? While you were reading, how did you want the story to end for Tina and Emily? For Robert?

A Conversation with CAMILLE PERRI, author of THE ASSISTANTS

What is your debut novel, *The Assistants*, about?

It's about a group of young female assistants who use their billionaire boss's expense account to pay off their student loan debt. Rupert Murdoch is going to love this book, absolutely adore it.

Tells us a little about the main character, Tina Fontana. She is well-educated, bright, and gutsy. Why is she still an assistant at age 30?

I see Tina as fairly typical of her generation—she's worked hard, tried to make good decisions, basically done everything she was told to do in order to be a successful adult, and yet she's nowhere near where she thought she'd be by now. She's very much an illustration of how I felt in my late twenties. Minus the stealing.

How does Tina, a "good" girl, first get involved in the scheme to skim money off her boss's expense account?

Tina sort of gets involved in this by accident. Sort of. Ultimately she does make the (clearly unethical) choice to cash a check that comes to her through a misunderstanding, and to use that money to pay off her student loan, but she really struggles with that decision. It's in no way easy for her to do something so dishonest. She convinces herself that it wouldn't actually be hurting anyone to cash the check—certainly not the multi-billion dollar corporation it belongs to—and it would give her a financial clean slate, a second chance at her own life, which is a temptation I believe many people with debt can relate to.

Have you brought any of your own past work experience to the novel?

I began this novel while I was working as the assistant to the editor in chief of *Esquire* magazine. One day while doing his expenses I remembered that my student loan payment was due. Not wanting to forget to make the payment, I immediately logged on to my account and when I saw those two windows open side-by-side on my computer, something clicked. It hit me how this debt that had been weighing me down for so many years was, in the larger scheme of things, particularly in the context of corporate money, relatively small. I thought: Hmm, if only I weren't an honest person. And then I thought: But what a great idea for a novel.

Income inequality is growing wider and wider. Do you think young people might actually fight back as those before them have failed to do?

I sure hope so. But it can be extremely disillusioning to be a young person today and to have faith in even our most progressive politicians. That said, this is an election year and we must be engaged. We're forfeiting our power if we succumb to apathy.

Do you think it is harder for this new generation to break in and move up the ladder in their chosen careers?

I'm sure every generation has faced its own unique challenges. I mean, it wasn't so long ago that women weren't allowed to wear pants and a black doctor was unheard of. Not nearly long ago enough. But I think what's unprecedented for Millennials is the skyrocketing price of a college education, and the over-reliance on underpaid underlings once they do enter the workforce.

Are all of the assistants in the novel women, or are there men among the underpaid, over-educated characters in the novel?

All of the assistants in the novel are women because I wanted to focus on the female experience. But of course in real life male assistants might find themselves in a similar predicament, only with less pressure to wear high-heels and smile.

Tina's boss, Robert Barlow, is in some ways a ruthless billionaire businessman, and yet Tina sees his good side, too. Why do you think he—and his real-life counterparts—are clueless about the plight of their underlings?

I knew early on that I didn't want Robert to be a clear-cut villain. He's not a bad guy. He's just very rich and very successful and with that comes a certain tone-deafness to how regular people live their lives. But we're all guilty of this in some way, of taking our own privilege for granted. Robert is simply a blown up (and hopefully comical) illustration of this.

As the writer, you don't seem to make a moral judgment in the novel about Tina's actions, leaving it to the reader to decide whether her embezzlement is serious or no big deal. Where would you come down on the situation if pressed? Is she justified?

I think the easy answer to this question is: No, Tina's actions are absolutely not justified. Embezzlement is stealing and stealing is wrong. But living in a country as we do where corporations and the .01 percent enjoy a government-sanctioned advantage over the rest of us, where secretaries pay more in taxes than the CEOs they work for, where Wall Street brought our economy to near-total collapse only to be bailed out with barely any significant punishment or change as a result . . . It makes the answer far less black-and-white.

As a lighthearted look at a very important workplace issue, _The Assistants_ seems to recall such groundbreaking comedies as _9 to 5_ and _Working Girl_. Has there been any interest in turning it into a film?

I take that as the highest compliment as those are two of my favorite movies from the 80s. There has been interest and I would love nothing more than to see this novel adapted for the big screen, but as of this moment no contracts have been signed. Stay tuned.

You were recently the Books Editor at Large for *Cosmopolitan*. Was this "day job" a help or a hindrance when writing your own book?

I had already finished and sold *The Assistants* when I began working at *Cosmo*. So maybe get back to me with this question for my next book.

Are you at work on a second novel?

I am. But all I will tell you is that it's got a lot more sex in it than this one.